THIEF!

The word exploded in Lissa's consciousness like a depth bomb, as her heart staggered and raced on.

Before her was the evidence she had searched for, yet feared to find. She had fallen in love with Lex Carson, the stranger who called himself a lawyer while remaining so much a man of mystery. He had stolen her heart—but now it seemed he had stolen far more: the sum of money she held in her trembling hand.

She knew she should turn from him in horror, but as she looked at him, her determination began to waver, her accusing eyes began to mist . . .

GIVE ME ONE SUMMER

A swift, pulsating story of danger and romance set against the colorful sea-swept background of the Maine coast.

Books by Emilie Loring

Published by Bantam Books, Inc.

EMILIE LORING

GIVE ME
ONE SUMMER

BANTAM BOOKS · TORONTO · NEW YORK · LONDON

GIVE ME ONE SUMMER

*A Bantam Book / published by arrangement with
Little, Brown and Company, Inc.*

PRINTING HISTORY

*William Penn edition published 1936
Grosset & Dunlap edition published March 1948
Bantam edition published June 1967
2nd printing
3rd printing
4th printing
5th printing
6th printing*

*Bantam Books are published by Bantam Books, Inc., a subsidiary
of Grosset & Dunlap, Inc. Its trade-mark, consisting of the words
"Bantam Books" and the portrayal of a bantam, is registered in the
United States Patent Office and in other countries. Marca Registrada.
Bantam Books, Inc., 271 Madison Avenue, New York, N.Y. 10016.*

TO
IRMA INMAN LORING

i

ONE! TWO! THREE!

The girl on the balcony of a house on the crest of a slope, counted the strokes of the village clock. Counted them again as they echoed from a distant ledge. She crossed her arms in their filmy flame-colored sleeves on top of the wrought-iron railing and watched a mist, like spindrift, veil the face of the moon which hung in the sky like a broken silver dollar and laid a path of diamonds on the rippling surface of the harbor. A dark ship floated in with the tide like a great red-eyed bird of evil-omen flying low over the water.

The air was soft as velvet, fragrant with the scent of peonies which rose from the garden and the breath of the pines and balsams which cast purple shadows on the lawns. How still the world was, so still that she could hear the croon of the tide, could hear birch leaves stirring with the sound of lapping water to the accompaniment of the shrill singing of locusts.

She might as well make a night of it here, she decided. She couldn't sleep. "Sometimes I wonder if you ever will sleep again, Lissa Barclay," she said to herself. The strain of the last few months when she had fought to hold her aunt in the world she loved had been heart-breaking. All that was over, the long night-vigils, the even longer days. Today—it was yesterday, now—she had rendered the last tender services she ever could render to Hetty Carson. Looking back it seemed more like ten than three years since she had come to this Maine village to make her home with her father's sister.

What next? she asked herself, as she watched two little fleeces chase a scudding cloud across the star sequined sky like chickens afraid of losing their mother. She answered her own question. The immediate "next" was already planned. Mr. Adams, a trustee of the Carson estate and Hetty Carson's legal adviser, was coming this afternoon to read her will. How could she have had much besides her jewels to bequeath? The income from a large property and Tarry Farm, the Maine estate, had been left to her for life only,

1

all was to go to her husband's nephew, Alexander Carson when she was through. Would he love the beautiful place with its miles of rocky shore, its gardens, cottages and boat houses, or would he give the White Queen's order, "Off with its head!"? It was an expensive estate to run in this tax-logged age. She knew. Hadn't she kept books on it during the last three years?

There would be two persons bitterly disappointed when they learned that the property went to him, Lisa's thoughts trooped on, her stepmother and half-sister. They had arrived at Tarry Farm four days ago. Hetty Carson had refused to see them.

"Buzzards! Buzzards!" she had muttered and closed her eyes.

Were they sleeping tonight or were they lying awake planning how they would spend the fortune they expected to inherit?

A thick cloud obscured the moon. Stars paled. Islands, distant hills, the anchored vessel, dimmed into shapeless shadows. A lighthouse loomed through the haze like a faint gray ghost.

Lissa dropped her head on her arms. The stillness was heavenly. Was that faint sound the dip of oars? It couldn't be. The only person likely to be on the water at this time would be Ozy, and he wouldn't be pulling his lobster-traps this early, neither would he be rowing, his dory would be running under engine power. She was hearing things. Darkness laid its soothing hand on her emotion-strained heart. She slept.

The French window behind her banged. She sprang to her feet. In her sleep she had drunk at some deep, cool spring in her spirit and awoke refreshed. An able-bodied breeze, smelling of salt kelp, was blowing from the harbor. Through a horizontal rift in a cloud, the moon's one eye gazed down upon the sleeping countryside with a knowing squint. Stars twinkled. A flame of scarlet spread in the eastern sky and gilded the upper edge of a fleet of silvery clouds. The lighthouse loomed as transcendently beautiful and unreal as the lamp-conjured palace of Aladdin. A cock crowed.

"I believe I slept," Lissa said and stretched lazily. One arm dropped as if weighted. She brushed fingers across her eyes and stared at the lighthouse. Had a flash, rapier-swift, shot from its great lens into the night, or had her eyes blurred from sleep, played a trick? How like her imagination to seize the bit in its teeth and gallop off on the trail of a mystery. It was a trick of vision, of course.

"You'd better go to bed, my girl, if you are beginning to

see, as well as hear, things," she told herself. "That light was discarded by the government three years ago."

A half hour later a streamlined cruiser glided smoothly into the harbor. In the pine-paneled main cabin four men bent over a table under a hanging light. The creak of anchor chains came through an open window.

One of the men straightened. A smile lurked in the depths of his gray eyes as they met the intent eyes looking back at him. He said;

"Here we are, my hearties. Two electrical engineers, temporarily; a lawyer, in quest of a vacation and an inheritance, presumably; and a playboy with nothing on his mind but the pursuit of pleasure, apparently."

Gravity routed the cool amusement from his voice and eyes. A muscle in his cheek tensed and relaxed. He tapped the map on the table with his forefinger and reminded in a low voice;

"Somewhere within the area surrounded by those pegs is the person we're after. I'm sure of it. And we are here to get him—understand—we are here to get him."

ii

"Now what, Mother Barclay?"

Standing by the mantel in her frock of soft white wool, Lissa Barclay addressed the crisp question to the small woman in black who huddled in a wing chair. As she waited for her stepmother's answer a ray of sunlight brought out the gold and red glints in her auburn hair. Her brown eyes glanced about the library in which she had read and dreamed and rebelled for three years. Now that she was about to leave it she loved the colorful, dignified room with its book-lined walls, its inviting green chairs and couch, its lamp-shaded tables with bowls of yellow roses. Fitful light from a lazy fire flickered on the portrait of a man above the mantel, a man with strong clear-cut features and a quizzical glint in the depths of his gray eyes. It brought out, also, the vivid flame and scarlet of tropical fish swimming in a crystal cylinder in the wrought-iron sconce against the wall. Beyond the long windows which opened on a broad terrace, the afternoon sun sparkled on rippling water, clear and blue as the sky above it; accentuated the red veins in the tawny rocks beyond which a pebbly beach glistened; shone on black and white cattle in a distant emerald green field. Through the wide open French windows came the whir of a mower and the scent of freshly cut lawns.

A girl, curled in the corner of the broad couch, removed a cigarette from her lips;

"Sure that that was old Adams, the lawyer, Lissa, and not a riproaring banshee who tore through laying us all flat with what he called Aunt Hetty's last will and testament?" she drawled. Her eyes were the color of larkspur, her hair spun gold, her mourning frock accentuated the rose-leaf perfection of her skin. Her thin lips curved in a cruel line as she looked at the woman in the chair and demanded;

"Well, Mrs. Barclay, as Lissa observed, 'Now what?' You're the next county to be heard from. We didn't renew the New York apartment lease thinking we'd have this place and a big income from Aunt Hetty with which to pay the bills we left behind us, and she left us nothing. We didn't even have a chance to tell our sob-story, she slipped out on us the very night of our arrival. Bring the wisdom of your years and experience to bear on the situation, Mother."

The blonde woman, whose personality was as colorless as a sketch done in fade-out ink, twisted a black bordered handkerchief in her plump white fingers. The corners of her mouth drooped as she looked at her stepdaughter who stood straight and curiously remote before the mantel with G-Man, the Irish terrier, squatted on his haunches beside her. His bright eyes had assumed an only-over-my-dead-body-you'll-touch-her expression as they followed the movements of the other two persons in the room.

Mrs. Barclay sniffed and transferred her reproachful glance to her golden-haired daughter on the couch.

"You needn't throw my age and experience in my face, Cleo. I'm still a young woman, only forty-five."

"Sometimes I wonder if you are forty-five, Mother Barclay, you are so casual," Lissa intervened. "I wish you would answer my question. With Aunt Hetty Carson's passing, this great point of land, one mile from a village, a village in itself almost, has gone into other hands. We must get out before the heir—Alexander the Great, Aunt Hetty and I nicknamed him—arrives, and he is likely to appear at any moment."

Mrs. Barclay leaned forward. Her eyes were dry now and angrily bright.

"I couldn't believe my ears when that man Adams read the will. Only a thousand dollars a year from a trust fund,

4

Hetty's jewels, her personal property in this house and an island with an old lighthouse for you, Melissa, and that tied up so you can't dispose of a cent of it without the approval of this Alexander Carson. Nothing for Cleo and me. Not even a ring. That divine set of aquamarines and diamonds of Hetty's would have been perfect on Cleo, all the blondes are wearing them this season. Such meanness, toward her brother's family, too. She never said a word of reproach to me for divorcing your father. That couldn't have been the reason she ignored me and my daughter in her will, she was his daughter, too."

"But, Mother Barclay, Mr. Adams explained that that was all Aunt Hetty had to leave. The large income from the property her husband left and this place were hers for life only, and that large income remained large because her husband's will provided that it be kept so by dipping into the principal if necessary. Something tells me that the heir, who is the namesake and nephew of her late husband, and trustee of my legacy—can you imagine a sillier arrangement—will find his inheritance a liability rather than an asset. The three cottages on the place are leased for the summer, but the rents won't pay taxes, interest and upkeep."

Alexander the Great was not the only person who would find his inheritance a liability, Lissa thought. How could she manage taxes and repairs on her island lighthouse and her living, on a thousand a year until she acquired a job?

Cleo narrowed her eyes to slits and inquired;

"Why wasn't the heir here yesterday?"

"Mr. Adams said he couldn't get here."

"Wouldn't take the trouble, probably. Have you met him? How old is he? What's his business? Perhaps he'll fall in love with you, Lissa, perhaps that was Aunt Hetty's scheme to let the Barclays in on the Carson property. I'll promise not to take your beau away this time."

Lissa hoped that her face did not reflect the sickening sense of humiliation which submerged her whenever she remembered that Cleo had lured the man to whom she herself had been engaged away from her, after which she had thrown him over. She declined crisply;

"Thanks for the noble offer, Cleo, but I'm not interested."

Mrs. Barclay brightened and suggested;

"Perhaps we ought to stay here at Tarry Farm and welcome the heir. If he has no family—"

"He might be overjoyed to adopt us, Mother means," Cleo interrupted. "What do you know about him, Lissa?"

Lissa remembered Hetty Carson's comment when told

5

that Mother and daughter had arrived at Tarry Farm. Their eyes now had the "buzzard" look.

"Not much," she answered Cleo's question. "Aunt Hetty resented his indifference to her—what she thought was his indifference—and the fact that the property was to go to him, and rarely mentioned him. I know that he is a lawyer, and that he studied for his profession in three universities. Can't you picture a man like that? Stooping, peering through huge bone-rimmed specs. Owlish, if you get what I mean. He lives in Washington."

"Perhaps we'd better stay until Alexander the Great comes, Mother. If he is a one-idea person—and that idea law—we may be of use helping him run this house, at least it would be a friendly gesture to turn the place over to him, it would show we have no hard feelings. I suppose Aunt Hetty gave you presents of money, Lissa? Doubtless you have a sizeable nest-egg tucked away?"

Anger sent a wave of color to the soft, uneven line of Lissa's hair. Was Cleo preparing to ask her for money now that Aunt Hetty Carson was no longer alive to help with overdue bills? She felt terribly alone in the world in which from now on she would have to make her way, in which she seemed tragically unimportant. As if he understood, the dog flopped to the floor and laid his black nose on her foot. The feel of him was curiously comforting. It helped her to answer lightly;

"A nest-egg! My savings would liquidate at about $10.95. Suppose I had more, I would have earned it, wouldn't I? When, three years ago, Aunt Hetty wrote that it was the duty of one of us to live with her, you refused to come, Cleo. I came, because I had promised father that if ever his only sister wanted me I would go to her. I've lived in this lonely house, this sea-coast town, for three years, and these last months have been heart-breaking, I felt so powerless to help Aunt Hetty cling to the life, which, ill as she was, she loved."

Lissa turned and stared down at the fire to hide a quick rush of tears. How could she have let herself go before those two hard women?

Cleo shrugged;

"And all the time you were having your clothes from the best places in New York. Stop sniffling, Mother."

The callousness of Cleo's words dried Lissa's eyes.

"Clothes don't make up for freedom. However, why think of that, it's past and I'm on my own. I wonder how often life, real living, I mean, begins with a death as mine has.

To return to the will, why are you two making a fuss over the legacy Aunt Hetty left me? You have a comfortable income from the settlement father made on you. You've been living luxuriously."

"Ever know anyone who had enough money?" Cleo's eyes made Lissa think of a cat, always on the watch, always suspicious. "Mother and I are up to our ears in debt. Of course you'll add your thousand to our assets?"

"I will not."

"Look here, Lissa, you've got to. I want to go to England for a year and I'll need every cent I can scrape up. I've been waiting until Aunt Hetty passed out so that you could stay with your mother and help financially."

Lissa laughed. It wasn't a pleasant sound even to her own ears.

"My mother! Your mother, you mean, Cleo. To me she never has been anything but my father's second wife. She never tried to be anything else to the three-year-old, frightened small child she acquired with her marriage. From now on, I live where I please."

Why was she standing here in the library arguing? Lissa asked herself. Beyond the long windows the sea sparkled an invitation. Heavenly day to shoot round the point in the flying outboard she hadn't used for weeks. Now that she was the owner of an island she wanted to land on it, take formal possession, plant a flag. Why not plant the pennant she had won on the last outboard race? What fun! She would take G-Man along as witness.

"Ahem!"

Fenton, the butler, who might have stepped from an English comedy, in his livery and his sideburns, stood in the doorway with a massive silver tray and its tea equipment.

"Good heavens! Fenton! When did you steal in? Your entrances are positively spooky! Put the tray here. I'll pour." Cleo motioned to a table near her.

Except that his long, tapering fingers tightened on the tray, the butler did not move. He said suavely;

"I'm sorry, Miss Barclay, if I surprised you, in future I'll try to clatter a bit before I enter. Will you pour the tea as usual, Miss Lissa?"

Lissa's lips twitched at his accent on "as usual." She shook her head.

"No Fenton. I'm going on the water. Come along, G-Man."

She left the room by a long window with the dog at her heels, dashed across a brick terrace patterned in gold from the reflected sun and ran down the path to the shore between

7

borders gay with gigantic late tulips, pink and bronze, white and lavender; blushing with huge pink peonies, and splashed with the scarlet of Oriental poppies. The pale green blades of late iris were treasure houses of color which a week of sunny days would release and spill through the border. The air was sweet with the breath of blossoms, spicy with the tang of kelp and the scent of balsam, spruce, pine and arborvitae. From a tree-top drifted the throaty call of a plover.

Yellow summer birds flew up from the fern-bordered pool around a fountain and slashed the air with gold as sunlight struck their backs. The dog dashed after them, returned, and with mouth open and tongue hanging, looked up with twinkling brown eyes. Lissa shook her head at him.

"You think it's a joke, don't you, to scare those birds? If you don't show more sense, I'll change your name. Don't you know that psychologists use the letter G as the symbol of mental ability? The more G a man has, the more likely he is to be a genius. Some day you'll start after something that won't scare. Then where will you be, Mister?"

The Irish terrier responded with a sharp bark and raced ahead. The slope to the shore was terraced. There were steps between each terrace and a Victorian wrought-iron seat to lure the passerby to linger and enjoy the panorama of garden, white lighthouse, and island-dotted sapphire sea set in a frame of purplish-green hills, their sides slashed by fissures, like scars on the face of a soldier which no plastic surgeon could efface. Sky as blue as the robe of a Madonna canopied the point of land projecting into the sparkling water. A great heron flapped slowly westward, long legs extended like a rudder.

Lissa resisted the temptation to dip into the boulder-enclosed swimming-pool near the shore and ran on to the boathouse. She changed to navy blue shorts, with a top of gay India print, white sandals, and caught up the green and gold pennant.

She stepped carefully into the flying outboard she had named The Scribbler, moored at the float. The dog followed and stretched out on the bow. She adjusted the carburetor and cleaned a sparkplug. A boat chugged alongside, a fisherman's dirty-white dory with a cabin which looked like a shoebox.

"Hey! Lissa! Hold on!"

She tossed back her hair and smiled at Captain Ozias, commonly known as "Ozy," whose forward thrust head gave the effect of a hound on the scent, whose ferret-like eyes seemed always on the trail of a mystery. She shouted to make herself heard above the throb of the engines;

"Howdy, Ozy. What can I do for the sheriff, ace-errand and lobsterman of the county?"

"Got to talk to you." He sniffed and caught the side of her boat. "Say, this is an awful tricky thing you're settin' out in. Shouldn't suppose your folks would let you go alone."

"Alone! I'm not alone with G-Man along as crew. Besides, what could happen to me? I hate to talk about myself, but I'm a fish in the water."

"Always jokin', ain't you? Your eyes are twinklin' with little gold stars. That's an awful deep dimple in your right cheek that comes when you laugh. You've been round here three years now an' I ain't never seen you down in the mouth. I hate to make you feel bad, but folks is gettin' terrible riled 'bout that dog of your'n."

Lissa suspected what was coming. Hadn't G-Man laid two strange bathing suits at her feet this very morning? It wasn't the first time he had brought loot. Apparently he had an irresistible penchant for garments dangling from clotheslines.

"What has he done now, Ozy?"

"You needn't yell, I kin hear you, your voice's clear as a bell. I guess you know without my tellin' what the critter's done. He's been stealing clothes again. You won't hev to go so far as you went before to return 'em. Those he snitched today belong to the folks who've moved into that cottage of your aunt's she calls the Treasure Chest."

"You mean he stole the bathing suits of the Millards, the tenants who came yesterday? They probably think that that is our usual welcome-to-our-cottage stunt. Thanks for telling me. It will save a lot of telephoning."

"Glad to help out, Lissa. Did you know them Millards had a boy? Thought your aunt never let in kids."

"She never has before, but this child is delicate; she decided that he couldn't do any damage to the cottage."

"Damage! By mighty, he looks as if a breath of wind would blow him away. 'Bout eight years old, I'd say."

"He'll gain in this air. How's business?" She waved a hand toward the lobster floats bobbing on the surface of the water near ledges like miniature boats.

"Not too bad. The summer folks eat a lot of lobsters. I got five traps sprinkled round this cove. They ain't doin' so well. Think I'll change an' buoy them on the other side of the island. I s'pose you'll be havin' your big lobster-bake as usual Fair week, an' need a lot? Just stopped in at your other cottage, Red Chimneys, to see if the folks there wanted to engage lobsters."

"Did they?"

"Yep. Say have you met that fella Packard who's hired it?

He's a smooth talker. His tongue feeds out words as easy as oil slippin' into a motor engine. I got to be goin'."

"Thanks for telling me where the bathing suits came from. Good-bye, Ozy."

iii

LISSA tuned up the engine and cast off. As the outboard shot forward it kicked up a jeweled spray that stung her face. She waved to the man who was watching her.

She called to the terrier;

"G-Man, what was the big idea when you stole those bathing suits? To make a smash-hit with our new tenants? If you don't watch out, you'll be in the dog-jail. Bad boy!"

The terrier gave a short, sharp bark of defiance and tucked his nose between his paws.

The water rippled under a gentle breeze. The rush of wind caused by the flying outboard tugged at Lissa's bronze lashes and blew her short auburn hair in a gollywog effect about her head. She drew the clear air deep into her lungs. She must make the most of it. Soon the ground roar of a big city, the wail of motor horns, the screech of fire sirens, would be in her ears instead of the swish of pebbles on the beach and the faint moan of a distant buoy. What city, she asked herself. She had been at Tarry Farm so long she almost dreaded to make a change. Maybe everyone had to wrench free from the pattern someone else had designed for her, maybe outside that pattern the world would be made up largely of crooked lanes and rough roads, but she had to get outside and take her chance.

She watched a thin drift of cloud wind itself about the top of a purple hill like a sari of rosy malines. Her eyes came back to the harbor. Its strength, its color, its beauty, tightened her throat. A war-vessel lay far out. A ship's bell was striking the quarter hour. The slanting sun set aflame the brass on a streamlined cruiser which rocked idly in a sea powdered with gulls. It was the last word in luxury, must be owned by a plutocrat, she decided. The blue absent pennant was flying at the starboard spreader. The club burgee was like a jewel against the sky. At the stern floated the yacht ensign, red and white and blue. The brilliant colors added the last perfect touch. She would round the point and look the cruiser over before she took formal possession of her island. Her island, but an island only at certain hours of the day when the tide covered the sandy ledge which connected it with the mainland.

The whitewashed walls of the lighthouse and the connecting one-and-a-half story frame building shone like mother-of-pearl against a towering background of balsam, pine and arborvitae. The island was patched with rocks, coarse emerald green grass, low-growing juniper, and groups of gulls.

As she looked at the iron deck above which the great eye of the tower glittered, she thought again of the beam of light. Of course it had been imagination plus. Why should anyone flash a signal? Bootlegging had gone by. Kidnaping was no longer classed among the easy-money rackets.

"My imagination's my fortune, kind sir," she chanted in a low, sweet voice and laughed. "I'd better use it on my plans for the future."

She throttled down the engine. She couldn't think constructively when the boat was shooting through the water. One couldn't live on a thousand dollars a year, plus the small amount she had inherited from her father, and maintain a lighthouse for a summer residence without working, could one?

After the settlement on his second wife and daughter, whom he had left, because, he had confided to Lissa, he couldn't stand their infernal bickering another day, her father had spent most of what remained of his capital traveling about the world with her. She had seen many, many countries but she had not made friends. He had been jealous of her interest in people; the moment she had found someone whom she really liked, he had moved on. Aunt Hetty had been like that, had disapproved of her outboard motorboating, of her devotion to the little church in the village, but she had persisted, they were outlets for her caged emotions.

She thought of her brief engagement to Johnny Grant, whom she had met after the death of her father when she was heartbreakingly lonely; and she thought of her humiliation when he had haltingly told her that he wanted to marry Cleo. She had recovered from her love for him months and months ago—had it been real love would she have recovered?

Never again would she allow herself to care for a man until he had been exposed to her half-sister's fascination. How could she trust one even then? Hadn't Johnny Grant seemed madly in love with her? She was through with men, she'd be one of those career-women whose biographies figure in the pages of magazines. From early childhood she had ached to be a writer and while living with her aunt the chance had come to try. She had devoted hours each day to creative writing. She wanted to write fiction, in spite of the fact that an editor had warned her to think well before she started on the rough and rocky road to authorship, that the woods, to say nothing of the park benches, were full of would-be writers.

She lived over the ecstatic moment when she had drawn a pink cheque from an envelope. Three dollars! It had seemed a fortune. She had sold something! Nothing much but some-one had wanted it enough to pay money for it. That was the acid test. Another much traveled manuscript had been in an editorial office six weeks; up to this one its flights had been in the non-stop class. She had had a nervous chill every time she opened the mail-bag for fear she would find it. Other stories had gone out and had done the homing-pigeon act, but not that one. If she did receive a cheque for it, she would deposit it in a travel fund.

Thrilled by the thought of achievement and freedom, she shot the outboard around a rocky point. Her breath stopped. A motorboat was almost upon her. Where had it come from? Had it dropped from the sky? Why hadn't she heard the put-put? Why didn't the dumbbell at the wheel slow down? Was it a villager or a summer resident out on a practice spin? Spin was the word. The top of something that looked like a head was visible. He was making thirty miles an hour, plus. She had the right of way. If she swerved the least bit, the one-man crew wouldn't know what to do.

"Sit tight, G-Man," she warned, as the dog, sensing danger, sprang to his feet.

She regarded the on-coming boat with the fascinated absorption she might bestow on an inch-worm looping its way across a man's collar to his neck. It was shooting straight for her! It couldn't be! It was unbelievable! It was! It would crash—

"Hi! Look out!" she shouted. Kicked off her sandals. Grabbed the pennant. Jumped.

She came to the surface, kept herself afloat with one hand while she drew the pennant about her neck and brushed her dripping hair from her eyes. Something had hit her forehead. Ooch, how it throbbed. Where was G-Man? There he was with his nose above water swimming toward her. Some distance away the motorboat which had crashed into hers, was drifting, it had lost power. Why didn't the man come back to see what damage he had done? Was he blind that he didn't see that her outboard had run amuck? It was buzzing round in dizzy circles. Funniest thing she'd ever seen. She laughed and swallowed an able-bodied wave.

She choked and coughed. She'd better keep her sense of humor battened down until she was out of this mess. Could she reach her boat? She started off in an easy crawl, she mustn't get winded, no knowing when she would catch the runaway. Suppose it charged in her direction? She speeded up, her arms flashed in the late sunshine. She could hear G-Man paddling beside her. The water was icy. She swallowed another mouthful. It made her a little sick. She shivered and her teeth chattered. Why, why didn't that idiot at the wheel of the motorboat come to her aid? She was getting winded. She tried to call but her throat was dry. She couldn't make a sound.

"Hi! Keep away from the outboard! We're coming!"

The words struck against her ear. She raised her head. A man in a launch was shouting through a megaphone. Must have come from the cruiser. Someone on board had seen the crash. G-Man shivered and whimpered as he gallantly kept beside her.

The hum of the boat was louder. A life belt dropped to the water. She clutched it with one hand. Caught the dog's collar with the other. They both went under. Bobbed to the surface. She was drawn along cautiously. A man's voice called;

"Steady! Steady! We'll have you safe in a minute."

Someone caught her under the arms. She looked up dazedly into a lean colorless face, into dark, troubled eyes. Hadn't she seen the man before somewhere? He was coatless.

"Women and dogs first," she gasped as she was lifted gently, but firmly, from the water. "Save G-Man, too."

Dizzy from the smart and throb of her forehead, exhausted by the effort to keep afloat in the cold water, she flung herself on the cushioned seat. The dog huddled in a wet dejected heap beside her.

"B—better f—follow that motor b—boat—m—man in it —m—must have f—fainted or someth—thing before he ran me d—down," she advised between chattering teeth.

"Don't worry about him."

"Nice voice," she approved mentally.

"I'll be all right in a min—minute. Soon's I s—stop shivering," she reassured the troubled eyes above her. Something soft and woolly covered her. She snuggled under it and clasped her arms about her shoulders in an attempt to stop their shaking.

"Drink this."

She pushed away the long firm fingers which held the silver cup of a flask.

"No, th—thanks. I'll be warm in a min—minute, I need nothing but a n—nice cr—crackling fire and dr—dry clothes. See? I've stopped shaking—almost. Don't make an invalid of me because of a silly accident. Accident!"

Memory brought her to her feet. She clutched the blue shirt sleeve of the man who had pulled her from the water. Color from the dripping pennant around her neck ran down her bare legs in little green and gold rivulets.

"What became of the motorboat which cr—crashed into mine?"

He held out the soft camelshair top-coat which had covered her.

"Stop thinking about that boat and put this on."

"Hmp! The ruling class," she told herself, and disciplined an urge to defy the authoritative voice. She dropped the pennant to the seat, slipped her arms into the sleeves and drew the coat close about her. She needed its heavenly warmth now that a strong, ocean breeze had sprung up.

"When we catch a mermaid—to say nothing of her dog—it's up to us to take care of her, isn't it?"

The laughter left his voice. His shocked gray eyes rested on her forehead.

"What a crack! Lucky it wasn't lower down. Prescott, make for the cruiser! We'll get something that will fix up this bruise."

"Aye, aye, sir!" the white-capped sailor at the wheel responded.

The man drew a fine linen handkerchief from his pocket, folded it and dipped it into the cold water rushing by the boat.

"Shut your teeth, this will smart," he said, and laid the compress on the wound.

The sting of salt on bruised flesh brought a rush of tears to Lissa's eyes, but it served also to clear her mind. The lingering daze vanished with the rapidity of fog in strong sunlight. Her rescuer must be the plutocrat who owned the cruiser. She brushed aside his hand.

"I'll hold it. I'm not going to the cruiser. If you want to help, catch that crazy boat of mine before it crashes into something! Watch it! It's going so fast that the number on the side is a blur."

"Prescott, cut over to the outboard. We'll try and kill the engine by throwing water on it."

"Aye, aye, sir!"

The sailor pulled his cap to a more acute angle and changed the course of the launch. Hands thrust hard into coat pockets, Lissa breathlessly watched her outboard careening in dizzy circles. Something was emerging from the water near it, something dark and glistening like the back of a seal. The tide was ebbing! The outboard straightened out. Made a bee-line for the ledge. Smashed into it with a shower of splinters and spray.

"That seems to be that," she observed with a catch in her voice. She loved that outboard. She was losing everything she cared for. She fought back a torrent of emotion. She mustn't let herself go. She mustn't.

Imagine cracking up over an old boat after what she had lived through these last months. She couldn't be so silly. She swallowed hard before she observed;

"That crash stopped the en—engine."

The man's eyes were dark with concern. Did he fear that he was about to have a sob sister on his hands? She'd show him. She laughed;

"But what's a crash in the life of an outboard? Let it stay there. I'll send for it. Now if you will round that point, I'll tell you where to land me." She drew a long unsteady breath. She had staved off a weep-fest that time.

The sailor looked interrogatively at the man who was slipping into a blue coat. His shoeless feet were braced to steady himself. The boat lurched and kicked up showers of spray as it sped through a sea the change of wind had roughened.

"Round the point, Prescott," he responded to the sailor's unspoken question. "Follow the orders of Miss—" He smiled at the girl and raised questioning eyebrows.

"Barclay," she supplied. She loved the buoyant note in his voice. What would he think if she added: "Lissa—to you." She removed the compress from her forehead. As he protested, she assured;

"It doesn't throb now, really. I'll pull a curl or two over it, see, and then the bruise won't show." She thrust the wet handkerchief into the pocket of her shorts. "It's bad enough to look like a drowned rat without adding a prize-fighter touch. I'll see that your handkerchief is returned spic and span."

Why was he looking at her so curiously? Surprised to find out who she was? As if in answer to her thoughts he directed:

"Make the Tarry Farm landing as quickly as possible, Prescott."

"Of course I'd like to get home, but shouldn't you render first aid to him?" Lissa nodded in the direction of the drifting motorboat. "He hasn't changed his position since I saw him shooting toward me. He may be terribly hurt by the crash."

She thought the sailor chuckled, she was sure that the man

now seated opposite her in the stern putting on his shoes said something colorful under his breath before he explained:

"That isn't the head of a man, Miss Barclay, it's a robot at the wheel. It's an automatic steering device which picks up radio waves, transmits their impulse to the wheel and keeps the boat pointed at a 'target' down the bay."

iv

"A ROBOT did all that damage?" Lissa demanded incredulously.

"Yes. Two guests on the cruiser are, well, call them engineers. They were experimenting with radio control of the motorboat. It was going like a breeze in a quiet, clear sea, when you shot round that point in your outboard. You know the rest, but, you don't know that terror, for fear I wouldn't reach you in time, took years from my life. When I saw you in the water holding the dog with one hand, and that crazy outboard likely to smash into you at any moment, I—" He ran his fingers under his collar. "I kicked off my shoes, flung off my coat ready to go overboard if you missed the lifebelt."

The memory of the instant when the motorboat had crashed into The Scribbler, sent chills along Lissa's veins.

"Let's forget it," she suggested. "I'm safe. G-Man is safe. Hell-dives are part of the day's work in a flying outboard. If The Scribbler doesn't dash her brains out against that ledge before I can rescue her, I may be able to have her repaired."

"The Scribbler?"

"That's the name of the flying outboard."

"We'll take care of it. Prescott will pick it up. I'd go back for it now but I want to get you home before you take cold. We'll have it repaired. Our robot is responsible for the damage."

"We, sounds like royalty. You'll have to take the question of reparations up with the Carson heir who has just inherited Tarry Farm. Who knows but the late accident may prove the foundation of my spectacular success. Heroine loses boat and acquires black eye. To borrow from the Duchess in Alice, 'the moral of that is,' turn casualty into cash; meaning it would make a grand opening for a story. I could turn the robot into a hero."

"What do you mean by spectacular success? Haven't picked up the motion-picture bug, have you?"

Lissa watched a lavender-winged gull dive into the tumbled, frothy wake of the launch as she answered:

"No, but one quite as deadly. I'm a working girl, did you think me a leisurist? Wonderful word, isn't it?"

She drew a deep breath. "Heavenly afternoon. The sun topping that brownish-green hill makes me think of a huge copper ball being balanced on the snout of a trained seal. It has turned the shore lines to red gold and the lighthouse to a tourmaline pink. How Nature loves jewel glints and tints. Like a woman, isn't she? See that dark ridge between the mainland and the island? As the tide recedes it will leave a road which will be usable for nine hours. I've never seen the mountains more purple nor the winding roads on them look so like silver threads, and man and boy 'I've watched three winters and summers come and go.'" She was working off her turbulence of spirit in chatter, she realized, but that was better than tears.

"I've never heard that last line declaimed better. Have one?" He offered a silver cigarette case.

"No, thanks. I don't smoke."

"Don't smoke! And you headed for screenland?"

"Why so surprised? I've met any number of wonderful girls in my travels who neither smoke nor drink. With some it's a sort of 'I am my brother's Keeper' complex, with others the courage to be different. You're wrong, I'm not headed for screenland. I mean to be a writer."

Was she too friendly? He was the first person, except Aunt Hetty and G-Man—he was a person if ever there were one—to whom she had confided her ambition. After all, one could hardly say "Hail and Farewell" to a man who had saved one's life, could one? One knew the moment one looked at him that he was a man of power. Someone to hold tight to in time of trouble. She liked him. Tremendously. Liked him better than any man she ever had met, and she had seen him for the first time less than half an hour ago! She did need a guardian! The launch rounded the point.

"There's Tarry Farm! Doesn't that half timber and brick English house look as if it had grown against the background of forest? Those streaks of color are the perennial borders of the path from shore to terrace. Aren't the cottages attractive? All leased for the season, too." She blinked back tears, said unevenly:

"I've thought myself a martyr these last three years to have to live here—it has seemed terribly remote in winter. Just as

I am leaving it, I realize that I love every inch of the place."

"Why are you leaving?"

She tucked the woolly coat more securely around her bare feet. G-man pressed close against her knees.

"I told you, Alexander Carson has inherited it. Apparently you haven't listened to my chatter."

"I can tell you every word you've said. So, this is Lex Carson's property?"

"Is he called Lex for short? Nice name. Do you know him?"

"Very well. He came in on that cruiser to—to take over his inheritance. He has spoken of you, but until you said you'd lived at Tarry Farm three years, I didn't know which one of the, quote, beautiful Barclay sisters—unquote, you were. I hoped that you were Lissa—or is it Melissa?" He was even better looking when he smiled, she decided, his teeth were so white and his gray eyes turned so dark and shining, and he didn't need to be any better looking than he was with his face in repose.

"Melissa for my grandmother but only one person in the world calls me that. I'm Lissa to my friends. Evidently you've heard all about my family from Alexander Carson?"

"I wouldn't say 'all.' I still have a lot to learn about you. Already I know that you are a writer."

"Intend to be a writer. They tell me it's a long slow road, that only about nine percent of those who start out carry through the first year. Even after that winnowing, the fatalities are staggering."

"Remember the old proverb, 'Leg over leg the dog went to Dover.' You'll arrive if you keep everlastingly at it."

"What else have you learned about me?"

"You mean this afternoon? That you have two freckles like tiny flakes of gold on the bridge of your nose—don't try to brush them off, you can't—that you're a grand sport, that your amazing eyes are pools of beauty."

"It listens lovely." Almost Lissa was tempted to believe him. Silly. Hadn't Johnny Grant said practically the same thing about her eyes? Only he had said they were "tops."

Cigarette between his lips he bent his head to the light cupped in his hands before he asked:

"Your half-sister Cleo was engaged to Johnny Grant, wasn't she? I hear she's a knockout."

Anger flamed through Lissa.

"Better take a leaf from the book of Ulysses, put wax in your ears before you meet her, then you won't hear the voice of the siren. It's fatal."

She was aware of his quick glance. Was he setting her

down as a jealous cat? The launch was almost at the float. She wouldn't have much more chance to reveal her disagreeable nature.

He tossed the cigarette overboard and stood up. Feet planted squarely apart to steady himself, he smiled at her.

"I don't need to take a leaf from the book of Ulysses, I'm immune to sirens."

"Sez who?" she mocked.

"Sez I," he mimicked. "Hope I haven't hurt you."

"Hurt me? How?"

"By referring to the engagement of your half-sister to the man to whom you were engaged."

She jumped to her feet and clutched the camelshair coat about her. Her eyes blazed.

"You have learned a lot about me, haven't you? How dare you refer to that—that maddening experience? I'm sunk in humiliation when I think of it."

His eyes steady and direct met hers.

"Then you still love him?"

"Love him! My love for Johnny Grant was as rootless as a mushroom."

"Thanks. It has suddenly become enormously important that I know."

"Why?"

The boat slid alongside the float. He stepped to the landing without answering her question and held out his hand.

"Come on! Why take along that messy pennant? What were you doing with it?"

Lissa looked at the wet stuff she was gripping which resembled nothing so much as a bunch of over-cooked spinach.

"I had gone very Admiral Byrd. I was about to plant it on my recently acquired possession, my island."

"Your island. The island with the light?"

"Yes."

He turned to look at the white tower.

"Sold by the Government, wasn't it?"

"Yes. Aunt Hetty bought it. She willed it to me." She confided in a hushed voice, "At dawn this morning I thought I saw the light flash."

"Isn't the tower kept locked?"

His face hadn't changed, but she had the curious feeling that he was taut as he waited for her answer.

"Yes. Of course it was a trick of vision. My eyes were tired."

"Of course, how could a person get in and why should he want to? Did you plant the pennant?"

"No. The outboard crashed before I could land."

"That disappointed-little-girl look in your eyes hurts me. I'll get another pennant and we'll plant it together. Shall we?"

"Don't talk to me as if I were four years old and had broken my doll. I'm a big girl now."

"Think I don't realize that?" He spoke to the sailor in the launch. "Prescott, pick up the outboard. Bring it in and wait for me here." He looked at her bare feet with their gem-like pink nails, then at the path that loped leisurely upward to the terrace of the big house. "You can't walk on those rough stepping stones without shoes. Where are they?"

"Kicked my sandals off before I dove. I have another pair in the boathouse. I have a frock there too. It won't take me a moment to get into it. Take your coat. Thanks for everything. Run along home, G-Man."

She threw the dripping pennant over one shoulder and lingered to watch the dog. He ran part way up the path, stopped and looked back.

"Go on!" she called, "and don't go near a clothesline!"

She ran ahead to the boathouse. She stared unbelievingly at the man who jumped the rail of the veranda and came toward her with outstretched hands.

"Lissa!"

"Johnny Grant! Is it really you?" For some unaccountable reason the sight of him set her a-shiver again. Had his eyes always been so colorless, his hair platinum blonde? Had he always swaggered a little?

"Sure, it's I, sweet thing. Don't look at me as if you'd been bumped awake. I'm stopping at the Inn in the village. Made a bee-line for you as soon as I heard that your late, if not lamented, Aunt Hetty had passed out and that you were free, Princess released from the dark tower stuff, what? That was only a brainstorm I had over Cleo—I'm crazy about you—"

He looked beyond her and called:

"Look who's here! Where did you drop from, Lex Carson?"

v

Lissa glanced at the man who had rescued her. There was a quality of strength and self control about him in sharp contrast to Johnny Grant's puffy outlines. His mouth was stern

20

as if trained to command, yet, boyishly tender when he smiled. His eyes were dark, intent, with quizzical lights in their depths. The picture of Alexander Carson as she had imagined him, stooping, peering owlishly through bone-rimmed specs, had been so deeply etched on her mind, that she doubted even now if she had heard Johnny's hail correctly.

"Are you really Alexander Carson?" she asked.

"If you don't know who he is, Lissa, perhaps you'll tell me why you've been sporting round with him in a launch, in those shorts? You look as if you'd been trying to qualify for Miss State of Maine with that striped thing over your shoulder. How did you get that vicious bump on your forehead?"

"I don't like that word 'sporting,' Johnny, and I don't care for the 'Hands up!' tone in which you ask questions."

"Nothing to get excited about, Grant. Miss Barclay's flying outboard ran amuck—she got a nasty crack on the head—and I pulled her out of the water. At a time like that, one doesn't insist upon introductions. I am Alexander Carson, Miss Barclay. Lex to you, I hope."

"Lissa! Are you so glad to see me that you've gone dumb?" Grant inquired with a pleased grin.

Lissa regarded him coolly:

"Pity you have such an inferiority complex, Johnny. That's sarcasm, in case you care. Been to the house to see Cleo?"

"I have not. It would be too soon if I never saw her again. I came to see you. The butler—that man is too English to be genuine—told me that you were on the water. He showed me how to get here in my car. I waited knowing you'd have to come this way. Jump into your clothes. I'm taking you out to supper."

From the corners of her eyes Lissa glanced at the man who stood straight and tall beside her. Was he thinking, as evidently Johnny Grant thought, that her one-time fiancé had but to whistle and she would drop into his arms? She declined crisply:

"Thanks, but I'm not going with you, Johnny."

"Sure, you're coming. You wouldn't break my heart, would you?"

"Your heart break, Johnny? It couldn't. Your heart is a graveyard of buried loves."

Grant grinned engagingly.

"That's a swell line. You're good, Lissa. Come on. Remember what corking times we've had hunting up new places to eat? We'll find tops tonight."

Lissa felt her color rise. Would he see it and flatter himself that she still cared? She grew redder at the thought.

"Not interested, Johnny. Please go."

"Better get going, Grant," Carson suggested pleasantly but uncompromisingly. "Miss Barclay is shivering again. The water was icy. Get into your dry clothes—Lissa."

As she took a step forward, Grant blocked her way.

"You're not going until you hear what I—"

"Your mistake. She is going at once." Carson's voice and eyes were dangerously cool.

"Who are you to say who will come and go here, Lex Carson?" Grant demanded.

Eager as she was to escape, Lissa lingered. Johnny's face was an angry red. Alexander Carson's had whitened. They looked ready to fly at one another's throats. She must stand by and stop it. Carson said quietly:

"I happen to be the owner."

Lissa had heard the expression, "his jaw dropped" and had thought it a phrase sacred to the use of writers. Now she knew it to be true. Johnny Grant's jaw not only dropped, it waggled.

"So you're the heir. Somehow I never connected the Lex Carson I met last winter in Washington—to whom in an incandescent glow, I confided the flop of my engagements— with Lissa's Aunt Hetty. What an inheritance! In spite of your high-hatting, I'll be noble and hand you a tip. Watch out for Mamma Barclay. She'll tell you what to do till you're ready to bash her over the head. What this country needs most is an advice exterminator. She'll have you roped and laid at the feet of the lovely Cleo before you know where you're at. It's already in the bag. You won't have a chance. You're a richer haul than I was, Gunga Din. Don't glare. I'm going. I'll be back, Lissa. I understand that you want to introduce the heir to his new relatives, so I'll step aside this time, but never again. No hard feelings, Lex, I'm too sorry for you. I'll be seeing you."

Lissa clutched Carson's sleeve.

"Don't follow him, please. He didn't mean anything—by that 'never again'—I mean."

"He meant enough to make you shiver with fear."

She laughed, an unsteady laugh, but it served to relax the muscles in the arm under her hand. She watched Grant's red roadster flame up the road before she removed her fingers.

"That wasn't fear. I never was afraid in my life. When you know me better, you'll discover that I always shiver at the strategic moment. Better than fainting, isn't it? The old time heroine belonged to that school of thought."

His laugh brought the color back under his bronzed skin.

"The fiction viewpoint sticks out in everything you say, doesn't it? Would a man dare love you, or would he suspect that his reaction to your charm would be merely good copy to you? Don't answer. That was a foolish question. Get into your clothes. I'll wait. I'm going to the house with you."

When Lissa rejoined him he was standing at the foot of the garden path, which was gay as an Oriental runner, with red and yellow, pink and blue blossoms of creeping plants set between the stepping stones. Hands in his coat pockets, he looked up at the house on the crest of the slope.

"Display seems to have been the architect's idea when he planned this place. The buildings are so much bigger than a person wants—these days. The upkeep must require an able-bodied fortune and employees by the regiment."

"It does. You haven't seen the half. Beyond the house are cattle barns, poultry houses, fields of grain, and fat silos. Your uncle and then his widow went in for model farming on a large scale, with Simonds, a dour Scot, as foreman. He and Fenton, the butler, are Czars in their departments." And because she knew what a staggering amount of money the upkeep required, Lissa could think of nothing cheering to add. She conquered an absurd urge to smooth out the two little lines between his brows and drew a deep breath:

"Isn't the air sweet?" She picked a bunch of rich blue bachelor buttons. "The first of the season. When the autumn flowers come, I think they are the loveliest and now that June is going, I'm all for tulips and columbines, peonies and iris. There's fickleness for you. Here's a boutonniere."

"Put it in, will you?"

She pulled the stems through the lapel of his coat.

"Aren't they a gorgeous color? The blue of the sea when it's deep and secretive and still. That doesn't mean that you are to stand there and admire them. You really should go to the house and be presented as the heir."

He strolled on beside her evidently in no haste to take possession of his inheritance.

"Plenty of time. Know what I was thinking when I watched you put the flowers in my coat? I was wondering if you were jotting it down as good fiction-copy."

"Jot that down! Old stuff like that? You're not supposing that I never have put flowers in a man's coat before, are you? Am I that unattractive?"

"Fishing, aren't you?"

The laughter in his eyes was reflected in hers.

"I'm not fishing. I'm expanding. For three years I have

been one of America's 53,000,000 rural inhabitants, and now the curtain is rising on a brand new life. Aunt Hetty was jealous if I appeared interested in anyone. Before that, I traveled with my father, who didn't care to have me make acquaintances. You've heard a lot about the richest girl in the world. I'm the poorest girl in the world when it comes to real friends. However, that's behind me. All my yesterdays have been dropped overboard. I intend to be madly, extravagantly, gorgeously gay—if one of my aversion to drinking parties and all that goes with them—can be. I'm a new person even before I'm in a new environment. Reorienting myself, I suppose you'd call it. Do you wonder that I'm excited and trying out a line I haven't had a chance to use?"

"I don't. Go to it. I'll stick around so that you may have me to practice on. All right with you?"

She ignored the question, which was more of a demand, in his smiling eyes.

"Do you know, Mr. Carson—"

"Lex. We are cousins-in-law, aren't we? Why be formal?"

"Lex, it is. I had a feeling when you pulled me into the boat, that you'd be like this."

"Like what?"

"Oh, understanding and good fun and hard as steel if you were crossed. By all the rules of fiction, I ought to hate you violently."

"Why? Because I have inherited this place? That's the reason I didn't tell you at once who I was. I thought you might be bitter because the property came to me. I wanted to make friends with you before you found out."

"Of course I'm not bitter. Why shouldn't your uncle's property go to you?"

"That takes a load from my mind. To return to your fiction complex, you might put Johnny Grant and me in a story and work it out. Do you believe in love at first sight— in fiction—of course?"

"I do, in fiction and in real life. It's the Shakespeare in me. Remember that once there was a boy named Romeo and a girl named Juliet?"

"Yes, I believe in it, too. Take this path slowly. There are a number of questions I want to ask. Your Aunt Hetty wrote that you knew this place from A to Z, were capable of running it, if I needed a manager."

Aunt Hetty had written that? Had she told him also that she had made him trustee of the legacy? No. Had he known it, he would have referred to it.

24

"Your Aunt and I patched up our differences via airmail and became rather fratty on paper," he went on. "She invited me to spend the summer with her."

"Here! At Tarry Farm? Strange she didn't tell me. Were you coming?"

"I was. I was winding up some business so that I could take a vacation for the first time in years, had interested Tod Kent in the location as a summer port for his cruiser, The Sphinx, when the wire came that she had slipped away. Then, I stayed and finished up, and here I am."

"And the whole darn Barclay family, too. We'll be out of your way as soon as possible. Tomorrow I'll turn my books over to you and—"

"What's the rush? The cottages are leased?"

"All three."

"Are they much care?"

"Not if we have plenty of rain. Wells supply the water. Tenants come from the city where water is inexhaustible and drain them usually the first month. If we have a dry summer, I have an attack of water on the brain. Stand here with your back to Tarry Farm, and you can see the cottages on the shore. The Treasure Chest is the brown shingled house at your right. At your left is Red Chimneys—that's my favorite—and beyond on a point near the island, Pirates' Den. Observe that each house has a motorboat moored in the offing. That is included in the rent. The cottages were Aunt Hetty's pride and she furnished them luxuriously even to books and boats. The tenants arrived at Red Chimneys a week ago."

"Are they husband and wife?"

"No, brother and sister, Ralph and Sidonie Packard. Romantic name that last, isn't it? Their references—Aunt Hetty was a stickler for references, informed us that Mr. Packard wanted a place in which he could be quiet and work. The inference was that he was a writer. Wouldn't it be grand if he would give me points?"

"If your eyes shine much more at the possibility, they'll explode the way the stars do. I recommended the place to the Millards who have taken one of the cottages. They are my friends. They have a delicate boy and I remembered what Maine air did for me when, as a kid, I came to visit Uncle Alexander after scarlet fever, his first wife was alive then. They lost two little girls, but you'd never know it from Madge, the mother, who is, I think, the bravest woman in the world. Jack, her husband, is a forester—when he works at it. He has a bit too much money to make his mark in

25

his profession. If ever you've been cynical about marriage you'll find your faith restored when you see them together Let me take you there to call, will you?"

"I will. G-Man stole their bathing suits this morning I would like your moral support when I make my apologies.'

"Mr. Adams is coming here tomorrow with the trustees final accounting. What you have told me about the cottages will help me appear intelligent. Yearly reports on the estate have been submitted to me so I know how the principal has dwindled."

"Have you seen Aunt Hetty's will?"

"No. That doesn't affect me."

"Doesn't it? Wait till you hear it, you'll be surprised."

"All right, let's skip that, I'll be surprised. Tell me about the other tenants. When do they come?"

"Your friends, the Millards, who have hired the Treasure Chest, came yesterday, and Major Fane takes possession of Pirates' Den on Saturday."

"What sort of Major?"

"An army officer on sick leave with two men servants. From what Aunt Hetty told me, I judge he is about fifty."

"Did she hobnob with the tenants?"

"Aunt Hetty hobnob! I forgot, you didn't know her, did you? She called upon them after their arrival, invited them to a lobster-bake during Fair week and let it go at that."

"Lobsters! The mere word makes me ravenous. Are there many about here?"

"Those lobster-trap floats bobbing in the cove are the answer."

"Do they belong to Tarry Farm?"

"No. To Captain Ozias—commonly called Ozy—who is fisherman extraordinary, as well as errand man and sheriff, to the community. Who is that crossing the terrace? He's waving his hand."

Lex Carson waved in return. Explained to Lissa:

"That's Tod Kent. As I told you, I came in on his cruiser. He is my best friend. He has more money than he can spend, added to which he has a public service complex. At present, he's engaged in research—for the Government. That explains the radio-control of a motorboat experiment."

"Research! For the Government in our harbor! How exciting. Tarry Farm has been a sort of Sleepy Hollow. Now it has suddenly come wide awake."

Eagerly Lissa appraised the man as he drew near. He was short, heavy, ruddy. His eyes were greenish hazel, his hair was red and laid close to his scalp in tight curls. His nose was retrousse to a degree, a comic-strip nose. Carson laid a hand on his shoulder:

"Miss Barclay, my friend, Tod Kent."

Kent's smile was of the ear-to-ear variety. Generous, heart-warming.

"Where did you find Lex, Miss Barclay? He was to meet me at the house above at four-thirty. I've been boring two ladies in its living-room ever since. Who hit you?"

His shocked question sent Lissa's fingers to the bruise on her forehead. She flinched. She smiled at the ruddy-faced man. She liked him, liked him immensely. This seemed to be her day for taking instant likes. Was it because she was on the threshold of a brand new life, looking for adventure? She shook her head and laughed:

"Don't look so accusingly at your friend, Mr. Kent, he didn't hit me. My outboard cracked up. Now that you have met my stepmother and sister, won't you present Lex to them?"

"Where are you going?" Carson demanded.

"To Red Chimneys to welcome the tenants and inquire if everything is satisfactory. I sent Fenton the day they arrived. I couldn't leave my aunt. Won't you both dine with us? You needn't change."

"Oh, I say, don't leave us," Tod Kent implored boyishly.

"We'll wait for her here. She can't shake us like that. Don't be long, Lissa, or we'll come after you," Lex Carson warned.

The two men watched her as she ran through cool green shadows under the trees. She turned and waved to them before she disappeared from their sight. Tod Kent drew a long breath.

"That girl has a warmth and fire and sparkle that warmed my old bones to the marrow. The French call it *joie de vivre*, don't they? Did you inherit her with the property, Lex?"

"No."

Carson's reply was curt. Hands in his pockets he looked up at the house on the crest of the slope, let his eyes travel along the shore.

"I'm staggered at the extent of this place, Tod. Feel as if the Empire State Building had toppled over on my shoulders."

"It is big. Does that island go with it?"

"No. Mrs. Hetty Carson bought it when the Government sold it and willed it to her niece." He lowered his voice. "Lissa told me that early this morning she thought she saw a flash from the lighthouse."

"Is the lamp working?" There was a hint of excitement in the question.

"No. Hasn't been for three years, but, a small electric torch inserted in that lens would throw a good-sized beam."

Kent's eyes bulged.

"Jiminy, we haven't picked up a loose-end here miles from where we expected to find one, have we? There must be a catch in it somewhere."

"Sure there's a catch. Lissa had been asleep and doubtless imagined she saw the flash. Loose-ends are not picked up so easily." Carson's brows drew together as he looked at the island. "Just the same, fella, we'll keep an eye on that light."

vi

WHIP-POOR-WILL! Whip-poor-will! Whip-poor-will!

The bird's call drifted from among the trees. Lissa loved it, it never depressed her. Some of the villagers thought it unlucky, had she heard it before she went on the water, they would have shaken their heads and insisted that it had foreshadowed the crack-up of the flying outboard. Of course it hadn't. There would be just as much sense in thinking it meant good fortune. That it had foreshadowed meeting Lex Carson.

She stopped running and walked as she visualized the events of the afternoon. Old Adams as he had read the will; the crash of the two boats; Alexander Carson's face as he had lifted her from the water; Johnny Grant vaulting the boathouse rail. Her heart had pounded in her throat when he appeared so suddenly. Was it possible that she was such a poor-spirited creature that she still loved him after his faithlessness?

She reached the question and Red Chimneys at the same moment. Admiration for the house which was a smaller model of the mansion above wiped Johnny Grant from her mind as effectively as a wet sponge erased chalk marks from a blackboard. Its two chimneys were the exact shade of the scarlet geraniums in the window-boxes. Lawns like green velvet surrounded it, a pine, twisted in the best Japanese manner, hung over the boulders which buttressed a sandy shore, a glassed-in porch extended almost to a pier which jutted into the water.

What were the tenants like, she wondered, as she had wondered each time her aunt had signed a new lease. Season after season they had come and gone in the three cottages without leaving the slightest impress on the lives of the occupants of the big house above them. Each year she had hoped that someone really interesting would come, someone who would provide a plot for a story.

She pressed the bell beside the wide open door.

"Help! Help!"

A woman's voice! "It can't be real! It's my plot fixation," Lissa thought, and dashed into the house.

"I'm awake," she told herself, in the instant she paused on the threshold of the chintz-hung living room. The flames licking the muslins at the window were real; the man beating at them with his hands was real, so was the woman shrinking against the book shelves.

"Why don't you help, idiot?" Lissa fumed mentally in the split second it took her to cross the room.

"Stand back!" she warned the man who was still beating at the burning muslins. "You can't put it out that way. Grab that small rug!"

She yanked at an untouched side of the curtain. It came down rod and all, a blazing mass on the floor. She snatched the rug from the man's hand and covered it.

"Now, if you'll stop being jittery, Miss Packard, and bring those two hand grenades from the hall, all danger will be over," she said to the woman.

"Stay where you are, I'll get them, Sidonie," the man ordered. Even in the excitement, Lissa noted his voice, remembered that Ozy had compared it to oil in smoothness.

"Hundred percent helpmate, aren't you, my girl?" she thought as the woman collapsed in a big chair and covered her face with her hands. She snatched the grenade from the man who seemed not to know what to do with it and flung it on the smoking mass. She administered another and watched the result.

"That settles that. You'll find those grenades at strategic points all over the house, Mr. Packard," she explained, the woman was too stupid to bother with. "Next time, get busy with those first, and save your hands. I'm the—the representative of your landla—lord."

Her smile stiffened as she met his eyes. She had seen the expression once before in the eyes of a suffering dog. Her glance dropped to his short, thickset hands. She shut her teeth on her lips to steady them. She spoke to the woman huddled in the chair.

"Get some oil, olive oil if you haven't anything else, and some gauze, and take care of your brother's fingers."

The huddled figure shuddered.

"I can't, it will make me faint to look at them."

"Then bring me the first aid kit in the large dressing room. Quick!"

Lissa waited until the woman had left the room before she suggested:

"You'd better sit down, Mr. Packard. First though, let's get that coat off. Hold out your arm."

Carefully she slipped a sleeve over one burned hand, then the other. She appraised the tailored clothes and the elaborate monogram on the blue shirt sleeve. Evidently this author earned enough to have plenty of jam with his bread and butter, no park bench for him. His teeth were set hard in his lips. He shut his eyes as he sank into a chair. Lissa filled a glass with water from a carafe in the dining room, came back, knelt beside him and held it to his lips.

"Drink this. No? Don't you like water? Hold your hands up, they won't smart quite so much. Ooch! It got every finger, didn't it? You'll have to let someone else do your typing, or perhaps you are one of those geniuses who talks his stories into a dictaphone?" she suggested, in the hope that the mention of his work might take his mind from his smarting fingers.

He opened his eyes, dark with suffering. There was something else in them too, something that flickered.

"My stories?"

"Yes. Aunt Hetty and I imagined you were a writer because you wanted quiet and privacy. Perhaps you're not. Perhaps—"

"But—I am a writer. You have been so kind—why—" he gritted his teeth, as if shutting back a groan, closed and opened his eyes before he added—"shouldn't you know? I'll be glad if you won't broadcast the fact—you've no idea how I'm bothered with autograph hunters. I hope to bury myself here and escape them."

Whip-poor-will! Whip-poor-will! Whip-poor-will! The sound drifted through the open window. Ralph Packard swore under his breath.

"There's that infernal bird again. It's been round here every night since we came. I counted twenty-five calls the last time. How my fingers burn!" He dropped his head back and clenched his teeth.

His sister entered the room followed by a houseman in a white coat. He was striking-looking in a dark Italian-bandit way, his eyes were close-set, one cheek was scarred. She was calmer, she even smiled.

"I'm sorry I lost my head, Miss Barclay. Fire always terrifies me. We'll take care of him now. Nino is an expert in accidents."

"He needs to be if he is traveling round with you," Lissa thought as she rose from her knees.

"Then I'll go." She smiled at Ralph Packard who was looking up with that curious blend of pain and something else in his eyes. Could it be mockery? "Don't trust those hands to home talent, Mr. Packard. Better have a physician look at them. There is an excellent one in the village. Please don't rise. I'm going. If I can help in any way, phone me, Miss Packard. Good-afternoon."

As she walked slowly through the orchard and up the flower-bordered path which climbed toward the house, she visualized the room she had left. At the time she had been too excited to notice details but now the slim figure of the woman in a colorful printed chiffon gown standing against a background of books came back to her. Not too young, late twenties, perhaps. Pretty, strikingly pretty. Her beautiful coifed hair was so blonde that it was silvery; her eyes were deep blue, her hands which had been constantly in motion, flashed with jewels. Her brother's hair was darker, she couldn't tell much about his face, except that his eyes were enormous and black as midnight.

He had seemed surprised when she had mentioned his stories. Had she not been interested in creative writing herself, she wouldn't have divined from the letter of application for the cottage, that an author was seeking a place in which to work. He must be well-known to have autograph hunters on his trail. Packard. The name didn't click in connection with fiction, biography or science. Perhaps he had assumed it as a disguise or perhaps he used it as a *nom de plume*. No. The cheque for payment of rent in advance had been signed Ralph Packard. It must be his real name. He might be publishing under another. He was extremely good looking perhaps in the early forties. She visualized again the living room at Red Chimneys, the Italian servant with the close-set eyes and scar across one cheek. She said aloud;

"I'd hate to meet you in the dark, Nino. I'll bet you'd cheat yourself at solitaire, if a houseman plays solitaire."

Quite suddenly her knees threatened to fold up. Her nerves shivered. Coming on top of the boat crash, the burning curtains had been a shock. She sat down quickly on one of the wrought-iron seats.

Time had galloped since she left the house for what had proved to be a spill in the flying outboard. From behind a dusky hill the sun was flinging up streamers of gorgeous lemon, pink and lavender. The sky was pale apple green where yellow blended with the blue. Fluffs of cloud were fringed with Roman gold. The color magician had transmuted the islands in the harbor to chunks of amethyst, and set them in a sapphire sea. Against one of them the brass trimmings of the cruiser gleamed blood-red. The lighthouse was rosy pink, its great glass eye shimmered like a plaque of burnished copper. The ocean breeze was crisp with brine from the choppy water of the bay. What a glorious world.

"I was about to organize a search-party for you," said Alexander Carson behind her. "What's happened? You're white."

Color and calm returned together. Lissa rose.

"I was waiting to get my balance after another hectic adventure. This is proving to be just one of those days, that's all. G-Man started the ball rolling merrily by stealing bathing-suits; the cat Blessed Evented—there were four kittens—in the cook's best hat and she says she'll be blowed if she'll stay in such a house; Mr. Adams read Aunt Hetty's will—its contents set my stepmother and sister in a rage. You saw the spill in the outboard, and to add the last perfect dramatic touch, there's been an accident at Red Chimneys. Where did you come from? Haven't you been to the house?"

"I told you we would wait for you. I've been smoking and thinking under the trees. Tod Kent has gone to the cruiser, he'll be back. We've accepted your invitation to dinner. What kept you so long? What did you mean by another hectic adventure? What was the accident?"

I would hate to be on the witness-stand being cross-examined by you, Lissa thought, as she met his intent eyes. She told him what had happened at Red Chimneys.

"You touched those blazing curtains! You need a guardian."

"I have one—I forgot. You don't know yet, do you?"

"To what are you referring? Do you always speak in conundrums?"

"No, I speak in facts. To return to the blazing curtains. What else could I do? The man was beating at them, you should have seen his hands—his finger-prints are changed for all time, and his fool sister—pretty but stooge variety—was shrieking her head off without trying to help. I've seen burning muslins before and I knew that the curtain rod came down easily."

"Let me look!" He caught her hands gently and turned them palms up. "No burns? Are you sure?"

"Sure. Total casualty for me, a few scorched spots on my frock. I'll have time to change before dinner. It will save cross-examination from the family. The less said about the affair at Red Chimneys the better."

"Agreed. I'll drop in there on my way to the boat this evening and inquire if I can help. The man beat at the curtains? Hadn't much thought for his hands, had he? What did you say the name was?"

"Packard, Mr. and Miss Packard. They are from the middle west. Apparently the whip-poor-will is unknown there. Mr. Packard's nerves were upset by his accident and the whip-poor-will's call shot them to pieces."

"Packard. I know some people by that name. Whom did they give as references?"

"I can't tell without looking up the correspondence. They are on the crest of the social wave if one is to believe Fenton. He approved of them, had a friend who worked for them."

"Admire that butler a lot, don't you?"

"As a servant, he's perfect, as a man I don't like him. I can't explain why. Except for a week-end off every month, he has remained on his job during the three years he has been here. Sometimes I've wondered if he were the younger son of a titled English family, working where he was unknown, to pile up a little fortune. His wages have been spectacularly high. Aunt Hetty liked him, he would talk with her about world affairs. I suspect he's something of a student. These last few months I was up a great deal with my aunt at night. I could see his lighted window in the ell from her balcony. Evidently he reads until very late. After he decided to stay, he told Aunt Hetty that he would like to send for his books and asked if he might have some cheap shelves built into his room. She was so glad to have him contented, she would have built a cottage for him had he asked for it."

"Let's hope the model Fenton approves of me. I'll be needing him."

He followed her across the brick terrace, through the open French window to the library.

"Mother Barclay, Cleo, this is Alexander Carson."

In the instant of surprised silence, which followed her announcement, Lissa glanced at the portrait above the mantel. No wonder she had thought she had seen Alexander Carson before. He was a young edition of his uncle.

Mrs. Barclay fluttered forward and welcomed him effusively. She presented her daughter.

Lissa burned with resentment as Cleo laid her hand in his and looked up at him. Sure of her charm, wasn't she? It didn't help that the bruise on her own forehead throbbed intolerably and reminded her that she must look as if she had been in a brawl.

"We've been waiting to turn this charming place over to you, Cousin Alexander," Mrs. Barclay purred, "and to tell you of a few things that must be done. We are packed and ready to go."

"But you mustn't think of leaving," Carson protested. "I'm counting upon you all to stay a month at least. I shall need you to show me the ropes."

Lissa resisted an almost irresistible urge to protest. He had invited them to stay a month! He'd been bowled over by his first look at Cleo, had he? He could have her. As for herself, she would rush through the inventory of the things in the house her aunt had bequeathed to her, and be off on her own adventure in living.

Carson stopped her as she reached the door.

"Don't forget our date," he reminded in a low voice.

"What date?" she asked in honest surprise.

"Have you forgotten so soon that you and I are to take formal possession of your island and the lighthouse? Take care of that bruise," he advised before he turned back into the room.

vii

SEATED on a corner of the flat desk in the oak paneled room which passed as the residence office at Tarry Farm, Alexander Carson frowned thoughtfully. Sunlight, which filtered through the slits of a Venetian blind, barred his tan slacks with gold, and striped the old-fashioned black frock coat of the thin bald-headed man with bushy gray mustache, who sat stiff and erect in a chair opposite. Carson tapped the paper in his hand.

"If this statement is correct, Mr. Adams, and of course it is, something tells me I'm in for a trimming!"

Adams fitted his fingertips together and nodded sombrely.

"I tried to make you understand the situation, Alexander."

"I'm not blaming you, sir. You suggested times enough that

I come here and make friends with my uncle's widow but it seemed like snooping round the property which, eventually, was to come to me. If my uncle had wanted me to know about the estate, he would have made me a trustee, wouldn't he?"

"You were too young for that at the time he died. Who would have thought when he made his will, that many of his gilt-edge investments would be wiped off the slate and that the income from others would be halved and halved again? We lawyers have learned something. We draw wills in terms of percentages now. We could have kept the head of the estate above water had it not been for the provision in the will that the income paid to the widow was to be kept up to a certain amount even if part of the principal was used."

"Did you speak to Mrs. Hetty Carson about it? With her consent you could have appealed to the Court to have her income reduced sufficiently to save mortgaging the cottages and city real estate."

"When we raised those loans, we thought things would come back. Instead firms folded up and left us holding leases and empty offices, and now the banks are getting restless. Perhaps you know what that means?"

"Know! I'll say I know! Didn't my father lose everything? He warned me before he died;

" 'Keep out of debt, Lex. Debt wrecks more homes than infidelity. Don't borrow. You won't need to in your profession, business is different. If you haven't money to pay for what you want, don't buy it.' I have remembered his warning and now it looks as if I'd be buried under debts not of my incurring."

"Who's rapping?" Adams asked impatiently.

Carson opened the door. A man stepped forward. A gaunt, gangling man, whose eyebrows, arched like the back of an angry cat, above eyes like those in a faded daguerreotype, contributed an expression of perpetual surprise to a face set between big ears which were full of spirals of black hair. He twirled a pencil on the end of a cable of gold chain, as he explained;

"I'm Simonds, the foreman. My wife and I came to welcome you to Tarry Farm, Mr. Carson."

His tone was aggressive, he spoke with a strong Scotch burr. One ugly-looking hand gripped the shoulder of a wisp of a woman in a blue and white print dress, and drew her forward. She tipped her head at a birdlike angle and looked up with eyes as black as her hair.

"Lem and I hope you'll be very happy in this beautiful home, sir," she said.

"Thank you, Mrs. Simonds," Carson responded cordially. "I'm new to everything here, and I shall rely upon you and your husband to show me the ropes."

She opened her lips to answer but Simonds forestalled her.

"There's nothing on this place I don't know all about," he assured pompously. "I run the stock and the fields and boss the men in all departments. Come along, Marty. Mr. Adams is here on business. We mustn't interrupt." He scowled in the direction of the trustee. "Run down to my office whenever you want information, Mr. Carson. You may find me and you may not. I'm a very busy man. Good morning."

He pushed his wife ahead of him into the hall and closed the door behind him. Carson looked at the door and then at Adams.

"He asked me to 'run down' to his office. Slightly swelled about the head, isn't he? He didn't look at you as if he loved you, sir."

"He doesn't. Hates me like poison. I tried to get Hetty Carson to cut his pay—it's ridiculously high—and of course she told him. He's picked up the share-the-wealth bug. He's Scotch and I'll bet he has the first dollar he ever earned. He's a crack-a-jack foreman, though."

"I liked his wife."

"Marty Simonds is an angel from heaven, a peppery angel, I guess some of them come that way. She must lead a drab life with him. One of the great unsolved mysteries of the world is, why some women marry some men and vice versa.

"Let's get back to business. Simonds, like the poor, will be with you always. I want to return to Boston as soon as possible. The financial condition of the estate is a tough break for you, boy. I talked with Hetty Carson two years ago, then again last year, stated conditions in the hope that she would agree to a reduction of her income, but, nothing doing. Why should she give up a cent to be saved for the man who was to inherit after her, she argued. She kept on buying blooded stock at high and selling at new lows. I felt that Fenton, the butler, egged her on. She wanted—and needed at the rate she lived—every dollar the will awarded her."

"And she got it." Carson ran his eyes down the column of figures. "It was some income. She closed her town house and lived here for the last three years. I realize that Tarry Farm is an expensive place to run but she couldn't have spent all that money on it."

"She didn't, not quite all. She put some of it into a trust fund for her brother's daughter, Melissa Barclay, not an iron-bound trust fund, there is a provision that the girl may draw

36

from it if the trustee agrees and who do you think was named trustee?"

"You, I hope."

"No, you."

"I! I? But, Hetty Carson didn't know me!"

"She thought she did. She told me that she had invited you here for the summer, said she wanted to see the man who would control her husband's fortune. She told me also that from your letters she judged you would be hard-boiled enough to combat Lissa's stepmother and half-sister, who, she was sure, would begin to chisel at the girl's income to say nothing of the jewels—she can't sell or give them away without your consent—as soon as they were hers. She knew, because they were everlastingly appealing to her for money with which to pay overdue bills."

"I shan't accept the trusteeship."

"Think it over. The money left to Lissa was taken out of the property, if you refuse to serve she may think you begrudge it to her. She earned it. She lived here for three years, managed the cottages, ran this great house, the servants like her. Hetty Carson was not a comfortable person with whom to live. She kicked up a row if Lissa made friends, and I guess it was simpler for her not to make them, though she did insist upon outdoor exercise and playing the organ at the little church in the village, but she never invited young people here."

"What a tough life for a girl like that."

"She could take it if anyone could. She has so many resources within herself. Life never can lick her. These last few months have been a terrific strain on her affection and emotions. In spite of weakness and suffering, Hetty Carson clung to life and to her niece. Lissa had all the last arrangements to make. I wouldn't be surprised if she went to pieces from reaction."

Carson looked at the papers in his hand but he was seeing a girl in a boat valiantly fighting back tears. Only sheer grit had kept her from going to pieces then. He said quickly;

"Of course I don't begrudge the money. How much is the legacy?"

"It will give her a little over one thousand dollars a year. Do you realize how much principal you have to get together nowadays to be sure of that income?"

"I do. I realize also that the income that comes to me from the estate won't carry the business property and this place. Well, I can sell it."

Adams' sombre eyes retreated into their caverns till they looked like the eyes of a prairie-dog peering from his hole.

"I hope you can, my boy, I hope you can. Real estate is coming back, but people aren't buying places the size of Tarry Farm, they cost too much to carry. In years to come this will be looked back upon as the tax-age."

"What can I do with it? I have a good income from my practice and a small one from a trust fund left by my grandfather. Can't touch the principal for five years, till I'm forty. There's no mortgage on this house. If I can't sell it, I'll scrap it. I will not break my back carrying a burden of debt. Lucky I had planned to take this summer off for a vacation, the first of any length since I opened my office. Vacation! Sounds like a joke. How soon will I have a free hand in managing the estate? I'm not familiar with Maine law."

"I'm filing the necessary papers now. The property comes at once to you. You can get busy looking things over and cutting expenses. I've asked Lissa to make an inventory of the personal property left to her. When she has it ready, we'll have an appraisal. She'll have a big tax to pay on the jewels."

"Where are they?"

"In a bank in Boston. I advise you to get rid of the blooded stock. That will cut down outside. This house swarms with servants. You can save there as soon as Mrs. Barclay and her daughters go."

Carson put his hands hard into his pockets.

"But, they are not going. In a lavish 'I'm the heir' gesture, I invited them to be my guests for a month."

"For the love of heaven, why? You don't like that whiny woman and her yellow-haired daughter, do you?"

"Not especially—but I like her stepdaughter; that doesn't mean that I shall accept the trusteeship. I couldn't keep one here without the others, could I?"

Adams hunched his thin shoulders in relief.

"You like Lissa? That's good news. You'll feel differently about the trusteeship when you know her better. She knew I was troubled about expenses here. I told her that these were uncertain times—as if that bright girl didn't know—and that perhaps she could persuade her aunt to go a little slow in spending."

"What effect did that have?"

"None, except that Hetty Carson immediately had living room and dining-room at the Treasure Chest done over, Wedgewood, I believe she called it, and paid an exorbitant price for a Holstein cow. She went in for Holsteins after her husband died because their black and white was in keeping with her mourning clothes. The expenses of running this place outside the house didn't come out of her personal income—the will provided that it was to be kept up as she wished it to be. The trustees had no power to hold her down."

"What a cockeyed will. Why appoint trustees? Why didn't her husband leave everything to her?"

"We've been useful in handling investments. I don't wonder you're bitter, Alexander. You're the son of my old friend and many a night I've walked the floor thinking of the raw deal that would be handed you."

Carson laid his arm about the thin shoulders.

"I'll do the walking now. I can take it. As you know, my mother died when I was a boy and I began young to accept responsibilities, to face problems and work out decisions. Better go off on vacation as soon as you get the papers through. Where are you staying?"

"At the Inn in the County Seat to be near the Court House. I'll be going. Sorry you've had so many problems dropped on your shoulders, Alexander. Phone me if you have questions to ask, though Lissa Barclay can give you more details about running the place than I can."

"I asked her to come here. She'll be along any minute now. Is your car in the drive? I'll come out with you."

He stood on the steps until Adams' sedan passed between the ornate iron gates which opened on the highway. Suppose he had told the old man that business problems were not the only ones that had been dropped on his shoulders, that he had been drafted by the Treasury Department to find and deliver a public enemy, who, it was suspected, was operating somewhere in the state? He had specialized in the legal science of criminology, but he'd never practiced the science of detection. The head of the Department knew that and had assigned him to the job. It was up to him to make good. He didn't like a man-hunt. But, the Government had organized a war against crime and one didn't refuse to serve one's country in time of war.

Grand day, it made anything seem possible of achievement, he thought, as he looked at the gold-edged hills, mere purple cut-outs, as they were reflected in a sparkling ultramarine sea. He had forgotten that the sky could be so luminous. The atmosphere shimmered.

As he returned slowly to the room he had left, he thought of his inheritance, and he thought of the burden it might prove to carry. He straightened his shoulders. If it did prove a burden, he would sell it, if he couldn't sell it he could pull down every building on this place—that wasn't mortgaged —and save taxes. It was being done—meanwhile there was a small army of employees to be paid.

Lissa turned from the window as he entered the room. He

39

closed the door and stood for an instant watching her.

Yesterday when her hair was wet, I didn't realize that it had so much gold in it, nor that it was so satin soft, nor that she walked straight into my heart when she looked up at me from the water, he thought. Perhaps it was her eyelashes, they're so long and curling at the tips and they sweep up so when she laughs, perhaps it was her mouth, it's such a gallant mouth, its lips are so naturally red and tipped-up at the corners and that dimple—oh well, what's the use in trying to explain myself to myself? "Fire and warmth." You said it, Tod. She had been lovely in white but there was something about the lilac cotton frock she was wearing that deepened the velvety brown of her eyes and accentuated the creamy delicacy of her skin. He asked;

"How is the poorest girl in the world after her ducking?"

"Not so poor, thank you. I'm sorry you remembered my sob-sisterish remark."

"Something tells me that I shall remember all your remarks. Why didn't you come to the library after dinner last night? I sent Fenton up twice with messages."

"He delivered them. I devoted my evening to denaturing the color of that." She pushed back her hair and revealed the bruise on her forehead. "It isn't quite such a lively purple as it was. I'll get by without the family knowing of my spill, unless you told them about it."

"Just a minute! Do I look like a person who goes about telling everything he knows?"

He loved her laugh. It was low with a trill running through it.

"On the contrary, you look like a person who would stand up under several third degrees without telling All."

She crossed to a filing cabinet, removed papers and laid them on the desk.

"Here are the leases and references for the tenants of the three cottages. Before you look them over, I want you to understand that I did not know that Aunt Hetty was gouging from your estate to leave that trust fund for me, nor that she was loading the care of the legacy on your shoulders. I knew she refused to take a cut in income—but I didn't know why. You, a lawyer, must know how to sidestep that trusteeship. Now you understand why I said that according to all fiction rules, I should hate you violently. In novels wards always fight with guardians."

"Sometimes they love them."

"I'm beginning to think you have a love complex. Seriously, if you need that money to help carry the property, you are to take it—understand?"

40

"I'm surprised, Miss Barclay, that you would make the unethical suggestion that a trustee use a ward's property."

"Don't laugh, it isn't a joking matter. But you won't be my trustee!"

"Oh, yes I will." When had he decided that, he asked himself?

"I don't need you. I've handled the small property my father left me. I'm twenty-five years old!"

"I've known women over that advanced age who have invested principal in Treasure Hunts and mines that existed only on paper. I'll stick. I won't interfere with you—unless you want to do something crazy. Do you need money?"

"No, and please don't give me any until after I leave here. You could say, couldn't you, that you would make no payments to me until the estate is settled? Why are you frowning? Is that another unethical suggestion?"

Carson drew his hand across his forehead. He had been wondering if she thought her stepmother and sister would begin to draw upon her to help pay overdue bills. Aloud he said;

"Have I smoothed out the frown? Don't worry. I'll hold the money. Let's skip the trusteeship. Tell me about the tenants."

"I've told you of the Packards. You know the Millards, so that leaves Major Fane who moves into Pirates' Den Saturday. The advance of half the season's rents has been paid. We got better prices than for several years. I read somewhere that it was getting to be a landlord's market instead of a renter's."

"Sit down, please, while I look over the leases."

He seated himself at the desk opposite her. Sounds from the outside world broke the stillness of the room; the monotonous drilling of a woodpecker on a nearby tree, the faint, far moan of a bell-buoy, the wail of a distant motor horn. A gay little peony-scented breeze danced in through the open window and was gone. Paper crackled as he examined leases. He frowned at a sheet of figures.

"The cottages are not paying for themselves."

Lissa leaned forward and crossed her arms on the desk.

"Paying! They are eating themselves up. Between taxes and repairs, interest, improvements upon which prospective tenants insist and their financial sob-story about what they can't afford for rent, those three houses are fast getting to be a liability. The Packards are the first applicants in three years who didn't ask for a reduction in rent."

"Did they come across with the advance promptly?"

"Yes. That reminds me. Did you call at Red Chimneys last night?"

41

"Tod and I stopped on our way to the boat. The Italian servant said that the doctor had been there and had given 'the boss' something to quiet him and that Miss Packard, much upset from the shock, had gone to bed."

"It's just too bad about that woman. She's really a girl, I suppose, though to me she seemed as if she had known the world and its ways for years. I'll wager she's concerned only in the spoils of her brother's work, not in the work itself."

"Why are you so interested in those two, Lissa? You didn't fall in love with the man, did you? You said you believed in love at first sight."

Her big, brown eyes were turbulent pools as she denied;

"Fall in love! I'm off falling in love forever. I'm now one of those persons who has to trust a lot to love a little. I told you yesterday that I suspected he was a writer. I thought if I were a perfect lady and laid offerings of fresh eggs and flowers at his sister's feet, he might answer a few How-to-be-an-author questions."

"Not above bribery, are you?"

"You would make a joke of it. Now I shan't need him."

"Why won't you need him?"

"Because I'm checking out at the end of the week."

viii

CARSON sprang to his feet and as suddenly returned to his seat.

"Why the Jack-in-the-box act?" Lissa inquired flippantly.

"Surprise, just surprise that you should think of deserting the ship. You can't leave Tarry Farm. I need you."

"Need me! You have invited my stepmother and sister to stay, haven't you? You don't know them or you wouldn't think you needed anyone else."

"They know nothing of the management of the estate. You do. You can help me. Give me this summer. One summer. Is that much to ask? If you are thinking of money—"

"I am. Know anyone who isn't these days? I'm thinking of other things, too. I have my living to earn while I am learning to write. Aunt Hetty paid me a small salary—"

"I'll double it."

"Double it! What would you want me to do to earn that money?"

"Just what you have been doing. Look after the cottages and the tenants, manage this house besides showing me where to cut expenses. If you will do that, I can concentrate on the business property. The fortune left by my uncle has been run ragged. I mean to devote what income there is to paying off the mortgages on the real estate."

"Same old battle-cry, Balance the budget. And you talk of doubling my salary! I'll stay on two conditions. First, the same salary Aunt Hetty paid, second, your promise that if you need it to carry the estate, you will use some of the money she left me."

"I will not."

"Then I'll not stay after this week."

"Lissa, don't be stubborn."

"Stubborn? I'm surprised that you are so out-of-date. The modern term is, 'rugged individualism.' Aunt Hetty takes money from you and hands it to me. I give it back when you need it. That seems logical to me."

"But I won't need it."

"Wait till you've lived here a week, you won't be so sure. Do I stay?"

"What a bargainer! Sort of a female Shylock, aren't you? I will not use it. You can't go," he announced triumphantly. "You'll have to stay until the property your aunt left you has been appraised. You and I must go to Boston to check up on the jewels at the bank—"

"They're not in the bank," Lissa whispered.

"Not in the bank! Where are they?" His voice was low as hers.

She looked at doors and windows before she glanced at the ceiling.

"Upstairs?" he demanded incredulously. "All of them?" She nodded. "How long have they been there?"

"Two weeks. Aunt Hetty wanted the thrill of handling them, and had them sent here."

"What an insane thing to do! Are they in your aunt's room?"

"No. In mine."

"Girl, you're crazy! I'll move my traps from the cruiser to this house this afternoon. As soon as the coast is clear after I arrive, give me the jewels. It isn't safe for you to have them. Does anyone know they are in the house?"

"No, unless Fenton suspected when an armed expressman brought them in."

"Nicely advertised, I'd say. The jewels are another reason

why you must stand by. We've got to guard them until I can get away from here. You'll stay, won't you?"

"If I can really help."

"Lissa, you're adorable."

"That's what Johnny Grant says. Where were we when you went off at a tangent about the jewels?"

"We were about to cut expenses," Carson answered drily. "Does Johnny converse with you about that, too?"

"You're positively motion-picturish when you scowl." She nodded toward the paper he held. "First question?"

"This lists fifteen men outside the house on the pay roll. Do we need so many?"

"Yes, if the place is to be kept up as it is at present. The men are not only farmers, there are painters and carpenters among them, two take care of the boats and boathouses. You've no idea how much care Tarry Farm requires."

"Light is beginning to seep through. I'll look over things carefully before I begin to cut. That's where you can be a tremendous help. I suppose you know all the families, how many dependents the workers have and where the cuts will hurt least?"

"I do and what I don't know Marty Simonds will tell me. She is the wife of the foreman. She's a dear!"

"I agree with you. Wish I could say as much for her husband. They dropped in on me this morning."

"You didn't like Lem?"

"That's expressing it too mildly. I had an almost uncontrollable urge to punch his head. Make a list of the employees, will you? Use this room as usual for your office. I'll make my headquarters in the sports room, that door leads to it, doesn't it? When you are writing, hang out a sign SILENCE the way they do in the libraries and I'll never intrude. I happen to know an editor, or two—"

There was suggestion in his laughing pause.

"Who is bribing now?" Lissa accused. "I don't write here. I've had a desk in the lighthouse for the last year."

"Don't work there alone. It isn't safe—"

A whistle low and clear drifted in through the open window on a blossom scented breeze. A fragment of a gay little tune, twice repeated.

"Who is that?" Carson demanded, though he had known the moment his eyes met hers, big and brown and startled.

"It's Johnny."

"Johnny again! For whom is he whistling?"

She looked up from beneath long lashes and laughed.

"Something tells me it's for me."

A red-hot wave of anger swept him.

"Tell that playboy to keep away from my secretary or there'll be a dead body round here." He laughed to offset the husky break in his voice—"Guess whose?"

"But even a secretary should have some hours off."

"Sure. How about taking possession of the island—don't listen to that whistle—this afternoon?"

"Perfect! At sundown? It will seem so much more romantic then. But what will we do for a flag? The pennant is ruined."

"I'll get one in the village. Let's take a picnic supper and watch the moon rise."

"We'd have to stay until nearly midnight for that. Yesterday morning the man in the moon had but one eye."

"What were you doing up so late?"

"Up so early, you mean. I couldn't sleep so I snuggled into a chair on my balcony and tried to think things out."

"Was that when you saw the light flash?"

"When I imagined I saw it flash. We'll go to the island by water. The bar road will be clear but I love a boat. I'll be at the pier at six with the supper and—"

"What do you mean—and?"

"You really should cure yourself of that habit of pouncing."

"I'm sorry. I thought you might be planning to bring a third party and I would hate that like the dickens. Don't forget that you are to be in the offing when I arrive bag and baggage this afternoon. After I've taken care of the jewels, let's stop at the Millards and say 'Welcome to our city,' will you?"

"I'd love it. I'll meet you there. I'm not likely to have a follower. Watch your step, or you'll have one. I know, I'm psychic," Lissa warned theatrically before she left the room in answer to the imperative summons of an automobile horn.

Lissa had been right, Carson thought in the late afternoon as he stood in the living room at the Treasure Chest. Mrs. Barclay and Cleo had been tireless in their attention. He had had barely time to secrete the jewels before Fenton had rapped on the door to say that madam and her daughter—would like him to join them for tea in the library. He had felt like a sneak as later he gumshoed down the service drive to the Millards' cottage.

He glanced around the room. If some of the loans raised on the city property had gone into decorating it, he'd admit that the money had been artistically squandered. The walls were Wedgewood blue, in a niche over the white mantel was a blue and white Wedgewood urn. Lamps were blue and white and the chairs were Adam upholstered in blue linen like the hangings at the windows.

His troubled eyes lingered on the fair-haired little boy on the couch. His throat tightened. That child must get well. As if he felt his intense regard, the boy raised heavy lashes and looked at him with translucent hazel eyes which seemed enormous in his white face.

"What's the matter, Lex, you're scowling."

Carson crossed the room and stood looking down at him.

"Am I, Andy? I was wondering how soon I can get you out in a boat fishing. How soon do you think that will be, Madge?" he asked the beautiful dark-haired, dark-eyed woman in the pink frock who entered from the glass-enclosed porch. She was followed by Lissa Barclay and a tall blond man with a lean, studious face, lighted by clear, friendly blue eyes.

Madge Millard sat on the end of the couch and smiled at the boy.

"How soon will it be, Andy?" Her voice was low, warm, with a hint of sadness.

"Mother! Mother dear, if only you wouldn't tease me to eat and would let me go to sleep and never, never wake up, I'm so tired," the child pleaded. Two big tears started from under his lids.

"Oh! Andy! No darling!"

Jack Millard caught his wife by the shoulders and drew her to her feet.

"Steady, dearest." He tightened his arm warningly. "What's that curious sound outside? A dog crying?"

Carson could see the tears in Lissa's brown eyes, felt the effort she made to keep her voice light as she said;

"That's my dog, G-Man. Shall I invite him in and let him apologize for stealing your father's and mother's bathing suits, Andy?"

The boy's lashes flew up. A faint color came into his cheeks.

"A dog! A real dog! Mother said the lady who owned the house wouldn't let me have a dog!"

"That lady has gone away on a long, long journey."

She opened the door. G-Man dashed in. For an instant he stood with black and tan body rigid, his wiry coat bristling, his V-shaped ears close to his cheek. Then with a bound he was on the couch. He stretched his long head on the boy's knees and licked his thin little fingers with a rough tongue.

"Oh, be careful!" Madge Millard warned.

Her husband held her as she started forward. "Let them alone, watch Andy."

The boy laid a clawlike hand on the dog's flat skull. G-Man looked up at him, mouth open, red tongue dangling, eyes sparkling like brown beads.

"Mother! Daddy! Look! He's laughing. He makes me laugh, too." It was a pathetic little laugh, but it was a laugh. Madge Millard turned her face against her husband's shoulder. He rested his cheek against her dark hair and whispered. She lifted her head.

"I know, Jack, I know, but—but he laughed! He hasn't laughed before—"

She was smiling when she knelt beside the couch.

"G-Man, funny name for a dog, isn't it, Andy?"

Lissa knelt on the other side as she explained;

"That name is supposed to mean that he has a fine mind, but I think it shows mighty little intelligence to go about stealing clothes, don't you, Andy? Say, 'I'm sorry,' G-Man."

At the imminent danger of sliding off, the dog sat up on his haunches, barked once and offered his paw. The boy raised himself from the pillows and caught it eagerly.

"You're excused, Mister G-Man. You're the bestest dog I ever saw." He dropped back and closed his eyes.

Lissa stood up. "I'm glad you like him, Andy. You'll have a fine time with him on the shore, he'll wear you out begging you to throw sticks into the water. Eat everything Mother wants you to, dear. There's so much fun ahead. Swimming and motoring and then the County Fair. You'll love that." The boy opened his eyes;

"Will there be a merry-go-round?"

"A grand one. So, rest and eat, won't you? You were sweet about the bathing suits, Mrs. Millard. If there is anything at Tarry Farm that will make Andy more comfortable, let me know and I will send it—I forgot. I'm no longer representing the landlady. It all belongs to Lex, now."

"Whatever belongs to me is yours when you and Jack need it, Madge," Carson assured. "Come on, Lissa. We have serious business on hand before sundown."

At the door she stopped to whistle. G-Man raised his head. Looked hard at her as if with all his might he were trying to talk, and laid his nose on the boy's thin hand.

Andy pulled himself up from his pillow, his eyes were like stars, his face was flushed. He said eagerly;

"He wants to stay with me! Please let him stay, Miss Barclay?"

"Of course he may stay, Andy dear. When you are tired of him, turn him out."

"I'll never get tired of him, never!" The boy put his arm around the dog's neck and cuddled his cheek against it. "I'll never get tired of you—dearest."

"He said 'dearest' in the exact tone in which his father speaks to his mother," Lex Carson remarked as he and Lissa walked along the path to the pier. "He's named for me, Alexander Carson Millard," he added gruffly.

"He's a darling. When he laughed the expression on his mother's face twisted my heart unbearably. Perhaps I don't know enough about it to judge—but it seems to me she's smothering the boy in a fog of fear."

"You can't blame her for being afraid of losing him. If only he will get well."

"I don't blame her for anything. Were I in her place, I wouldn't have half her courage. I go panicky if G-Man has the sniffles, I'd probably be shot to pieces if anything happened to a child of mine. Of course that boy will get well." She drew a deep breath. "Can anyone help getting well in this air? He'll be swimming and racing and eating before this summer is ended."

"Lissa, you're adorable!"

"That's been said before, begins to sound like a refrain. If we don't hurry, we won't get the flag planted, and that's our reason for coming, isn't it?"

"I wouldn't say it was the only reason," Carson qualified. "Here's the boat. Jump in!"

ix

STANDING beside Lissa on the deck of the lighthouse, Lex Carson looked across at the Treasure Chest, a brown shingled cottage, snuggled against a dark green background of pine and arborvitae. Was Lissa right? Was Madge, in her terror of losing the boy, smothering him with fear? Would the realization of her apprehension keep Andy's mind focussed on his weakness?

"I think you've got the right idea," he said aloud.

Lissa, with arms crossed on the iron rail, responded lazily;

"Thanks for those kind words, but which one of my world-beating ideas were you approving? I have a lot of them."

"I mean about Madge being too anxious about the boy.

They have a competent nurse but his mother rarely leaves Andy."

Lissa's eyes were on the Treasure Chest.

"Watch the lavender smoke from that chimney. It rises straight until it gets above the tree tops then spreads like the hair of a mermaid under water and drifts to the east. That means a gentle western breeze. It seems hardly fair to her husband. You look dazed. My nimble mind has leaped back to Mrs. Millard's devotion to her son."

"Jack doesn't mind."

"Doesn't he? I wonder. If you loved your wife very much, would you like to be pushed aside for your son, no matter how much you loved him?"

"But the boy is sick."

"So is the man, sick at heart, as he looks on at her suffering and is powerless to help."

"How do you know so much about a man's heart?"

"I don't know, but I'm always imagining myself in the other person's place and I think your friend Jack Millard could do with a little coddling. Almost any man needs a woman who has time to make him believe he is her dream prince. Unless I miss my guess, there are two blonde sirens in the neighborhood who are not extremely busy at the moment, who'll be tempted to try their practiced hands on him."

"Don't be so cynical. Do you think that a man who loved beautiful Madge Millard would look at another woman?"

Her eyes flashed up to his, a soft color rose to her hair. "Now I understand what you meant," she said.

"What do you mean by 'now I understand what you meant'?" he demanded sharply, in an effort to rid himself of the uneasiness her reference to two blonde sirens had set pricking in his mind. Of course she referred to Sidonie Packard whom he had not met, and Cleo whom he wouldn't trust as far away as he could see her. Equally, of course, Jack wasn't in the least danger, but, it would do no harm to suggest to Madge that she go out with her husband more, he could argue that she would come home fresher and with more strength to give to the boy. Lissa's voice interrupted his troubled thoughts. It took him a second to realize that she was answering his question.

"I'm sorry. I was speaking in what you call conundrums. Do you know, I didn't believe you'd make it."

"Make what? You hop from subject to subject so fast I can't follow you."

"My nimble mind again. I referred to your arrival at the Treasure Chest unaccompanied. You did it! I hope you had enough to eat. The cook is unused to preparing picnic suppers for men."

"She's a grand cook and it was a grand supper and I liked having it on the rocks so near where we took possession of your island. The Stars and Stripes look great, don't they?" he indicated a small flag fluttering below them.

"Perfect. They are beautiful anywhere but never more throat-tightening than when floating between sea and sky. How salty the air is. I feel as if I owned the world and a little bit of heaven when I'm up here on the deck of the lighthouse."

"You look like part of the sea and sky in that turquoise blue jumper, Lissa, your amethyst scarf and skirt tie you to earth, though. There's a touch of drama in the way you wear your clothes. You have an instinct for the right colors for your gorgeous hair, haven't you?"

"You're rather snappy, yourself. I like that coarse-weave blue shirt and the tannish-yellow pull-over the color of your flannel slacks. The perfect costume for the well-dressed man on a picnic."

"I strive to please." Gravity routed laughter from his voice. "I wonder why this light was given up. When Tod Kent planned to bring The Sphinx here, he studied charts. This harbor is of easy access night and day and affords anchorage for the largest vessels. It's frequented by many small craft too, isn't it?"

"It is, but the powers that be decided that the site was too low for the light and that the sound of the fog bell was masked in some directions by neighboring hills. Isn't Tarry Farm beautiful from here? How plainly we can see Red Chimneys. There goes the sun! It has left a flamingo sky. See the thin clouds scurrying! They look like long-legged crimson birds with wings outspread. How the brass on the cruiser glistens. All the little islands in the bay have turned dusky purple. The blue of sea and sky is darkening. I love it! Don't you?"

"I do. Let's sit on the outermost rock of the point till the glow fades. It will seem like setting out to sea."

"That's a thought. I want you to stop a minute in my workroom first, though. You didn't really see it when we came in. It was the service room of the lighthouse and I still call it that."

She lingered at the head of the winding iron stairs. Asked, over her shoulder:

"What did you pick up in the lamp-room?"

"Have you eyes in the back of your head? My sandal buckle was loose."

The truth, but not all the truth, Carson admitted to himself as he followed her down. Why tell her that he had picked up a cigarette stub? She had said that she had imagined a flash from this long unused light yesterday morning. He pressed the stub in his pocket between his fingers. It might have been a flash, not imagination.

He looked with interest at what had once been the service room of the lighthouse. There were wicker chairs cushioned in red and pink hollyhock chintz; shelves of books, an old gilt-framed mirror, a filing cabinet, a typewriter on a table desk beside a window, a gay knitting-bag on a hook. Oil cans, dust pans, funnels, lamps, shone like gold.

"Who keeps this brass polished?" he asked.

"One of the men on the place. It was part of the equipment of the lighthouse. Fenton came over when my aunt bought the island and gave it the first rub-up. Everything had to shine like that when the Government operated the light. Aunt Hetty and I selected the furnishing for the rooms. I didn't know then that she intended to will it to me."

Carson crossed to the fireplace, looked at the map above the mantel, then down at the birch logs piled on the andirons.

"What item did you clip?" He indicated a corner of a newspaper sticking from between the logs. A diamond-shaped piece had been torn from it.

"I didn't tear that out. When I want an item for my files, I cut it. Probably the man who brought old newspapers from Tarry Farm and laid the fire saw an ad he wanted to answer."

The hole in the paper pricked at Carson's mind. Suppose the person who had dropped the cigarette in the lamp-room had torn out an item which interested him? Suppose the two were in some way connected? A crazy idea, but when one was on a quest like his, one didn't pass up even a crazy idea. He said aloud;

"I can't hand much to the man who laid this fire, Lissa, I'll take it apart and lay it so that it will burn the instant you touch a match to it. Meanwhile, get me a drink of water, will you? Those eggs stuffed with anchovy were grand, but they've left me with a terrible thirst."

"I never saw a man yet who didn't itch to re-build a fire someone else had laid. I suppose it's the Boy Scout influence working in them," she flouted gaily.

As she left the room, he removed the birch logs, pulled out the newspaper. He tore off the corner from which the piece had been removed and the date at the top of the page.

"Last February," he said to himself. "Last February."

As the sound of pumping stopped in the kitchen, he thrust

the scraps into a pocket of his slacks. When Lissa entered with a glass of crystal clear water, he was replacing the birch logs. He stood up.

"You won't have trouble starting that fire, Lissa. This is wonderful water. Do you compose your masterpieces at that desk by the window?"

"You're laughing at me. I'll never write masterpieces. I'll leave the miseries, ironies, vain hopes, and frustrated dreams to more experienced writers. I want to write the kind of story—it will be just as much a part of the real world— that will cause persons who see 'Melissa Barclay' on a cover to plump down their problems—and incidentally the price—and seize the book. If, when they reach 'the end' they forget to go back for their problems and march blithely toward the day's work pepped up and refreshed, refreshed— it's a great word, isn't it—I shall feel that I have achieved something. Wasn't it Emily Dickinson who said; 'If I can stop one heart from breaking, I shall not have lived in vain'? That's the way I feel about my writing."

"You're too young, too gay in spirit, Lissa, to know so much about breaking hearts and problems."

"But I've had such a lot of time in which to observe and think. One can learn much in twenty-five years, most of them motherless, many of them spent traveling about the world with a temperamental father and three with a woman like Aunt Hetty Carson. Even after that discipline, I still believe that the beautiful things of life are as real as the ugly things of life; that gay courage may turn threatened defeat into victory; that hitching one's wagon to the star of achievement lifts one high above the quicksands of discouragement. In short, that it's a great world to the valiant."

"Optimist, aren't you?"

"I hate that word, because so many of the people who use it put a sting in it. Be honest, have you ever known gloom or depression to solve a problem? Problems aren't solved that way. Instead it settles over one's spirit like a fog and that fog attracts more fog and there you are in the middle of it groping for a way out, but if, instead, you keep in the sunlight of courage, even if a gale of misfortune blows you off your feet and whirls you along, at least you will have the thrill of seeing where you are going while you ride it."

"What cult taught you that?"

"It's not the philosophy of a cult or ism, it's just plain commonsense. Why do I tell you my innermost thoughts, I wonder? I never talk to anyone else—except G-Man—about myself."

"I hope you'll always tell me your innermost thoughts,

52

Lissa," he declared on a sudden note of tenderness. "We'd better go, or we'll lose the rest of the sunset."

"Lock up, will you?"

Hand in hand they climbed over boulders. They stopped to poke a backing crab out of a tide pool in which it had been marooned. Seated on the top of a great rock that dropped precipitously to the water which fringed it in white, they looked off to sea. Lissa sighed rapturously;

"Isn't it heavenly?"

"It is at present, the sea is as bland and smooth as a campaigning woman politician, but she's a fickle jade. When she's in a temper the waves must lash at the light tower till it shudders under their fury."

"They do and in the migrating season ducks dash themselves against the lantern and drop on the rocks and provide game dinners for the keeper. Can't you imagine sailors in years past, peering through fog or storm for this light? I'm glad I own it. There goes Ozy in his dirty old dory to pull his lobster traps. I go out with him whenever he'll take me, in spite of the fact that his boat smells horribly of oil and the dead fish he uses for bait."

"Does he get many lobsters?"

"Yes. He has the sole right to set traps in this cove. Perhaps it isn't a legal right, but the villagers never trespass. How large The Sphinx looks from here. How long is she?"

"She's a 63 footer."

"The owner's burgee is being run up. Mr. Kent must be going on board. I like that man. Wasn't he amusing at dinner last night? In spite of his way of turning everything into a joke and his lazy manner, I have a feeling that I wouldn't care to have him on my trail were I defying the law."

Carson looked at her quickly. Suppose he were to tell her the truth? That The Sphinx was anchored in the harbor that its owner might be on hand to assist him in his manhunt? She might help. She was used to working out plots, and there were plots a-plenty tangled up in Tod Kent's reason for bringing his cruiser to this harbor. It was worth considering. He attested;

"Tod may appear lazy, but he has an enormous capacity for work and infinite resource and sagacity. I'm glad you like my friend, but don't like him too much, will you?"

"Never, never again will I like a man 'too much,' " Lissa rejoined passionately. She added in a lighter voice;

"The vivid color is fading, sky and sea are darkening, Venus glows like a lantern lowered from Heaven. Listen! The music must be coming from the cruiser's radio."

From across the water drifted a man's voice singing;

" 'Somewhere a voice is calling
" 'O'er land and sea
" 'Somewhere a voice is calling, calling for me.' "

Lissa fought a surge of emotion. She rested her elbow on her knee, and held her chin tight with one hand. It mustn't quiver, it must not. Why should that song make her wonder if life were worth living? Make her think of Lex Carson's face as he had said; "Do you think that a man who loved beautiful Madge Millard would look at another woman?" That was what he had meant yesterday when he had boasted that he was immune to sirens. He loved her. It didn't make sense. It was just that her nerves were a-shiver after the strain of the last few months.

" 'Night and the stars are gleaming, tender and true,' " the rich passionate voice sang on;

" 'Dearest, my heart is dreaming,

" 'Dreaming of you.' "

Lissa covered her eyes with her hands and the storm broke. Her body shook with sobs.

With an exclamation of concern, Carson flung his arm about her and drew her close. His warm protecting tenderness swept away the last crumbling dam of self control. She turned her face against his shoulder, clutched his pullover and cried her heart out to the sound of a man's voice singing and the ebb and flow of the tide.

She struggled to control her sobs, drew long, ragged breaths. It was wonderful to lean against someone, she had lifted and braced others so long. She felt his cheek against her hair, heard his husky voice;

"Cry it out, beautiful. You had it coming to you."

She made a desperate effort for composure, flamed with self-contempt when she realized that she had been clinging to a man who loved another woman.

Hadn't she become engaged to Johnny Grant when she was lonely. Hadn't that affair been a farcical flop? Here she was feeling sorry for herself again and quite ready to drop like a ripe apple into the arms of a man with disturbing eyes and a boyish smile. If only she had known that he loved Madge Millard before she had promised to stay at Tarry Farm. Impatiently, she drew away.

"Don't move till the storm is over," Carson commanded and pressed her head back against his shoulder. He gently dried her long bronze lashes with his handkerchief and tucked it under her hand.

"Better use this."

She freed herself from his arm. In between raggedly drawn breaths, and dabs at her nose and eyes, she explained;

54

"I—I don't k—know why I w—went to pieces l—like that. I never d—did it before. I—I can't remember c—crying like that in all my—my life. It just sneaked up on m—me."

"There's a first time for everything. Give me the handkerchief. I see a tear you've missed."

He touched her cheek tenderly. Lissa's breath caught.

"Don't—don't be nice to me. I—I should be shaken and scolded."

"Okay, I can do that, too. Come on, it's getting dark. Let's go."

It was high time they were going, Carson told himself, if she looked at him again with those eyes like great velvety wet pansies, he would kiss her and then where would he be? Even in this age of easy kisses, she was not a girl who would welcome a kiss from a man whom she had known only twenty-four hours, not while her heart and pride were still raw from Johnny Grant's defection.

"As you suggested, we'd better go," Lissa reminded in a voice still roughened by tears.

"Come on!"

He held out his hand to help her but with a shake of her head, she thrust hers into the pocket of her turquoise blue jumper. Side by side they climbed the rocks, still pink in the lingering afterglow, skirted the lighthouse and clumps of junipers. Stars were pricking through the darkening sky, boats blossomed with riding lights, a million little flying, creeping, hopping things swarmed a rhythmic accompaniment to the soft swish of the tide.

"You haven't spoken for five minutes. You're not going to sleep on your feet, are you?" Lissa inquired with exaggerated concern. She looked up with a smile that was like sunshine after showers. Her voice still caught between words, "Don't, because we're on the runway to the float and you might walk off into the water. It would be such cold water, I should have to plunge in after you." She shivered delicately. He untied the painter of the motorboat.

"I wasn't asleep, I was thinking that a little more than twenty-four hours has passed since your outboard went crazy. I feel as if we had been friends for years—we are friends, aren't we, Lissa?"

"It's rather too soon to know. I—"

"Hi, Lissa!" Johnny Grant hailed her from the red roadster which stopped with a grinding of brakes in the road beside the pier.

"Cleo told me you were here. I came over the bar road to take you home." His blonde hair shone like pale gold above his white polo shirt. Lissa looked up at him, called:

"I'll go with you, Johnny. Lex must be bored to death—"

Carson caught her as she took a step forward. Swung her into the motorboat and jumped in.

"When I start out on a party with a girl, I take her home," he announced and threw on the self-starter.

"Hasn't the girl anything to say about it? I'm going with Johnny," Lissa defied and kicked off her sandals.

Carson seized her as she stepped up on the seat. He pulled her down, kept an arm tight about her shoulders as with one hand on the wheel he steered the boat.

"Planning to swim to your Johnny, were you? Nothing doing."

"Let me go! You're holding me!"

"That's the underlying idea."

"I won't be told what I can do!"

"Your mistake! You're being told what you can't do. Stop twisting!" The motorboat bucked a wave which drenched them with spray. "Now see what you did! I don't know this harbor and I may smash into a ledge. We'd look pretty funny, wouldn't we, perched on a ledge all night?"

He glanced over his shoulder at the pier. Laughed and removed his arm.

"If you go overboard now you'll have to call for help, and you'd be too proud to do that, wouldn't you? Sit here beside me, Lissa, and give me steering orders. As has been said before, I don't know this harbor."

"You seem to be getting on without help. Do you know, you don't belong in this country. You ought to be across the water with the other dictators." She retreated to the stern.

"Oh, but I'm needed here. Didn't your aunt leave you to me to take care of?" The laughter left his eyes. "And from what I have recently observed, you'll need some care, lady."

He didn't speak again until they reached the Tarry Farm float. Then he announced curtly;

"Your friend in the red roadster is breaking all speed records across the bar. Now, you are quite free to go with him. Good-night."

He jumped back into the motorboat and steered for the cruiser.

SUNSHINE poured into the breakfast room at Tarry Farm. The French windows, which formed one side, had been folded back to leave it open to the terrace. Beyond the terrace, stretched a panorama of loping, mist-girdled hills; sky, turquoise and pearl, pierced by an ivory tower; sea, sapphire and malachite; islands, emerald and amethyst and faint topaz. Gold flickered on the soft green walls and ceiling. A breeze, fragrant as balsam boughs, cool as dew, soft as the breast of a dove, stirred the mauve linen hangings and fanned the flames under the old-fashioned silver chafing dishes on the maple buffet till they danced like tiny scarlet and vermillion dervishes.

Lissa at the table, in a pale yellow linen frock, absent-mindedly dropped a lump of sugar into her coffee. Three weeks had passed since she had told Lex Carson she would stand by while he needed her, three weeks since she had collapsed in his arms and cried her heart out, and he in love with Madge Millard! It was also three weeks since he had held her in the motorboat. She must have had a brainstorm when she started to swim back to Johnny Grant. She had been determined to break the charm of Lex Carson's eyes and smile. Lot of good the attempt had done her. She could feel the warmth and hardness of his arm about her shoulders now.

"Did you speak, Miss?" Fenton hovered beside her. "I thought you said 'ooch!' Miss. Perhaps the coffee was too hot?"

"Perhaps it was, Fenton. Are the others coming to breakfast?"

"Yes, Miss. Mrs. Barclay and Miss Cleo sent word to the pantry that they would not have trays in their rooms as usual. The morning was so beautiful they would breakfast here. Mr. Carson returned last night, Miss."

Lissa looked quickly at the butler who was filling a glass. Had he intended that last sentence to be as significant as it sounded?

"Oh, I see. Is he coming to breakfast?"

"He is, Miss. Before the ladies and he arrive, I'd like to say a word to you, Miss."

Had he more complaints from the house-staff to report, Lissa wondered. These last three weeks had been a battleground. Mrs. Barclay was determined to take over the management of the house. Now that Lex was at home, he could settle the question this very day, choose her stepmother or herself to take charge. She had had several phone calls and one letter from him about her legacy. They had been crisp and businesslike, not even a friendly inquiry as to how she was getting on. Why should he care? She had been snippy and disagreeable to him on the motorboat. Besides, hadn't she gone cry-baby on the rocks? Men hated tears. Mrs. Barclay had stirred up so much trouble that it had taken hours that she herself wanted to devote to writing to placate the maids.

"What is it, Fenton?"

The butler glanced over his shoulder at the sun-flecked terrace, toward the door before he confided;

"It's about the jewels, Miss. They're not safe here."

Lissa did a bit of rapid-fire thinking. Her voice was as amazed as her eyes as she demanded;

"What jewels, Fenton?"

"I see that you don't wish me to remember that the late Madam had her jewels brought here, Miss." His face was as bland as his voice. "I spoke only in the interest of the estate. There's a lot of breaking and entering of summer houses, I hear, Miss."

"See our little early bird, Mother," Cleo exclaimed, as in a frock as blue as her eyes, she posed on the threshold. Mrs. Barclay in a dusty-pink gown stood beside her. They had discarded mourning shortly after the reading of Hetty Carson's will, Lissa remembered.

"What worm are you out for, Lissa, my girl?"

"Not the one you're stalking," Lissa snapped and was promptly ashamed of herself. Would she never become callous to her sister's digs?

"And what worm am I stalking, Miss Barclay?" Cleo's voice was as sweetly puckery as the core of a persimmon. She lifted a silver cover and peered into the chafing dish. "Scrambled eggs again! I wish someone would make the cook variety-conscious."

Mrs. Barclay at the table lifted plump, white hands and dropped them to denote futility.

"I've tried, Cleo, you know I've tried, but what can I do when Melissa—Oh, here you are, Alexander. I hope you've come to stay! Sit here beside me, dear boy. Fenton, serve—"

"I'll serve myself, thanks. Good morning, Cleo. Hello, Lissa."

Lissa nodded curtly in response to the buoyant greeting. What business had he to look so carefree when the whole darn load of managing Tarry Farm was on her shoulders? She glanced at him from under the fringe of her lashes, as he lifted silver covers at the buffet. He was in white from collar to shoes. Did that mean that he had come to stay?

As if he had divined her question, he drew out the chair beside her and deposited a plate in front of him.

"Home is the sailor, home from the sea," he announced blithely—"home for twenty-four hours at least."

"Are you really, Lex?" Cleo, in a chair across the table, tucked her sandalled feet under her and beseeched with eyes as well as voice—"Let's do something to celebrate."

"After I've—what's the commotion in the pantry, Fenton?"

The butler put his fingers to his lips.

"Ahem! It's the cook, sir. She insists upon seeing you, sir."

"Seeing me! I haven't anything to say about—the cook." There was a hint of panic in his voice. He looked helplessly at Lissa who kept her eyes stubbornly on her plate.

"Of course, you shouldn't be bothered, dear boy," Mrs. Barclay twittered into the breach caused by her step-daughter's silence. "I would have spared you this, but Melissa insists upon—"

"Let the woman come in, Fenton," Carson snapped with a suddenness that caught Mrs. Barclay with both voice and lower jaw suspended.

"Yes, sir! Mrs. Loosch will be glad to speak to you, sir."

The butler opened the door to the pantry and admitted a huge woman dressed in white.

Carson dropped his napkin on the table and stood up. Did he think he could take what was coming better on his feet, Lissa wondered and disciplined a chuckle. He didn't know the half yet, Mrs. Loosch was good when she got started.

The woman's eyes were mere slits of brightness above her apple-red cheeks. She crossed arms bare to the elbow on her breast and braced her feet for battle.

"Fenton says you wish to speak to me, Mrs. Loosch?"

Carson's smile and courteous inquiry perceptibly reduced the cook's temperature. She changed weight from one foot to the other before she answered;

"I do, sir. I want to know from whom I'm to take orders. Miss Lissa makes out the menus for the day—I never before worked under a person so pleasant and so efficient—then Mrs. Barclay or her daughter comes to the kitchen and gives different orders. Not that I take them, sir. I'll be blowed if I will, but it's very upsetting, sir, not to know who's managing this house." Her fat-encased heart pumped her breath to the tune of excitement.

Lissa glanced at the faces in the room. Fenton's lips were touched by a secretive smile. Mrs. Barclay's eyes were sparking blue fire. Cleo was looking at her brilliant-nailed fingers as they rolled a crumb on the satin surface of the maple table. Lex Carson stood straight and tall before the fireplace. Two sharp little lines cut between his brows, color stole to his hair as he announced in a voice which made Lissa think of tempered steel;

"You're to take orders from Miss Barclay, Mrs. Loosch. When I came here I asked her to continue to manage the house and grounds as she had done while living with her aunt. She consented. Mrs. Barclay in her desire to help me, didn't understand. I hope this will satisfy you, Mrs. Loosch. You're a grand cook and I'd hate to lose you."

Mrs. Loosch's grievance went limp as a deflated parachute in response to his boyish smile and praise.

"I'll try to please you, sir. I know a gentleman when I see one—and a lady too." If a glance could burn, Mrs. Barclay would have shriveled like a gelatin film exposed to flame. She backed toward the pantry door.

"Just a minute, cook. I'd like to have the tenants in for dinner this evening. Could you manage five courses in your top style, than which I'll bet there's nothing finer?"

Mrs. Loosch simpered.

"Sure, I can, sir. If Miss Lissa will plan the menu, I'll see that it's cooked to the queen's taste. It'll be grand to cook for men again. I never did like catering to women. They don't eat. They pick."

She flung a flaming glance at mother and daughter and departed kitchenward.

Mrs. Barclay sniffed into her handkerchief.

"Terrible woman. I wonder if she's a safe person to have in the house. I didn't mean to make trouble, Alexander. I wanted to help. Melissa is away so much. She spends hours and hours on that island—"

"And running round the country in a red roadster with her ex-fiance," Cleo interrupted smoothly.

"I—" Lissa on her feet, snapped her teeth on a fruious denial. What did Lex Carson care whether or not she was running round with Johnny Grant? She asked;

"Has the mail come, Fenton?"

"Yes, Miss. It's on your desk in the residence office, Miss."

"Have you also given Lissa sole authority over the distribution of the mail in this house, Lex?" Cleo demanded. "Everything that comes is sifted in her 'office' before it reaches us. Sometimes I suspect she's carrying on a clandestine correspondence with a man who is not an ex-fiancé, someone whom she picked up when she was wandering about the world, someone of whom she's ashamed."

The anger which Cleo's insinuation roused was transmuted into a nervous desire to laugh as Lissa thought of the reason the mail was "sifted" in her office. She didn't intend that either her stepmother or her sister should know how often manuscript-filled Manila envelopes winged home to their nest. She could endure their digs on other subjects, but sneers at her determination to be a writer would jab at her very soul.

"If you wish to keep your mail separate better have a bag of your own, Lissa," Carson suggested in a cool, clipped voice.

"That's a thought," Lissa agreed. "Come along, Fenton, and I'll give you the family mail to distribute."

She heard Cleo and her stepmother talking in unison as she left the room. Heard Mrs. Barclay inquire;

"Do you think it quite proper to have a dinner party so soon after dear Hetty's passing, Alexander?"

"But this isn't a party," Carson disclaimed impatiently.

Would they give Lex a chance to finish his breakfast? He wouldn't repeat the experiment of a day in his happy home after this morning's blowup. Not a chance.

In the room which she and her aunt had jocularly named the residence office—they had picked up the term from the description of the home of a motion-picture star—Lissa sorted the mail. She handed a bunch of letters to the butler. What was he thinking? She'd like to take a sight-seeing bus through his mind. She had the feeling that there might be secret passages and shuttered memory cells it would be exciting to explore.

"Thank you, Miss. If you will allow me to say so, I think Mr. Carson's suggestion a good one. If you say the word, I'll have the postmaster lock your mail in the Tarry Farm bag, and leave the rest outside, Miss."

He glanced at two large Manila envelopes on the desk.

"I think I know what you're doing, Miss, and I wish you success. I'm sure you'll make a great writer—in time, Miss."

Lissa frowned at the door he closed softly behind him. Fenton the omniscient. He knew that she was writing, that the jewels were in the house—how could he know about them?

She slid the Manila envelopes under the blotter before she answered a light tap.

"Come in!"

"The plump Mrs. Loosch certainly gave you an A1 reference," Lex Carson approved as he entered. He closed the door and crossed to the table-desk. Perched on one corner he demanded;

"Look here, you think it's all right to have the tenants in to dinner tonight, don't you? It isn't a party and even if it were, I wouldn't be showing disrespect to Mrs. Carson's memory. I never knew her."

"It's quite all right. Aunt Hetty was violently opposed to any sort of mourning. Perhaps you have noticed that I have not worn black. She felt that it was a depressing factor in the world."

"Then that's all right. I've asked Mrs. Barclay to phone the guests—I thought an invitation to dinner would come better from her—got to kowtow to the conventions once in a while."

Lissa picked up pad and pencil.

"Whom are you inviting?"

"The Millards, Packards, Major Fane and Tod Kent. That will make an even number. To date I've had no chance to get acquainted with my tenants and I want to know them. Forgiven me yet for keeping you from going home with Grant, the night we were at the island, Lissa?" As she turned to lower a Venetian blind, he went on, "You needn't answer, I understand. Have Cleo and Mrs. Barclay been bothering you a lot about the housekeeping? Think you can stick it out?"

"I'll stick it out. I like to finish a job I begin."

"Don't be so grim about it, beautiful. Makes me feel as if I'd chained you to a treadmill. I told Fenton—"

"Fenton! That reminds me!" Lissa came close. "Fenton knows that Aunt Hetty's jewels are in the house."

"How the dickens can he know?"

"I told you, an armed expressman delivered them."

"I see. He put two and two together." He drew his finger across her brow. "Smooth it out. No occasion for worry. The jewels are back in the vault."

"Really, Lex?"

"Really, Lissa. Have you a list of them?"

"Yes. I made one for Aunt Hetty when she looked them over."

"I'm asking because some of the jewels must be sold to pay the inheritance tax. Go over the list and check the pieces you can best get along without, and I'll attend to selling them for you."

"Get along without! That's the funniest thing I ever heard. I've done very well for twenty-five years without owning one jewel."

"Don't you like rings?"

62

"Mad about them. I'll keep Aunt Hetty's and the set of emeralds and diamonds, they're being worn with red hair this year, I understand. We'll sell some of the pieces that would make me feel as if I were wearing diamond plasters if I put them on. How soon do you want the list?"

"Give it to me this evening after the guests have gone. I'm off again in the morning. Play with me today, will you?"

Lissa opened her lips to say, "I'd love it." Closed them. Apparently she was putty, just putty when he smiled at her. Didn't he love Madge Millard?

She declined hastily.

"Can't. I've got to work. No one has to tell me that no matter how one's mind sparks with ideas, unless one writes, nothing gets written. I've learned that still living truth. I'm writing a novel. Don't laugh."

"Why should I laugh? I presume that even the most successful novelist wrote a first one. I understand why you have the mail delivered to you first, so you may let out what you call homing pigeons, isn't it? I know you're not carrying on a clandestine correspondence. I wish I felt as easy about that red roadster. I—Come in!"

"Long distance phone for you, Mr. Carson," Fenton announced from the threshold.

"All right. How are you going to the island, Lissa?"

"I'll walk across the bar. Need the exercise."

"I'll come for you. My roadster isn't red. It's dark green, with lighter green cushions, they're being used with red hair this year, I understand. It's a snappy number. You'll like it," he prophesied and went into the hall.

xi

Humming in a sweet, husky undertone, Lissa ran down the path between borders filled with a wealth of canterbury bells dangling from their stalks like huge pink tourmalines; spikes of anchusa, blue as the sky; Madonna lilies by the pearly, fragrant score and stately towers of delphiniums, amethyst, azure and indigo purple. Roses, there were, clumps of them; pink and yellow, crimson and white, they scented the air. Shrubs in the background threw grotesque shadows.

Lex Carson's defense of her, in the face of her family's complaints, was what had set her spirits ballooning, she decided. Why had he invited the tenants to dinner? As she had listened to his plan, she'd had a curious feeling that there was more behind it than a desire to become acquainted with them. Two were his friends. Why shouldn't he want to entertain in the house he had acquired so recently? How like her to imagine an ulterior motive. She'd better put Lex Carson out of her mind and concentrate on her novel, it needed thinking about and then some.

Too hot to think. She pulled off the green kerchief tied gypsy fashion over her hair. Gorgeous day but too hot to run. The air shimmered with heat. A cicada shrilled and from a distance another answered.

As she crossed the bar which connected mainland and island, she felt like an atom crawling in infinite space. Innumerable shades of blue in sea and sky in ever-changing values encompassed her. A blue heron, fishing for his breakfast, balanced on one slender leg in sun-kissed shallows. Against a dark bank on the horizon, the white sail of a fishing boat flashed as it caught the sun.

The sight of the dark bank plunged her back to reality. If three summers in Maine had taught her anything, they had taught her that the bank on the horizon meant fog. Would she have time to get in a few hours' work at her desk at the lighthouse before it crept up? Why worry? The wind might change and blow that dark bank out to sea. If Lex came for her—

Resolutely she forced him and the memory of the morning friction at Tarry Farm into retreat and brought forward the plan of her novel. Long ago she had discovered that the power to close the door on problems was one of the perquisites of creative writing. One dwelt in another world when one was at work on a story.

The service room of the lighthouse was like an oven when she entered. She left the door wide. Opened the window beside the typewriter desk and let in the smell of the sea and the monotonous moan of the buoy. It was too hot to work. She sharpened a bunch of pencils. Went to the kitchen and pumped clear, sparkling water into a glass. Drank it. Back in the service room, she rearranged pink and white Shirley poppies in a green bowl. That accomplished, she glanced around for something else to do and met her own eyes in the mirror.

She made a little face at the flushed, auburn-haired girl, who grimaced at her in return. She accused;

"Stalling, just stalling, aren't you? Your story stuck yesterday and you dread to tackle it because you don't know how to push it ahead. Go to it, my dear, go to it."

She sat down before the typewriter and resolutely kept her eyes from the window, that alluring window, beyond which the sea sparkled and beckoned, and outboards, scooting round the harbor like a flock of prehistoric waterfowl tempted her to join them. She opened her manuscript at the page where the story had stuck, read it, went back three chapters and read up to it again. The characters just wouldn't carry on.

Sheer terror stopped her heart. "Am I all through?" she asked herself. "Has my imagination petered out? Can't I write any more—ever?

"You're the world's worst quitter if you get panicky over a thing like that," she scolded herself. "The story started off too easily. You've barely scratched the surface of your mind. Dig in, gal, dig in."

Hands clasped behind her head, eyes on a dog-shaped stain on the wall, she thought of how the male lead had dashed up a flight of stairs in pursuit of the clue to a mystery which threatened his love interest and how on the top stair he had stopped, one foot extended, like a mechanical toy which had run down. She couldn't budge him. Suppose she had sent her hero down in the first place, instead of up? She'd try it.

She slipped a sheet of cheap yellow paper into the machine. She sent the man to the street and "click" the story was off again. Her cheeks burned, her fingers flew as they kept pace with the thoughts that flooded her mind. The keys changed tempo with the mood of her story. Once she held her breath as she touched them as softly as if she heard cautious footsteps. Once she laughed. She stopped to brush fingers across her wet lashes. Once she frowned.

She rested her hands and looked at the world outside. The hills were girdled by a crawling, gray mist. The sky was gray. The islands had turned to gun-metal. The buoy sounded muffled. She pulled down the window to shut out the smell of fog, and the depressing moan. Closed the door, lighted the fire, the fire Lex had laid, she remembered. She glanced at the clock. The bar would be passable for two hours more. She must finish the chapter while her mind was tingling from the impetus of the story.

She typed on and on until tired, but triumphant, she curled up in the wicker chair and read aloud what she had written. She nodded satisfaction and exulted;

"Sending our hero down instead of up did the trick. It started the story off again with a bang. I'll thumb-tack a reminder on the wall;

"WHEN STUCK GO INTO REVERSE."

She slipped the manuscript into a drawer and hooded her typewriter while she planned the next chapter of her story. It should have a surprise ending. O Henry was the master of surprise endings. It would help to study his method. There was a set of his stories at Red Chimneys. She'd borrow the books and reread them.

Someone outside! The sound snapped Lissa out of the world of imagination into the world of fact. Had Lex come for her? She opened the door.

"You hav a vera nice place here, signorina," approved an oily foreign voice.

Against the casing leaned Nino, the Packards' houseman! In one hand he held a lighted cigarette. Behind him fog twisted and billowed in thick coils. Its cold grayness accentuated the sinister effect of his close-set dark eyes, and the deep scar on his cheek.

"What do you want?" Lissa demanded.

"Vera sorry to trouble you, signorina, but the water at our house no longer run. Signorina Packard must washa the hair. I phone beeg house to tell you. They say you here, so I come."

"Did you look at the engine?"

"No, signorina. I no engineer. I houseman. I hear the pump going."

"Probably the belt has slipped. Go back and look at it. If it has, pull the switch and stop the engine. Then slip the belt onto the wheel. It doesn't take an engineer to do that. Start the engine, then if the water doesn't run, phone the village electrician. You'll find the number tacked up in the pump-house."

"I go, signorina. May I first go up the stairs and see the great lamp?"

Through Lissa's mind flashed her appraisal of the man the first time she had seen him;

"I'd hate to meet you in the dark, Nino."

This wasn't the dark but it might as well be. Fog filled the world.

"No. No one is allowed in the lamp-room. You'd better hurry back and attend to that engine."

She banged the door. Turned the key on the inside. She leaned against the casing. Listened. Not a sound outside but the hollow warning of the buoy.

"Just what have you gained by locking him out and yourself in?" she inquired aloud.

The sound of her voice helped dispel the spooky effect of

the fog-whitened windows. The room vibrated with curious little sounds; a vine tapping outside; the wicker chair creaking as if stretching after being relieved of her weight; a beam cracking; the tick-tock of the brass clock; soft whispers among the scarlet and orange embers on the hearth.

She tried to pick up the plan of her story, but the advent of the scar-faced Nino had blown it to smithereens. She'd better start for home before the fog became more dense. In front of the mirror she tied the green kerchief over her hair. A golden glow flickered on the wall. Headlights! An automobile horn wailed like a lost spirit with a cold in its head. A fist pounded on the door. A voice called;

"Lissa! Lissa! Are you here?"

She turned the key and flung open the door. Hatless, in a yellow slicker glistening with moisture, and with another over his arm, Lex Carson frowned at her.

"I've been blowing the horn like mad. Why didn't you answer? I almost turned back, thought perhaps when you saw the fog coming, you beat it home. You're shivering. Put this on. Why were you locked in?"

She slipped her arms into the slicker he held. "I wasn't locked in. Someone was locked out."

"Who?"

The question cracked like a boy's mammoth torpedo flung against a wall. Should she tell him, Lissa asked herself, and answered on the same thought-wave;

"The Packards' houseman, Nino."

"What did he want?"

"He came to report that the water had stopped running at Red Chimneys."

"Suppose it had? What could you do about it?"

"Tell him what he could do about it. After that he asked to go up and see the 'great lamp.'"

"Did you let him?"

"Let him! You do ask a lot of foolish questions, don't you? Of course I didn't let him. Listen! Isn't that the put-put of a motorboat leaving the island pier? He's gone. Let's get away from here. The fog is rolling in thicker and thicker. It will be tricky crossing the bar road."

"Pity you didn't think of that two hours ago," Carson reminded as he locked the door.

"But it came so quickly. One moment it was a dark bank on the horizon, and the next, the world was blotted out. I wish that Italian houseman would drop his stub at home. It isn't an addition to my doorstep." She pushed the fragment of a cigarette with her foot.

"Hold on. I'll take it along and fling it into a bush as we pass. Pretty fussy about your doorstep, aren't you, Miss Barclay," Carson teased. "Hop into the car."

The lights of the roadster glowed feebly, the eaves of the building, the foliage on nearby shrubs dripped, dripped, dripped.

Seated beside Lex Carson in a weird unreal world, Lissa glanced at his strong hands on the wheel, at his profile, as head bent slightly forward, he peered into the mist. His usually brown skin looked chalky in the ghostly light. Beads of moisture tipped the short hair at his temples.

"Keep your eyes on the road, will you, Lissa? That last fog-shrouded shrub we passed almost gave me heart-failure. Thought it was a man stepping in front of the machine. Two pairs of eyes are better than one in this thick whiteness, especially when one pair is familiar with the road."

Had he felt that she was looking at him? Lissa teased gaily;

"Eyes front, it will be, your Honor. If you don't watch out, some day you'll be a judge and wear a black gown. Already you have acquired the stern judicial manner. Here we are on the bar road. We haven't come a moment too soon. Hear the oily lash of the tide."

"How the darned fog rolls and twists. Makes me think of the evil genie which was everlastingly rising from the sea in the old fairy stories. Speaking of stories, did genius burn this morning?"

"It took a lot of work to get the fire started. My hero went dead on me. I tried blood transfusion, artificial respiration. He wouldn't breathe. Then I seized him by the shoulders and faced him the other way. After that, he went so fast I couldn't keep up with him."

She peered around the side of the windshield into the cold whiteness ahead.

"We're almost across. Then the wood road and we're at home. Can't get there too quickly to suit me. The monotonous swing of those two windshield wipers makes me dizzy. I feel smothered, oppressed, as if something were closing in on me, as if I must scream."

"Don't." He gave her an oblique smiling glance. "I need both hands on the wheel."

She remembered how he had held her in the motorboat and shrank as far away as the green leather seat permitted.

"I shan't scream. That was a figure of speech. We're across the bar road. Doesn't the moisture dripping from those ghostly pines sound like rain? There's something moving ahead! It's a person! Hear the call? He's lost! No, it's a woman's voice!"

Carson pressed the accelerator. Stared incredulously at the slender figure that ran forward. Stopped the roadster. Jumped out.

"Madge!" he exclaimed. "Madge!"

"Oh, Lex! Lex, dear! I'm so—so glad to see you, I was lost!" Madge Millard half laughed, half sobbed.

That fervent "dear" was like a steel hand twisting Lissa's heart. Did Madge Millard love Lex? Next time she felt herself go all soft and quivery inside when he smiled at her, she'd put that word into her memory phonograph and give it a whirl. Meanwhile, she was sitting like a bump on a log. With one foot on the running board she suggested;

"Take Madge home, Lex. I'll walk. I want to stop at Red Chimneys and make sure the engine is running. I could find my way from here in the dark."

"Of course you won't walk, Lissa. Don't make me feel more like a sob-sister than I feel at present," Madge Millard protested. "When I started from the Treasure Chest—I go to the farmhouse every day for eggs—there was only a faint mist. Then suddenly everything became blurred, unreal, weird. I was confused and lost my way."

"I don't wonder," Lissa sympathized, "but now that you're safe, charge the adventure up to education. You wouldn't have seen a typical summer here unless you had experienced one fog. I'll see you at dinner tonight."

It seemed but an instant to the man and woman looking after her before she disappeared in the mist.

"You'd better follow her, Lex," Madge Millard suggested anxiously. "She'll lose her way."

"No. She knows these woods and trails better than I do. Get in and I'll take you home."

He drove on through the mist with the eyes of his mind following Lissa, with Madge saying how much she liked the Treasure Chest and how wonderful Lissa had been to Andy and didn't he think she was about as charming a girl as he'd ever met?

"The most charming," he attested crisply.

"Care for her a lot, Lex?"

"Mad about her."

"Thank heaven you're in love at last. Jack and I have worried about you. We've suspected that you'd had a disappointment which made you cynical about women."

He smiled. "You're right about the disappointment but not about its lasting effect. I can laugh now, but it was a tragedy when it happened. I invited the girl with whom I was terribly in love to my Class Day. She fell for my roommate. I was a cynic about girls for months. Then, I took up law, got tremendously interested in my work and kept women outside my life. I haven't met a girl I wanted to marry until I pulled Lissa Barclay out of the water."

"Then—then why let her spend so much time running round with that light-weight, Johnny Grant? The Packard man also is too devoted."

"I'll have to take my chance, Madge. I can't stay here for the present—I've got to get the mess of my uncle's estate cleared up. After that—" he abruptly switched the subject. "How's Andy?"

"He has made a wonderful gain. Everyone is so good to him, even your butler, Fenton, comes to inquire for him, brings him something the cook has prepared especially to tempt his appetite. Andy has taken the greatest fancy to him. I—I—can hardly believe it, his improvement, I mean." She steadied her voice. "It seems like a miracle."

"I knew this place would fix him up." His color rose as he suggested;

"Now that the boy is better, why not play round more with Jack? I think he's lonely. He—he, well—you know he's friendly and likes people and—"

He was bungling what had started out to be a simple suggestion that she devote more time to her husband.

Her hand gripped his arm, her face was white, her eyes were terrified.

"Are you trying to tell me something, Lex? Something about a woman and—and Jack?"

"No! No! It's only that Jack seems sort of woman in his mind—he loves the boy as much as you do—and I thought —well, you know how I feel about Jack—you and he are my dearest friends—and I can't bear to see him hurt. Here we are at the Treasure Chest."

He caught her hand as she stepped from the roadster.

"You do understand what I meant about Jack, don't you, Madge?"

"Better than you think, Lex," she answered and went into the house.

In the residence office at Tarry Farm, Lissa frowned at the pad on which all phone calls for her were listed. No record of a call from Red Chimneys. She had stopped there on her way home. The servants in the kitchen had been surprised when she inquired if the water was running. Sure, they said, did she think it had stopped?

She visualized the Italian houseman in the doorway of the lighthouse. Why had he come there? Why had he wanted to see the lamp-room? She laughed! Already her imagination was hot-footing on the trail of scar-faced Nino.

FENTON was serving coffee on the terrace. In mid-afternoon
the fog had blown out to sea. The sun had blazed down on
a steaming world long enough to dry it. Now the glassy surface of the harbor mirrored a three-quarter moon and a
scatter of shimmering stars. The still air was sweet with
the breath of lilies. Silver tinkled against china to the accompaniment of low voices and soft laughter.

Lissa, in a fan-back chair, looked up at Tod Kent perched
on the brick wall of the terrace. Moonlight turned his white
dinner jacket to silver and silver-plated his red hair, it even
threw a kindly shadow on his retrousse nose. He responded
with an understanding grin.

"Admiring me, are you? Just one more victim to my deadly
charm?"

"Too bad you haven't more self-confidence, Tod. Why not
consult a psychoanalyst? He might help."

"That-a-girl! Glad to hear you laugh. You were so serious
during dinner I thought of suggesting that you sob out your
sorrow on my shoulder. It's being done. Now, what is there
about that mild ribbing to turn your face as red as one of
those roses in the garden?"

"Your eyes are playing tricks. My face didn't turn red.
It's sunburn being shown up by the moonstone blue of this
frock."

"Is that so! The customer is always right. How come that
you're alone for a minute? Packard didn't talk or look at anyone but you during dinner. With Lex devoting himself to the
fair Sidonie, those two were on the crest of the social wave
and"—he lowered his voice—"if you ask me, that's what
they're out for."

"Sidonie is lovely and that glittering gold frock of hers
is the answer to a maiden's prayer."

"It may be, but it isn't a patch on the blue and silver
rag you're wearing. It does things to your eyes and your
gorgeous hair—added to beauty you have brains, which, boys
and girls of the radio audience, puts the pep into beauty. I've
met 'em beautiful and dumb before, but Sidonie is the

dumbest yet. I have a hunch she's afraid to talk. Look at her now with her brother. I'll bet she's scared stiff of him."

Lissa's eyes rested on the girl to whom Ralph Packard was talking. She remembered her hysterical incompetence at Red Chimneys when the curtains were burning. A person of that type would be dominated by a stronger nature and there was no doubt that the brother was the stronger of the two. That didn't necessarily mean that she was afraid of him. She protested;

"If you see signs of fear in Sidonie Packard's manner with her brother, you've a keener imagination than I have, Tod. They're all going in. Cards, of course. It is the first time I've seen our tenants together. Varied, aren't they?"

She rose and leaned against the terrace wall as she appraised the guests. Cleo and Jack Millard were standing in the shadow of a palm. The glow of a cigarette lighted his fine eyes, they were too fine to be wasting a glance on the girl beside him. Moonlight reduced Mrs. Barclay's age by a decade, as she listened with flattering attention to Major Fane. Without doubt he was treating her to a detailed account of his late operation, she, herself, had heard it twice. His white dinner clothes made him appear short and stocky. His shiny bald head—which wind and weather had burned a fiery red —with its fringe of iron-gray hair, made Lissa think of the sun, with a ring around it. Her eyes moved on to Lex Carson talking to Madge Millard. She winced. Even from the distance, she could see the tenderness of his expression.

"I'd like to know the stories woven through the life of each one of the tenants, wouldn't you, Tod?" she asked. "They look smooth enough on the surface, but I have a feeling that beneath some of them there may be seething retorts of emotion ready to blow-up at a spark, undercurrents sweeping them along. Curious that I should feel so about this group. Previous tenants have come and gone without stirring my imagination."

She was aware of Kent's quick look at her.

"You have me scared, Lissa. If I stay here a moment longer, you'll ferret out the dark secret of my young life and shove it under your microscope. I'm going. I'll grab Madge for a partner before Lex gets her. Those two play contract like nobody's business."

Lissa's thoughts followed him. He knew of undercurrents in the lives of some of the guests here tonight, she was sure of it. He had betrayed the knowledge by his quick look at her. Which ones? Did he know Lex loved Madge?

"Do you and I have to go inside this perfect night?"

Ralph Packard's smooth query brought Lissa's thoughts

rightabout face. She looked up at the man whose dark eyes made her think of smoldering coals. He extended his hands with their square, reddened finger-tips.

"It is really painful for me to hold cards."

"O-o-o!" Lissa crooned compassion. "You must be careful of your hands. We are not needed at the card-table. There are enough without us. I agree with you, it is too fine an evening to go in. What shall we do?"

"Look at the harbor from one of the upper balconies of this house. Ever since we arrived, I have wanted to see the world—this fragment of it—from one of these windows. Red Chimneys is all right, but I like to look off from high places. May I?"

"You may. We'll go to the balcony of the conservatory at the head of the stairs."

Lex Carson stepped out of the French window of the living room. He loomed superbly tall against the lighted background.

"You're the one in a hundred who can wear a white dinner jacket without looking like a deck steward," she thought as he approached her.

"I missed you, Lissa. Be my partner, will you?"

"Too late, Carson. I've engaged Miss Barclay to personally conduct me to the upstairs balcony from which we are to view the moon."

Ralph Packard's velvet voice was not quite so smooth. The pile had been rubbed the wrong way. He produced a flashy cigarette case, all red enamel, and gold. A monogram in diamonds glinted on the top as he snapped it open and offered it to his host.

Lex Carson looked down at the case. Why was he hesitating, Lissa wondered? She saw a faint color come into his face before he helped himself to a cigarette. Packard snapped a jeweled lighter.

"Thanks. Sorry I'm too late, Lissa," Carson regretted. "Perhaps you'll play later. I like this cigarette, Packard. I'll bet a hat it didn't come from this part of the country."

"No. I import them. Have them made especially for me."

"I judged so from the monogram. By the way, I don't know why this cigarette should remind me of it—I hope the water is running without a hitch at Red Chimneys?"

"Running! As far as I know it is. Why did you ask?"

"Your man reported that the engine was running wild. Probably didn't want to disturb you about it, so phoned to us. If you gaze at the moon too long, Lissa, I shall come after you. Remember, you are my responsibility." He stood aside for her to enter the house.

"What did Carson mean, when he said you were his responsibility?" Packard demanded of Lissa as later he leaned against the rail of the conservatory balcony.

His head was dark against the moonlighted sky. The tip of his cigarette and the shine of his eyes were sharp accents in the face she couldn't see clearly.

Below, the garden lay fragrant and still. The spray of the fountain turned to silver mist before it tinkled back into a molten pool. Tree tops and shrubs were tipped in silver, and across the harbor the lighthouse was a silver shaft. Lissa leaned her elbows on the railing.

"An enchanted world, isn't it? The moon gives a lovely light."

"You haven't answered my question about Carson. Why are you his responsibility?"

Eyes on the distant island she answered;

"Am I to believe that you have been at Red Chimneys over three weeks and do not know that my aunt left a trust fund for me to be administered by Lex Carson? If you don't, you're the only person within a radius of three counties, who doesn't."

"I remember now. Sidonie was quite excited when she heard about it. Told me that not only was there a trust fund but a legacy of fabulous jewels. Why aren't you wearing some of them? I'm not jewel-wise but I know enough to know that those three broad bracelets are genuine—rhinestones. Afraid to keep the real jewels here?"

Lissa held up her left arm and moved it till a million facets caught the light and shot forth a million iridescent sparks. Why should he be interested to know where the jewels were kept?

"I hope you don't mind my question, Miss Barclay," Packard went on. "It was my story-hound scenting the trail of plot material. I presume when you leave Tarry Farm you'll be swept into a whirl of dinners and gayety in your social circle?"

Curious, the earnestness with which he asked the trivial question, Lissa thought before she answered;

"Not I. Socially, I'm the poorest girl in the world. I have traveled so much that I have no 'circle' of any kind. Cleo is the socialite. She has scores of friends, the kind who have several country places, yachts and polo ponies and chateaus in France and Italy, she belongs to what the fashion journals call the International set. When I return to the city I shall get a job and probably be able to afford one small room—until—gorgeous thought—I begin to sell stories. And speak-

74

ing of writing, is genius burning? Can you write at Red Chimneys?"

"I tried typing but my fingers are still too tender. I had the grandest idea for a story, tried dictating it to Sidonie. She took it in longhand, and pretty bored she was about doing it, too."

"Let me type it for you from her copy," Lissa offered eagerly. "Think what a lot I would learn. You've been so modest, never telling me the name of one book or article of yours. I know you must write well, you talk so well. I won't let anyone know what I am doing. Not afraid I'll steal your ideas, are you?"

"Of course not. I'd prefer to read Sidonie's copy to you. It's crude. Between you and me, that sister of mine hasn't a language cell in her brain."

Or any other, according to Tod, Lissa thought. She said hurriedly;

"I have a typewriter in my work room on the island. I'll stop for you on my way over tomorrow. Together, it won't take us long to make a copy."

"I shall be eternally grateful for your help. How the lighthouse shows up from here. It has been discarded by the Government, hasn't it?"

"Yes, but—" Lissa caught back the incident of the flash she had been about to confide. That was her story. She intended to use it in her novel.

"Why did you break that sentence?"

She met his eyes. She had seen the same flicker in them the afternoon he had been burned. She had thought it mockery. Was he secretly amused at her attempt to be a writer? Some successful authors were like that, contemptuous of beginners. She'd met them.

"An idea for a story derailed it. Don't they ever come to you like that? Let's go down. After all, I'm a hostess of sorts here."

Sidonie Packard was standing at the foot of the curving stairway as they descended. Lex Carson was holding her shoulder cape of green maribou.

"Ralph, I have a horrid headache. Won't you take me home?" she pleaded.

Her eyes were as glittering as her frock. Two spots that were not rouge, burned in her cheeks.

"We'll go at once, Sidonie." Packard took the cape from Carson and placed it over her shoulders. "Say good-night to the others for me, will you? I must get my sister home. She's apt to go to pieces when her head aches. I'll be waiting for you tomorrow, Miss Barclay."

Lissa and Carson stood side by side until the tap of heels across the terrace died away. He slipped his hand through her arm;

"Come with me."

In the sports room with its motley collection of stuffed fish, moose heads, guns, golf clubs and tennis rackets, he closed the door and drew a chair to the desk.

"Sit down, Lissa. I want to talk to you."

"I'd rather stand." She backed to the mantel as he approached. Why was he so colorless? His eyes probed hers as he demanded;

"Where are you meeting Packard tomorrow?"

Why should his question start her pulses racing? She brought up her shock troops of defense.

"I shan't tell you. You may have authority over my money, but not over me."

"Granted, but, won't you tell me if I say, 'please,' beautiful?"

She steeled herself against the smile in his eyes, the caress in his voice. She thought, "that's the way he looks at Madge."

"No. My friends, if not my money, are mine to enjoy as I please. I refuse to have my dates checked up."

He came a step nearer. His color was high now, his gray eyes black with anger.

"Making a lot of dates with Johnny Grant too, aren't you? Perhaps you're thinking of getting engaged to him again?"

Lissa flung back her head.

"Perhaps I am. What can you do about it?"

"I'll show you what I can do about it! Come here."

His hand on hers seemed an irresistible magnet drawing her. Ecstasy in the feel of it, torment as she remembered Madge Millard. She gripped the edge of the mantel, clung to it.

"No. I—"

A tap on the door.

"Reprieved!" he said with a note in his voice and a look in his eyes which caught at her breath.

She opened the door, smiled radiantly at the man on the threshold.

"Come in, Tod, dear. I'm just going." She turned and flung a folded paper on the desk. "There's the list of the jewels, L—Lex. Good-night."

Kent frowned at the closed door, then at Carson unfolding the paper.

"Have I gone haywire or did she call me dear?" he looked askance at his friend before he reminded;

"You told me to come here as soon as the card-party

folded up, Lex. I came but I have a feeling that my arrival was—to put it mildly—inopportune."

"It's all right."

Carson thrust the paper into his coat pocket. Kent watched him, as he turned the combination of a safe and withdrew a tin box. He placed it on the desk, opened it.

"I've got something," he said. "It may have nothing to do with what we're after, but something queer is going on round here."

He opened a roll of tissue paper and displayed portions of three cigarettes. With long, delicate tweezers, he picked up the shortest stub and laid it on the desk.

"Exhibit A. Found in the lamp-room of the lighthouse the day after Lissa saw the flash."

He placed another stub beside it.

"Exhibit B. Nino, the Packards' houseman, dropped this on the doorstep of the light this morning."

He held up the third piece.

"Exhibit C. I took this from Packard's case this evening." He laid it beside the others. Kent looked at them.

"What's it all about?" He turned the cigarettes over with the tweezers. Looked up with incredulous eyes.

"Jiminy, Lex! They're monogrammed R. P."

"They are. From now on, watch the light on the island from midnight to dawn—every night—don't trust it to anyone else. Understand, Tod?"

Kent's voice was rough with excitement as he answered;

"You bet I understand."

xiii

At the open French window in the sports room at Tarry Farm, Alexander Carson watched a ruby-throated hummingbird still fluttering wings above a mass of pink petunias in a huge vase on the terrace, saw it thrust, and dart away. He crossed to the desk and looked at the calendar. The middle of August. The days seemed speed-mad.

Besides working on the problem which had been apportioned to him by a Department confident in his ability to solve it, he had sunk his intelligence teeth into the job of straightening out the estate he had inherited. He squared his shoulders, he wouldn't allow discouragement to shake him off. He knew what he should do and he intended to do it. It would take longer than he had thought to put things on a paying basis, but it was up to him alone to keep the property which should be an asset, from sucking him into financial quicksands.

He had had so little time to devote to Lissa. During the week-ends he had spent at Tarry Farm she had avoided him. He had had only a few words with her since the night she had intimated that she might again become engaged to Johnny Grant. Had she meant it?

He'd better stop thinking of her, if he could; she was in his mind, in his heart, in his very soul. Resolutely he switched his thoughts to the estate, which was proving a maze of new responsibilities. Mrs. Carson's will had been probated and he had been appointed trustee of her niece's legacy; he had sold enough of the jewels to pay the inheritance tax when it was due; his uncle's estate had been turned over to him.

Yesterday he had announced a cut in wages to all on the place to take effect next week. He had to cut even though he might keep the house open but a few weeks longer. The outside expenses would go on and he couldn't afford them as they were at present. He had told Fenton, the butler, to inform the house-staff. He had called in the men who worked outside and had been listened to in grim silence. When he had finished, they had walked out without a response. He didn't need a psychologist to tell him that they resented the cut. There had been a look in the eyes of the hairy Simonds, he hadn't liked. If they but knew it, they were lucky that it was only a cut, not dismissal. He answered a knock on the door.

"Come in. Good morning, Mrs. Barclay."

The small woman in a pale gray linen frock had lost the faded look he had noticed the first time he saw her. She was really pretty and young looking. If she hadn't an advice complex and that infernal twittery way of talking, she might be fairly attractive.

"Good morning, Alexander. No, thanks, I won't sit down." She declined the chair he pushed forward. "I know that I'm intruding on your business time but do you realize that you invited Cleo and me to stay with you a month and that we have been here longer than that now?"

Carson did some rapid-fire thinking. He had come to intensely dislike the woman and her daughter, but he was away so much that he didn't have to see them often. If they went he would lose Lissa—she couldn't stay at Tarry

Farm without her stepmother—if he hadn't lost her already.

"Not getting bored here, are you, Mrs. Barclay?"

"Bored? My dear boy! This is the most enchanting place. The summer residents for miles round have made us welcome, Cleo knows so many people, and last evening we dined with the tenants at Red Chimneys. Mr. Packard seems fascinated by my lovely girl. I shall depend upon you, Alexander, to look up his financial standing, should his attentions to her become serious. With Tod Kent and his cruiser at our disposal, how could we be bored?"

"Then don't think of going at present. If you can bear it, stay on until after Labor Day—by that time—"

"You are not thinking of closing this divine house then, are you? Maine is so gorgeous in the autumn. You mustn't do it, Alexander. You really should stay through October."

The sharpness of her eyes offset the softness of her voice. He evaded;

"It is too soon to decide what I will do. I shall keep the place open the rest of the summer anyway." He opened the door to the hall. "Sorry to hurry you but I have an important appointment. It's settled, isn't it? I may count upon you to stay a while longer?"

"Dear boy!" She patted his sleeve. "Of course you may, just as long as you need me. I'm glad to be of use to someone. My girl is so independent that sometimes I feel like a fifth wheel and Melissa is such an unstable person. By the way, while on the subject of my stepdaughter, I hope she is getting the little income dear Hetty left her? She is so reticent that I can't learn from her if it is being paid."

She was sounding him to find out if her stepdaughter had anything she could borrow, Carson suspected. His voice was confidential as he answered;

"It's unfortunate, but the estate is in such a mess that it will be months before Lissa will receive her little income regularly. In the meantime, if you could help her out—"

She gasped as if water had been dashed in her face. "I'll see what I can do. I'll talk with you later."

As the door closed behind her, Tod Kent appeared at the open window.

"Coast clear?" he inquired in a sepulchral whisper.

"Yes. Come in."

Carson crossed to the mantel and stood back to the fireplace. Mrs. Barclay's estimate of Lissa stuck in his mind like a thorn. Was she unstable? She was stepping out a lot with Johnny Grant. Why in thunder did he mind what that woman said? She was a nettle. She left a prickly spine in him each time she came near.

Kent, perched on a corner of the flat desk, glanced up over the lighter he was applying to a cigarette.

"You look as if you'd been given a shot of poison, Lex, or a dose of advice. Mrs. Barclay has that effect on me too. She should head an advice clinic. How does a woman get that way, everlastingly telling everybody what he should do? She and the lovely Cleo dined with the Packards last evening."

"So I hear. Was Lissa there?"

"No. She's been seeing a lot of Packard, though. They have something up their sleeves which interests them both. They make sort of a mystery of it. Mother Barclay is not taking 'Melissa' out in company with her golden-haired daughter, believe it or not."

"I believe it. How do you know Lissa wasn't at Red Chimneys last night?"

"Because I was. The Millards also were guests. Unless I miss my guess, the fair Cleo is out to annex Jack, if I know her type, and I do. Sidonie, the beautiful but dumb, was a nervous hostess. Kept looking at her brother. He was as smooth as cream, but all the time I had the feeling that if one scratched his civility too deep, one would find a tough guy."

"Something tells me you're right. Let's skip him. I got word today that some of the stuff we're following up has cropped up hundreds of miles from here."

"Got by us! What do you know about that! I've watched that lighthouse every night as you ordered. Not so much as a glimmer from it. That proves that the flash and the cigarette exhibits have nothing to do with our hunt."

"Soft pedal. Someone's at the door. Come in," Carson called. "Glad to see you, Ozy."

Captain Ozias' ferret-like eyes snapped as he entered the room. His thrust forward head waggled as he held out a large, over-stuffed, legal looking envelope.

"Special Delivery. Say, Lex, you ought to tell folks that there ain't no such animal in this village for the rusticators. The summer houses is all too fur away from the postoffice."

Carson glanced at the postmark and laid the letter on the desk.

"Nothing of importance. Sit down, Ozy. You look hot and bothered. I'll have Fenton mix you a drink."

Fright distorted the face of Captain Ozias.

"No! No thanks. I ain't never going to drink nothing again."

Kent slid from the desk and joined Carson in front of the mantel.

"What's the matter, Ozy? Been seeing sea-serpents? Nice, slimy, wiggly sea-serpents?"

"No, 'twasn't nothin' like that, Tod."

The captain peered furtively over his shoulder before he approached the two men and confided in a whisper which carried to the remote corners of the room;

"I ain't a reg'lar beer-drinker, boys, but one evenin' long 'bout the last of June, I was kind of tuckered, I'd had so many errands to do, so I went into the open-all-night eatin' place in the village and got my supper. The first glass of beer tasted good, an' I had a second. 'Twas terrible late, most midnight, but I felt fine an' come round to the island in my dory to pull my lobster traps, 'cause I knew I wouldn't hev a chance next day an' if you leave the critters trapped too long they're likely to eat off each other's claws. Kinder playful that way at times."

"You didn't fall overboard, I hope?"

"Course I didn't fall overboard, what d'you take me for, Lex? Trouble wasn't in my legs, 'twas in my eyes. When I got out to the lobster floats each one was twins. I checked up on 'em all. Where I'd buoyed one trap, there was two."

"Nothing in that to frighten you. Someone else is poaching on your fishing ground. That wasn't beer in your eyes, Ozy."

"Mebbe 'twas't, mebbe 'twasn't, Lex, but, I was so upset to think that two mugs of beer had made me fuzzy that I went home without pullin' the traps. Reckoned I'd get a few hours' sleep before I touched 'em. I went out 'fore sunup next mornin'. 'Twas kinder misty—an' how many do you think was there?"

"Look not upon the beer when it is foamy, Ozy. How many did you find?" Tod Kent chuckled.

"Jest five floats, one in each place where I'd let down a trap. No twins. Do you wonder I'm off drinks from now on? I'd seen double. I got to get goin'. Beats all the number of errands you summer folks have. Anything I kin do fer you boys?"

"Nothing, thanks. Sure you won't have an orangeade? There would be no extra floats in it, I promise."

Captain Ozias shook his head. "You think it's a joke, Lex Carson. I'll tell you it ain't a joke to see double. Tell Lissa she can count on all the lobsters she wants for the bake next week, an' tell her I'll be on hand to open 'em as usual."

Kent waited for the door to close before he laughed. "Poor old codger, he'll never touch beer again. Someone is poaching on his ledges, of course."

"It must be someone from away then, Lissa says that no villager would trespass."

"Good morning, Lex."

Framed in the opening of the French window stood Madge Millard.

"Come in," Carson welcomed.

"You here, Tod?" she exclaimed as she entered. "The sun is so strong outside. I didn't see you in the shadowy room. If you two boys are in conference—I'm posted on business terms, please take notice—I'll come some other time. I was on my way to the farmhouse for eggs and thought I'd take a chance on finding Lex. He's so absorbed in estate matters that he hasn't been to see us."

Her nervous chatter was so unlike her that Carson glanced at Kent. He gave an imperceptible nod of understanding before he assured;

"Lex and I had finished conferring, if one can call listening to Ozy, the sheriff, a conference. I'll be seeing you. Bye-bye."

As the sound of his footsteps on the terrace died away, Carson said gravely;

"Come into the room, Madge. Don't stand there by the window as if you were afraid of me."

"Afraid of you, Lex! You're the last person in the world of whom I'd be afraid. You've been so wonderful to Andy and Jack and me. You've been like a rock to cling to when it seemed as if I couldn't bear anxiety a moment longer."

Her yellow frock was like a patch of sunshine against the dark wood of the mantel. She was pale. Her voice had broken on the last word.

"Andy's not worse, is he?"

"No. Better, amazingly better. I never can be grateful enough to Lissa Barclay and her dog. That girl is the sweetest thing, I don't wonder you love her, Lex. She has taken Andy out in her yellow roadster every day with G-Man sitting like a sentinel between them. He adores her. He said to me only yesterday;

" 'Lissa isn't afraid for me, Mother, she makes me feel that I'll be strong and well and rough like other boys some day. Gee, I'd like to feel rough.' "

"Is Andy's admiration of Lissa what is troubling you, Madge? Are you jealous of her?"

"No! No, Lex, how could you think that? It's—it's Jack. Remember that you warned me that—that he might be lonely?"

She rested one arm on the mantel. Head averted, she said;

"Don't think I blame Jack. You were right, I haven't been very companionable."

82

"I ought to be shot for putting such a fool idea into your head. Who's the woman?"

"Cleo Barclay. You would have known if you hadn't been away. She is always dropping in for tea and taking Jack off in her car to tell her about some unusual tree she has discovered. She says she's writing a book about trees and needs his expert advice."

Carson checked a laugh as he saw the expression of her eyes.

"Cleo writing a book! That's the funniest thing I ever heard. You know that Jack adores the very ground you walk on. Cleo Barclay is a blonde, and an artificial one at that. Ever know him to fall for a blonde? He likes 'em dark. You ought to know that."

She raised her head and smiled through a mist of tears.

"I do! I do! I got panicky, and went all to pieces. Now that anxiety about Andy isn't pressing on me like a leaden weight, I've lost my bearings. Lex, you're a dear! You know how I love Jack. It cut to the quick when that girl—"

She hid her face against his shoulder and broke into a passion of tears. He put his arm about her tenderly.

"Cry it out, Madge! You've had a good cry coming to you for months." He had said that to Lissa, he remembered. "You—"

"Look at me, Lex! Look! I walked here!" called a high boyish voice.

Madge Millard raised her head. Lex Carson's eyes flashed to the open window. Lissa Barclay and Andy stood there looking in.

xiv

SWIFTLY the boy's mother crossed the room, dropped to her knees beside him, encircled him with her arms. Her face was radiant.

"You walked! All the way from the Treasure Chest, Andy? How marvelous! Tired, dear?"

He straightened his thin shoulders. His eyes reflected the blue of his linen blouse and shorts as he disclaimed;

"Tired! Course not, but, your roadster's outside so I guess

I'll ride home." He spoke to the dog, who with head on one side, was watching him. "Coming, G-Man?"

The Irish terrier looked at Lissa. She nodded.

"Run along, G-Man. Send him home when you take your nap, Andy."

"I will. There's Fenton! Hi, Fenton!" the boy hailed. The butler who was passing on the terrace stopped.

"How are you today, Master Andy?"

"I'm fine. I walked here. I'm getting strong, Fenton. Gee, feel my muscle!" He held out a thin, tanned arm. The butler closed his hand about it and nodded approval.

"It's coming along, Master Andy. It's surely coming along."

"I guess there'll be no trouble with my holding on with that arm when I ride in the merry-go-round at the Fair, will there, Fenton?" he asked anxiously.

"Not the slightest in the world, Master Andy. And if Madam, your mother, is willing, I'll ride beside you and show you how to sit your horse."

"May he, mother? May Fenton take me on the merry-go-round?"

"Of course dear, it's kind of Fenton to think of it. Come home now and get your rest."

With her arm about the boy's shoulders, she lingered in the embrasure of the window.

"Thank you, Lex, for—for everything. I can't begin to thank you, Lissa, you've been so wonderful—" Tears choked her voice.

"Don't thank me. I love being with Andy. For three years I lived with Aunt Hetty who had forgotten how to be young. Playing round with him makes a fair average."

Lissa's voice died away as she and the mother and boy crossed the terrace.

She had gone without a word to him. Lex Carson paced the floor. He visualized her startled eyes as they had met his above Madge's head against his shoulder. Of course she would misconstrue the situation, equally of course, she couldn't understand that Madge had had to cry, had needed terribly a shoulder against which to sob out the pent emotion of months. Unfortunate, darned unfortunate, that it had happened to be his and not her husband's.

Could there be any truth in what Madge had told him about Cleo Barclay? He wouldn't put it past her to try to fascinate Jack. She was the family-breaker type, and he was attractive enough and rich enough to be fair game for her. What a crazy suspicion. He wouldn't fall for a girl like that. He couldn't believe it. Not of Jack. He'd better forget it— quick.

Impatiently he picked up the special delivery letter, ripped t open and pulled out a newspaper. His eyes flashed to the date.

"February! It's come! About time," he said under his breath.

He spread the paper on the desk. Took from the safe the two scraps he had torn from the newspaper in the lighthouse. He compared the dates. The same. He tried to fit the torn-off corner on the newspaper. It didn't match. He compared dates again. Okay. It might be a later edition which had omitted the item he was after. Only one more page. He had it! He had it! The printed lines ran parallel!

He read the item framed within the diamond-shaped opening in the scrap he had brought from the lighthouse. It didn't make sense. He picked up the long envelope in which the newspaper had been mailed. Waste of money to have sent it special delivery, waste of Ozy's time—

Ozy! A light blazed through his mind. Ozy! Ozy had said "one evenin' long 'bout the last of June—"

He seized the paper and reread the item which stood out as if boxed within the diamond-shaped opening.

"I'll be darned!" he said under his breath. "I'll be—darned."

Someone knocking. He caught up the papers and thrust them into the safe. His pulses raced. He had to steady his voice before he called;

"Come in."

Simonds, the foreman, entered. His gaunt, gangling figure was attired in good looking clothes which proclaimed him dressed for an occasion, not work. The man had come to make trouble, Carson was sure of it. He motioned to a chair.

"Sit down, Simonds, and tell me what's on your mind."

"No. I'll stand." The foreman twirled the pencil at the end of his gold chain. "It won't take me long to say my say. The men won't accept a cut in wages."

"What does that mean? Don't beat about the bush. Give it to me straight."

Simonds thumped one hairy fist on the top of a crimson leather chairback.

"It means this. We listened to your talk of cutting wages. You've come into one of the biggest fortunes ever willed in this state—I hear you're rich in your own right, too. They say you're a smart lawyer. Well, let me tell you, there isn't a lawyer in this country smart enough to cut the wages of the bunch of men working on this place. What've you got to say to that?"

"What I said yesterday. The wages will be cut."

"Oh, no they won't. Because we won't take them. We'll

give you time to think it over, if you still say 'cut,' at the end of the week, we'll walk out."

"If you walk out, not one of you ever will walk back. There are fifteen of you, fifteen families will be without a weekly pay-cheque. Better think it over."

The big Adam's apple in Simond's throat bulged and contracted.

"I guess you're the one to think it over. About sundown when the prize cows haven't been milked nor fed, and the poultry is clucking its head off for food, you'll think us men worth the wages we were paid. Good morning. You know where to find me when you want me."

"Yes, I know where to find you. At your 'office.' And, Simonds, be sure that the men understand that if they walk out, they walk out for good."

He opened the door to the residence office in response to a quick tattoo on its panels. Lissa stood there. Her eyes were like stars. She waved an envelope.

"It's come, Lex. An acceptance of my story, after, I'll confess now—the twenty-fifth trip. I believed in that story. I don't dare open it myself. Will you—"

The radiance faded from her face as she saw the foreman. He spoke quickly;

"You'd better make the new boss listen to reason, Miss."

Lissa's eyes followed him as he strode into the hall and banged the door behind him. They came back to Carson still standing before the mantel.

"What did Simonds mean?"

For an instant his voice failed him, a pulse drummed in his throat. The expression of her eyes when she had turned away with Madge and the boy had been like a steel clamp about his heart, squeezing it intolerably. The relief, the incredible relief, that she had come to him in her happiness! He said, with an effort to keep his voice light;

"Simonds and the men threaten a walk-out if I persist in the pay-cut."

"Will you?"

"I must. I can't afford to pay what I offered, which is more than they would get if they were working for the county, but I couldn't let them down too much."

"I wonder if Marty Simonds knows of the planned walk-out?"

"Let's skip them, Lissa. Let's talk about you and the short story."

"The short story." Her eyes blazed with excitement. "Imagine my forgetting it for anyone. I came to you directly I found this in my mail. Remember I told you that you were

86

the only person to whom I talked about my work—that is, before I met Mr. Packard?" She held out an envelope. "Open it, will you? That story has been in the editor's hands over three months. I'm too shivery. Know what I've planned to do with the cheque? Start a travel fund."

"Lissa, don't take it so seriously. Suppose it shouldn't be an acceptance?"

"If it isn't, I can take it. But, what else can it be after all this time? The manuscript hasn't come back. Open it!"

Carson slit the envelope and drew out a sheet of paper. His eyes followed the typed lines.

"Hurry up! Read it!" the girl prodded. "It is an acceptance, isn't it?"

"An acceptance—of sorts." He read aloud—

"Dear Miss Barclay;

We like your story, HIGH HARVEST. You have a great theme. The denouement is a bit too obvious but with your permission we will change that. As we are not at present paying cash for contributions, we are giving you four yearly subscriptions to our magazine. Trusting that this will be satisfactory, we are,

Very truly yours,
The Editors."

Lissa's face was blankly incredulous, then it crinkled into laughter, though Carson could see the glitter of tears in her eyes.

"Four subscriptions! For my grand story HIGH HARVEST! It's too—too funny! Suppose I can sell them for my travel fund? Perhaps you'll buy one?" The sentence rippled into a shaky laugh.

"Steady, Lissa. You'll have hysterics if you don't watch out."

"I? Never. Writers who get there don't have hysterics. I've always claimed that success in writing—provided of course one had what it takes to make a writer—is like success in marriage, largely a question of good sportsmanship, of keeping on keeping on, of giving one's best and trying, everlastingly trying to make that best, better. The offer struck me as funny, that's all."

"Will you let it go for four subscriptions to their dinky magazine? Will you let them change the ending?"

"No, to that last question. It isn't a dinky magazine. It has good backing but I think too much of my ch—child—" her voice caught, "to let it go for that."

"Apparently you've made a smash hit with the theme. What is it? Mind telling?"

"No. The idea came from a sort of back-to-the-family article I read. It may be because my own family life was such a hodge-podge that it seems to me that there is no more important, no more up-to-the-minute need, no higher career for a woman than that of wifehood and home-maker, to answer 'Here!' when a child comes home and calls, 'Where's Mother?' It takes in everything, economics, business and government laws, a communal viewpoint, and comradeship, courage, sacrifice, and last, but not least, a sense of humor. It calls for a sporting instinct if anything does."

"What's the matter with that theme? It's vital."

"Speaking with the Voice of Rejection Slips, it has a 'Woman's-place-is-in-the-home' taint which is out-of-date at present, and my story is worth four magazine subscriptions, nothing more."

"Lissa, don't feel so hurt. I—I can't bear it, darling."

"Don't call me that! First, Madge, then me. When I saw this letter I was so excited I forgot the tender scene I interrupted a few moments ago."

"Lissa! You're wrong. I'm too old-fashioned to go in for wife-snitching. You're not consistent. You said you believe that the beautiful things of life are as real as the ugly things of life, yet you won't believe that a man's love for you may be true and steadfast."

"I believe my eyes, too. I was silly enough to have put you on a pedestal. Now you've fallen off and—and—crashed and there isn't a piece of the person I thought you were, big enough to pick up."

She had put him on a pedestal! She had liked him that much! She wasn't in love with Johnny Grant, she couldn't be. He could explain. He'd make her love him. He'd wait until her anger had cooled, meanwhile he'd try diplomacy.

"I'm sorry you feel like that, Lissa, because I'm in a jam. Tod and I need your help."

"My help! Is Tod in love with Madge, too?"

"Forget that—please. I'll take up the matter of whom I love, later. What I am about to tell you is strictly confidential. Can I trust you?"

She crossed her throat with a pink-tipped finger.

"I promise."

He glanced into the hall. Closed the door. Returned to the desk. A soft breeze sifted through the Venetian blinds and stirred a lock of the girl's auburn hair. A sparrow chirped outside.

"I am a lawyer, Lissa, but because I've specialized in criminal law I've been drafted by the Treasury to work on a case."

"Are you a—a G-Man, Lex?" Her brown eyes were wide and startled.

"Nothing so dramatic. Do you remember that in a world-famous case ransom money was traced by a map?"

He unlocked a flat drawer in the end of the desk. Lissa, beside him, looked down. Her eyes flew to his.

"Why—why—it's a map of this state and New Hampshire!"

He nodded and indicated colored pegs which outlined a large area near the coast.

"What do the pegs mean, Lex?"

He closed the drawer. Locked it and dropped the key into his pocket.

"Stand beside me." His voice was low. "Face doors and windows. Keep watch for shadows outside, while I tell you that somewhere within that pegged-in area is a man or men whom the Government wants."

"I'm a-shiver with excitement. What are they? Bootleggers? Kidnappers?"

"Neither. Nothing so rough. White-collar workers. Counterfeiters."

XV

"COUNTERFEITERS!" Lissa echoed incredulously.

"Yes. Did you have time to notice that the pegged-in area covers several counties on the coast? A year ago, it was discovered that counterfeit coins and bills were seeping through the two states. The map was set up. Whenever a piece of bad money was reported, the town from which it came would be pegged. Two hundred thousand bogus dollars and unlimited small coin has been rounded up. So far the gang —my mistake, organization is the word now—hasn't tried to pass anything but small stuff, but undoubtedly there are bigger bills ready to float."

"Has no one been caught trying to pass the bad money?"

"There are ten persons serving time now, but they say they don't know where it came from, though they confess they bought it, sometimes one hundred dollars' worth of bogus bills and coins for ten dollars in good money. We're after the man who, we are sure, is the brains of the organization.

One of his aliases—he has a number, is 'The Ace.' He was arrested about four years ago, and fingerprinted, but was not convicted."

"Then you're a detective?"

"No. I'm a lawyer—with a few cells in my brain which start pricking when there's a mystery in the air. The Treasury Department heard of one case I solved and drafted me on this. Not being a professional, it figured I could get at things better than one of its men. The fact that I was the residuary legatee of Tarry Farm gave an excellent reason for my vacation in the very middle of the pegged-in area."

"Are Tod Kent and the electrical engineers here on that business?"

"Yes. The harbor was the best port for the cruiser. We can spread out in all directions from here. Tod helped me once before and the two men who pass for engineers are really criminologists. Somewhere within that pegged-in area are the plates of a complete counterfeiting outfit, I'm sure of it. One whisper of our errand and all our work to date would go blooey. You realize that, don't you?"

Lissa's eyes were brilliant and eager and friendly.

"I do. I realize also that this county is in the middle of the area. You wouldn't have told me this unless you thought I could help, would you? Of course I will, I promise. I hope I shan't feel like Mata Hari doing it. I—that's Fenton's discreet knock. What does he want? Sure you locked that drawer?"

"I did, don't look at it. Not that Fenton would know what it meant if you did. I told him yesterday what I would pay the house-staff and asked him to lay the cut before them. He's probably here to report another walk-out. Come in!"

Fenton closed the door behind him. He looked at Lissa and then interrogatively at Carson, who responded to his unspoken question;

"It's all right, Fenton. Miss Barclay knows that I asked you to interview the house servants. Shoot. What's the verdict?"

"We accept the cut, sir. The maids realize what a power for good in the community the late Madam was, sir, and that they have been highly paid and we're all glad if we can help you get your business affairs straightened out, sir."

It was an instant before Carson could swallow the lump the unexpected decision brought to his throat.

"Tell them I appreciate their co-operation, Fenton."

"Yes, sir, they'll be glad to hear that you are pleased, sir. As I told them, 'Man may not live by bread alone.' There's something in the world besides money. Anything else, sir?"

"Only that the men outside have threatened to walk out."

"Is that so, sir? If you will excuse me for asking about something that is outside my department, what will you do about the cows, if they do, sir?"

"Cows?"

"Yes, milking them, sir. We are exhibiting at the County Fair shortly and we'd lose a ribbon or two if they get out of condition. I helped select some of them. My father had the care of the prize cattle on Lord Byram's estate in England. I got to know a lot about them. I'm—I'm very fond of cows, sir, in short, I have a sort of passion for them. I'll do the milking—if necessary. The late Madam wouldn't allow mechanical milkers to be used."

Carson was aware of the flash of laughter in Lissa's eyes. Had she visualized as he had the butler's immobile face and sideburns bent over a milk pail?

"Thank you, Fenton, if the men do walk out and things get screwy, it will help to know that you're standing by. But, I can't believe they will. They have too much to lose."

"I wouldn't be so sure, sir. One specked apple in a barrel can do a lot of damage to the other apples, and if you'll excuse me for saying it, sir, Simonds, the foreman, is badly specked. I presume that the party at the pool and the lobster-bake will come off next week as planned, Miss?"

Lissa looked at Carson. He assented;

"Of course, that is unless we are boycotted and can't get the goods for it."

"The barrels have already been delivered, sir. Captain Ozias will bring the lobsters and clams, there's no danger of him striking. If you will excuse my saying so, I have seen this walk-out coming. I know human nature, sir. If that's all, I'll get back to my work. Thank you, sir." The door closed behind him.

"Fenton's a trump. How long has he been here, Lissa?" Carson asked.

"Three years. During that time the others on the house-staff, except the cook, have been from about here. When Aunt Hetty decided to make her all-year home at Tarry Farm, she decided also, that in so far as possible, the money to carry on the place should be spent in this county. It was her idea of community service. The village girls have come here, been perfectly trained as waitresses, parlor, personal, upstairs maids and laundresses, have even been taught to cook; have departed to give place to others. Their wages were high, but —perfect service was demanded in return. Aunt Hetty believed that the mental discipline and efficiency acquired by such rigorous training would be invaluable when they took up other work and that the how-it's-done knowledge would cost them nothing to carry around."

"I call that community service—plus. Didn't Fenton protest at the program? It must have made extra work for him."

"It did, but he appeared to be as proud of results as Aunt Hetty was. I trained the upstairs and he the downstairs maids. He was a stiff disciplinarian, but the girls liked him. His salary has been spectacularly high, but you have cut it and he stays on. I feel as if I should go down on my knees and apologize to him. As I told you before, I've never really liked him."

"Why?"

"I don't know why. I couldn't state a single incident upon which my aversion was founded. He did all the buying for the place—Aunt Hetty would give him cheques and he would pay cash. She wouldn't allow us to have a bill. Why do you look at me like that?"

"Like what?"

"As if you were staring through my head at something that startled you. Your face went white."

"Thought someone moved outside the door. It was a risk to tell you what I'm after where we might be overheard. Do you wonder I'm suspicious of every sound? If anyone is outside, keep your eyes away from that drawer." He looked into the hall, closed the door.

"No one there. I'm getting jumpy. Hope I'm not developing nerves. Go on. You said that Fenton turned cheques into cash and you wondered—"

"I wondered if perhaps he put some of the money into his own pocket. He didn't. I kept the house books and his expenditures and receipted bills balanced to a cent. My dislike of him has been tempered since he has been so kind to Andy. Now it has been turned to admiration by his loyalty. I think loyalty is the grandest quality in the world."

"Is that why you're sticking to Johnny Grant?"

The question was on the air before Carson realized that he was asking it. It brought a pink stain to Lissa's face.

"What do you mean by sticking?" she demanded truculently.

"Oh, running round with him, swimming and dining and—well, just sticking."

"I don't like that word. You've cross-examined me before about my—my friendship with Johnny, and as I told you then, I don't consider it your business. I'm not swimming and dining with him any more than I am with Tod Kent or the two electrical engineers—I forgot, they aren't engineers, are they—or—"

"Ralph Packard?"

"How did you know?" She set her teeth hard in her lips as if disciplining them for having allowed the startled question to escape.

"I'm not so submerged by business problems that I don't know and care what happens to you, beautiful."

"That's nice of you. Especially when you have other persons in whom you are so deeply interested."

She took a step toward the door, turned; reminded in a low voice,

"Fenton said that Simonds is 'badly specked.' He may be one of the men you're looking for."

"I was thinking that myself," Carson agreed. "Bring me the leases and references of the three cottages, will you?"

His eyes followed her as she left the room. Would he never learn? Just when she appeared interested and friendly he had gone haywire and lugged Johnny Grant into the picture. His inductive reasoning might pick up clues and link one into another till it solved a crime mystery but it was a total loss when it came to helping him with the girl he loved.

Lissa returned and dropped some papers on the desk.

"What's happened?" he demanded. "You're white."

"The leases of Red Chimneys and the Packard references are gone."

"Gone! Don't you keep the filing cabinet locked?"

"Why should I? There has never been anything in it that anyone would want."

"Except that lease and the references, evidently. You may have mislaid it. It isn't important. I'm interested in the Pirates' Den lease and the references of Major Fane."

"Those are among the papers on your desk."

"Then that's all right. I'll keep the leases in my safe for the present. Better keep the filing cabinet locked after this, Lissa."

"I'll lock it this minute."

He waited until she had left the room before he scooped up the papers she had dropped to the desk. He thought as he placed them in the safe without looking at them;

"Lissa couldn't have suspected from my bluff that the absence of that lease and reference is just one more link in the chain of evidence. This has been what she would call, 'Just one of those days.' "

"I'm not so submerged by business problems that I don't know and care what happens to you, beautiful."

During the night the words echoed and re-echoed through Lissa's mind. She couldn't sleep. How had Lex Carson dared say that to her barely ten minutes after she had seen Madge in his arms? After her experience with Johnny Grant, she'd been a weak sister to have taken him seriously for a minute. Why shouldn't he think a girl would believe anything he said, who, after seeing him making love to a married woman, had rushed to him with the news that she had sold a story? When she had seen that envelope on her desk, she had forgotten everything but the fact that her story was sold—which it wasn't—and that Lex must hear the wonderful news.

Suppose he had sounded sincere? Hadn't Johnny said the same sort of thing to her and didn't he fall in love with Cleo the first time he saw her? She knew now by the way it had hurt when she saw Lex's arms around Madge that she had not been in love with Johnny. He had hurt her pride, not her heart. He had been just someone who eased her loneliness after the loss of her father.

No wonder Lex's words haunted her, she excused herself, the tenderness of his voice and eyes had drawn her like a magnet. She had saved herself by thrusting the memory of Madge between them. There was no excuse for allowing herself to care for Lex Carson, she'd had warnings.

She sat up and hugged her knees. She must thrust Lex and Madge from her mind. She'd much better think of the reason for the arrival of The Sphinx in the harbor. The memory sent little icy chills skittering through her veins. It was incredible that government investigation had narrowed to an area on the coast and that she was in the very middle of the storm belt. If only she could help. What an adventure to have a part in! Who would have suspected Lex Carson, with his clear amused voice, his quizzical eyes, his perfectly cut clothes, his social technic, of being a secret-service man—call it by any name you liked—that was what he was. Was it possible that the papers missing from the filing cabinet had anything to do with his quest? No. He had been interested only in Pirates' Den lease. Was he suspicious of Major Fane?

What a waste to spend time in bed when the very air outside might be tingling with sinister signals, beating with the wings of mystery. It was almost morning, she wouldn't stay in her room another moment.

She slipped a shimmering green satin lounge coat over her pale blue pajamas, thrust her bare feet into silver mules and scuffed her way to the balcony.

The sheer beauty of the world outide tightened her throat. The east was crimsoning. Glow from a hidden flame turned silvery clouds to saffron islands and tinted the edge of those higher up with rose. Stars were silver-gilt. The quiet sea was indigo, the riding lights of the cruiser paled as the mounting glow turned its brass trimmings to swaying flames. The lighthouse loomed like a blood-red tower. A gull soared like a faint white spirit faring forth to greet the rising sun.

Arms on the balcony rail, thoughtful gaze on the glittering eye of the light, accompanied by the chirp, chirp of crickets, Lissa reviewed what Lex Carson had told her of the hunt for the counterfeiters. His startling story strengthened her in her belief that she had seen a signal from the lighthouse the night before he had come to Tarry Farm, that the flash had not been part of a dream.

Who could have given the signal? There wasn't a person in the village whom she would suspect of dishonesty. She had told Lex that Nino had asked to go to the lamp-room but he hadn't seemed disturbed by the fact.

"Simonds, the foreman, is badly specked."

The words echoed through her mind as distinctly as if Fenton were beside her saying them.

Simonds! Did he suspect that the law was on his trail? Was he planning this walk-out to switch attention to that? Attention would be switched good and plenty if fifteen employees deserted Tarry Farm. No matter how evil Lem Simonds might be, Marty, his wife, knew nothing of it, she was sure. She would give the foreman and men time to think it over. If they didn't take back their threat to walk out at the end of the week if Lex didn't accept their terms, she'd talk with Marty. Marty was a power with the wives and daughters. She'd better stop thinking about it and get some sleep.

"And so to bed," she said aloud.

The glow had reached lawn and gardens now. Great heads of hydrangeas, just coming into bloom, blushed faintly in the light. Moisture on trees and shrubs sparkled like pink diamonds. Trap nets that blood-thirsty spiders had woven cunningly in the night were scattered on the lawn like filmy handkerchiefs dropped by fairies fleeing as dawn crept up on them.

She stretched up her arms, lifted her face and filled her lungs with the dew-washed air.

"Thanks for this lovely world, God," she whispered. With a backward glance at the lighthouse, which appeared to regard her with a knowing eye, she entered her room.

LISSA slowly walked along a road bordered by yellow tansy and white yarrow blooming against the blended grays and browns, the gleaming marble and silver-flecked granite of a stone wall, which dipped and mounted and dipped again as if determined, old as it was, to keep pace with the modern black highway, which ran ahead to cities and villages it would never reach.

At dawn six days ago, talking over the proposed walk-out with Marty Simonds had seemed a brilliant idea, she told herself, but as she neared the foreman's vine-smothered cottage set in a tidy, colorful garden, it didn't seem such a world-beater.

She crossed her arms on top of the white fence. G-Man beside her stuck his nose close to the pickets as he furtively regarded Goldie, a big tortoiseshell cat with back hunched, who stared at him with hypnotic topaz eyes.

"Morning, Marty!"

The wispy woman in a black and white print dress, on her knees attacking weeds in the border of purple petunias and orange-king calendulas against the house, nodded and smiled and kept on with her work. As Lissa watched her, her courage oozed. Opening up the disagreeable subject didn't seem so simple. She deployed:

"It's a lovely day, isn't it? I've never seen the sky bluer nor the water more like a mine of shimmering sapphires. Listen to that thrush!"

Marty Simonds' busy hands stilled, as a firm, flute-like sound was followed by ascending and descending notes of incredible sweetness, rising higher and higher in the scale only to climax in a clear silvery tinkle.

The woman on her knees released her breath in a soft sigh.

"Isn't it wonderful! So rich and mellow and poured out so easy, as if the bird couldn't help its coming. Wish some of the radio singers would take lessons of a thrush. What have you been doing, child?" She tipped her head and looked sidewise at Lissa with bright, dark eyes.

"What I've been doing seems stodgy after listening to

that heavenly song. I've just come from the shore. I wanted to be sure that everything needed for the lobster-bake was on hand, that the rocks were the right size and that the men understood that they were to be red hot before they were put into the bottom of the barrels, that they hadn't scrimped on cheese cloth in which to wrap the tinker mackerel, and that there were buckets and buckets of clean salt water, plenty of canvas and heaps of rock weed. Everything was okay and the lobsters, clams and fish are ready to cook."

"Got potatoes ready to go in?"

"Yes, sweet, white, and green corn. The watermelons are packed in tubs of ice."

"I guess you've thought of everything. The weather an' the lobster-bake weren't what you came here to talk about, were they, Lissa? When I saw you coming in that lilac cotton, you know is my favorite color, I knew you had something serious you wanted to talk over with me."

"I've told you before, Marty, that you're psychic, and I've told you also, that talking things over with you has kept me from blowing-up emotionally heaps of times during these last three years."

She opened the gate and barely escaped squeezing the dog's nose as she quickly closed it.

"You can't come into Marty's garden, G-Man, until you've learned to be a perfect gentleman. Have you forgotten that the last time you were here you treed Goldie and ran off with Marty's black cape she was airing on the line?"

She turned her back on the Irish terrier's reproachful eyes, ignored his sharp bark of protest, and sat down on a yellow wheelbarrow. Hands clasped about one knee, she watched the woman's knotty fingers work with expertness and despatch in spite of the tortoiseshell cat who was rubbing its back against them.

"It would be a help if flower plants would grow as fast and luxuriantly as weeds, wouldn't it?"

Marty Simonds sank on her heels and brushed back a wisp of gray hair with earthstained fingers.

"Isn't that just the way with folks, Lissa? Don't their faults grow faster than their virtues? Leastwise, sometimes I think that's the way it is round here." She vented disapproval of her neighbors on a stubborn root. Lissa plunged.

"That's really what I came to talk to you about, Marty. The walk-out at Tarry Farm."

The sudden capitulation of the weed sent Marty Simonds back on her heels. It dangled from her hand as she demanded;

"What walk-out?"

Lissa told of Carson's decision to cut wages and of the foreman's threat. She concluded;

"Your husband accused Lex Carson of pleading poverty, but, it's not true, Marty. I've kept accounts for Aunt Hetty for three years, and I know that expenses are terrific. The men have given him until tomorrow to take back the cut. If he doesn't, they'll walk out. I supposed you knew about it."

"Know about it! They wouldn't let me know. I've scolded too much about their fool ideas. I'll bet their wives don't know." She threw tools into a garden basket and rose with the agility of a girl.

"What will you do?"

"Talk to the women. They're all knitting crazy. Making dresses. Do you think they'll stand for an idle man hanging round the house asking what they're making, an' why they're making it, an' don't they think they'd better be canning or braiding? I know how it is. How long did you say the men are giving Mr. Carson to take back the wage-cut?"

"Until tomorrow noon."

"They picked a good time. The County Fair opens tomorrow an' the wives'll be busy gettin' their exhibits arranged. You should have told me before, Lissa."

"It seemed so like telling tales that I waited, hoping that the men would realize how well they had been paid through the years, be sports and take the cut. Even then, Lex Carson is paying them more than he can afford."

"I like that young man. Nice mannered. Lem and I went to the big house to welcome him when he first came and he called on me one afternoon, couldn't have treated me better if I'd been First Lady. If I had youngsters, I'd starve manners into them if I couldn't make them learn any other way. Surprising what starving will accomplish with those who love their food." Her laugh was brittle. "After honor, good manners is about the best asset a person can have. Your aunt realized that. What a lot she did for our young people. She gave them something better than money—they earned a nice little pile of that too—when she gave them the training they got at Tarry Farm. They're showing the result of it in the choices they're making as they go on in life. Land sakes, how I am running on."

"I love to hear you 'run on,' Marty. I think you're wonderful and—and I'm terribly fond of you."

Marty Simonds blinked a mist from her snapping eyes.

"You're a sweet child, Lissa, perhaps sweet isn't just the word, spicy fits you better, neither is fond the word that expresses my feeling for you. Run along an' get ready for the lobster-bake. I'll be on hand to help dish up as usual. I suppose Ozy'll be there to open the lobsters—he won't miss the chance to hear what's goin' on. Don't tell him about the walk-out or t'will be all over town by night. Everybody'll blame Lem, he isn't very popular, but except for the fact that he's terrible close with money, he's a good husband."

Simonds was close with money. Did he love it enough to pass bad money? The thought sent the blood in a quick tide to Lissa's hair. Marty was looking at her sharply. Could she possibly suspect what she was thinking? She asked hurriedly;

"Do you really think you can stop the walk-out?"

Marty Simonds picked up the tortoiseshell cat brushing against her skirt. Her laugh was like a dry cough.

"My tongue's in good working order. All I need besides that is plenty of gas in the flivver and time. Don't worry, child. Run along and get ready for your party."

Later, as Lissa fastened the green belt of her white frock, she stepped out on the balcony of her room. Time had slipped away since that dawn when, arms folded on this very railing she had wondered what she would do next. Now, the borders of the path to the shore were a riot of gorgeous color. Mammoth zinnias, gold, rose, lemon, nodded in the soft breeze; towering lilies swung in the air like rusty red bells; shafts of purple and lavender monkshood made a soft background for phlox, clumps of it, salmon, white and cherry red and off in a bed by themselves where their jewel tints would not be dimmed by the strong colors in the border, hundreds of gladiolas raised their dainty faces to the sun.

Weeks had passed, she thought again, and still she had no definite plans for the future. How could she plan until she knew how long she would be needed at Tarry Farm? She certainly would be needed if the men walked out. Would they walk out? She chuckled as she visualized Marty Simonds' expression as she had said;

"Surprising what starving will accomplish with those who love their food."

Would she starve Lem into subjection? Apparently she loved him even if he were "close." Love did strange things to people. There was Johnny Grant who had been so desperately in love with Cleo, hanging round the house in which she was living, apparently not caring at all for her, but again devoting himself to the girl to whom he had been first engaged. And Lex in love with his friend's wife.

There she was again, thinking of Lex and Madge! If she didn't watch out, she'd begin to be sorry for herself. Love wasn't the only thing in the world, was it? Not when one had an ambition and determination to be an arrived writer, not when a new life lay ahead with fascinating adventure lurking in the offing, not when this perfect afternoon had been made for the swimming party and lobster-bake.

There wasn't a cloud in the clear turquoise sky except for a few piled like a snow-drift on the western horizon, probably for the sole purpose of adding a spectacular effect or two when the sun set. The sea was smooth. The green of distant hills fused into hazy purple as it neared the peaks which were reflected in the still water as in a gigantic blue mirror. The lighthouse on her island shone like a mother-of-pearl shaft with one great eye. It wasn't an island now, the ledge which connected it with the mainland was a sandy road upon which two automobiles were parked. A picnic party, probably. From the shore rose white plumes of steam from cooking shellfish and seaweed. She sniffed. Delicious smell! It made her ravenously hungry.

She ran down the broad stairs singing under her breath;

> " 'There is a green hill far away
> Without a city wall.' "

She had played the hymn on the organ in church last Sunday. She broke off with a laugh as she remembered how the congregation had dragged on the last line as if they couldn't bear to let it go.

"Lissa! Wait!"

Cleo hailed her from the threshold of the library. The rich woodwork of the room behind her accentuated the delicacy of her pale blue sports suit, the gold of her hair the rose-leaf perfection of her skin.

"She looks positively angelic—sweet as sugar—and her eyes are like glowing sapphires," Lissa thought. No wonder Lex Carson said she was a knockout. She, herself, felt like a splashy oil-painting beside a delicate water color.

"What do you want, Cleo? Make it snappy. I ought to be at the pool. I'll have to do a marathon now to get there before the first guests arrive."

"Got any money, Lissa? I'm being hounded by shops to pay overdue bills. Let me have five hundred dollars, will you? I can throw that to the pack and it will stop them for a while."

"Five hundred dollars! I haven't it, Cleo." Lucky she had asked Lex Carson not to pay her salary or income until she was ready to leave Tarry Farm.

"I've got to have it! How much have you?"

"Oh, perhaps the magnificent sum of ten dollars."

"I don't believe it. Hasn't Lex paid your income?"

"Aunt Hetty's estate is still being settled."

"Then you'd better get another trustee. If the present one spent more time on your business and less at the Treasure Chest—appropriately named—it holds his treasure, doesn't it—perhaps he'd push your business along."

Evidently Cleo knew of Lex's devotion to Madge. In spite of her certainty that the insinuation had turned her heart to a hunk of hard, cold ice, Lissa said lightly;

"You'd be a find for a newsreel outfit, Cleo. You belong to the ancient and honorable order of sees-all-hears-all-suspects-all."

Cleo's face flushed with anger.

"I see enough to know that you've fallen for Lex Carson and fallen hard. Is Johnny Grant coming to the lobster-bake?"

"I haven't invited him. Johnny isn't what you'd call intuitive but even he may suspect from that fact that he isn't wanted."

"I want him, I'll try him for money. If he won't loan me five hundred, well, there's a last resort—fortunately."

"What do you mean, Cleo? You—"

"Ahem!"

The sound was the first intimation of the butler's presence. Cleo whirled angrily;

"For heaven's sake, Fenton, where did you come from?"

"I'm sorry, Miss Barclay, if I startled you. I clattered a bit before I entered. You are very nervous, aren't you, Miss? You are wanted on the phone, Miss Lissa."

"Who is calling?"

"He wouldn't say, Miss. Quite mysterious, the party was. Shall I tell him you won't answer till you know the name?"

There was a thread of eagerness in his voice. Lissa had suspected that somewhere deep in the butler's impenetrable calm was concealed a well developed bump of curiosity. Now she knew it. She was curious about the message herself. What mysterious "party" would call her? Was it Simonds to ask her help to prevent the wage cut?

"I'll answer on the office phone, Fenton."

As she crossed the hall, Cleo reminded;

"Don't forget about Johnny Grant, Lissa."

"If you want him at the lobster-bake, do your own inviting. There are two phone lines to Tarry Farm."

What scheme was the lovely Cleo about to put across now? Would she ask Johnny for money? Her eyes and voice had been desperate. She must owe a great deal, Lissa thought as she lifted the phone. The voice at the other end of the wire scattered all speculation as to her sister's debts.

"That you, Lissa?"

Ozy! Wasn't he coming to open the lobsters? Whom could she get to take his place this late in the day? She put her mouth close to the transmitter;

"Don't tell me that you can't come to the lobster-bake, Ozy!"

"Sure, I'll be there. I just wanted to know if Lex is home."

"He went away two days ago. He said he would be back in time for the bake, but that he might be late."

"By mighty, that's bad. Will Tod Kent, the fella that owns the cruiser be there?"

"Yes."

Lissa didn't need the aid of television to get a picture of the little man with his forward thrust head and his bright eyes at the other end of the wire.

"He'll have to do, I guess. Don't let anyone know I inquired for Lex. Sure, now. I'll be on hand as usual to open the lobsters."

Lissa was aware that Cleo had entered the room. Was Ozy helping Lex and Tod? She said hurriedly into the transmitter;

"All right, I'll expect you. Good-bye!"

As she cradled the phone Cleo asked;

"Who was the mysterious party? Your voice was shaking with excitement."

"It's a wonder I spoke at all. When I found it was Ozy at the other end of the wire, I thought he was phoning that he couldn't open the lobsters. Then where would I be? He'd have to be mysterious, mystery is that man's first name."

"Is he coming?"

"Yes."

"So is Johnny." Cleo's eyes glinted above the cigarette lighter. "I told him you wanted him."

xvii

In her flame-color swim suit, Lissa sat on the rim of the pool of sun-warmed water and watched Tod Kent mount the steps to the high diving board. For an instant his figure was outlined against the clear blue sky. He dove.

"That was clean cut," Ralph Packard approved as he established himself in a beach chair behind her. "Kent is so heavy that I always expect he'll land flat and be knocked into a cocked hat."

"But he never does." She turned to look at him. "In that white suit you might have stepped from the Well Dressed Man page. Don't you ever swim?"

"Sometimes with your sister. I'm not keen for it. You're lovelier than ever today; in this light your hair looks as if it were on fire."

Lissa turned her head away. When he spoke in that voice it had the effect of a grade-crossing bell clanging a warning. During the summer she had seen him almost every day, she had typed two stories for him. In all that time she had kept up the bars of formality. He had been "Mr. Packard" to her. Once he had called her "Lissa." She must have shown her annoyance as ever since he had said "Miss Barclay." Why should she object to his familiar use of her name? she asked herself, and could find no answer. Each time they met, he had made her feel that she was becoming of increasing importance to him. Not that she thought him really in love with her—it was merely a where-have-you-been-all-my-life mannerism. Lots of men had it, evidently thought it made them invincible in the love game. It had quite the opposite effect on her. It froze her. Why did she give his manner a moment's thought? He and Cleo had motored, swum, danced and dined together, to Mrs. Barclay's evident satisfaction. She said lightly;

"Miss Packard is marvelous in that swim-suit of sequins. It gleamed in the water like a strange tropical fish all shiny flame-color scales. That costume belongs to Hollywood, not here. Never before has anything so gorgeous swum in this pool."

Her eyes roved on to where Cleo, in a black satin water frock, which was a perfect foil for her delicate coloring, was animatedly talking to Johnny Grant who sat beside her on the rim of the pool. Was she cajoling for five hundred dollars with which to pay those overdue bills? What was the "last resort" she had threatened if she didn't get it?

"I'd give a dollar a word to know what you're thinking. First you smiled and now you're frowning."

Ralph Packard's voice brought Lissa's eyes back to him. Curious about his voice. It hadn't the quality one would expect from a man of his polished appearance and profession. Smooth as it was, it wasn't, well, cultured was a snobbish word, but that expressed it. She acknowledged gaily;

"Pity I can't find an editor who is in accord with you who

will give a dollar a word for what I write." She remembered the four magazine subscriptions and disciplined a catch in her voice. "At the moment you made your munificent offer, I was deciding that Major Fane, standing behind your sister's chair, is not at all my idea of what a Major in the United States Army should be, even a Major on sick-leave. Instead of being tall and trim with a the-world-is-mine manner, he's short and stocky and slightly furtive. Ever notice his eyes? They're opaque. I wonder what goes on behind them."

"I forgot when I made an offer for your thoughts that you are fiction-minded. Are you keeping notes on all of us?"

"I am. The Major is Case History No. I."

"What number am I?" There was a slight edge to the question.

"Haven't reached you yet, but, I warn you, you're under the microscope, so is your sister. I finished typing your short-story yesterday. I left it on my desk in the lighthouse. We can go to the island and get it after the bake, if you want it tonight."

"I do—"

"What ho, beauteous gal! Where's Himself?"

"Okay for the lighthouse," Packard whispered before Tod Kent followed his hail.

Lissa didn't like the whisper. It made her feel that she was conniving at something clandestine. She answered Kent;

"If you mean by Himself, Lex—he hasn't returned from Boston and points north. He said he would be late getting here, but that he would come."

"Running out on us is getting to be a habit with that lad. He didn't tell me he was going."

"Are you Carson's keeper?" Packard inquired smoothly.

Lissa noted the quickly subdued flash in Tod Kent's eyes before he answered jovially;

"Wish I were. I brought my boat to be here while Lex was on vacation—he hasn't had one for years—and he's hardly been at Tarry Farm two days in succession. He and I had planned to finish up this party on the cruiser. Hope you'll all come. Marty Simonds is making cabalistic signs at you, Lissa."

"That means that the clams are done to a turn. Tell the men to dress, will you, Tod, and I'll round up the girls."

Ralph Packard's confidential whisper recurred to Lissa, as in her knit frock, she left the boathouse. The more she thought of it the less she liked it. It had turned the friendly act of stopping at the island for the manuscript into a secret date.

She looked at the white cloth spread on the pebbly beach.

On it piles of green tin trays, paper plates, cups and napkins flanked glass pitchers of melted butter and pans heaped with clams that had been steamed till their shells gaped and their round, plump bodies were succulently tender.

Apparently she was the one member of the family who felt a sense of hostess responsibility. Ralph Packard was sitting close to Cleo, and Mrs. Barclay was cooing at Major Fane, who was devotedly—if clumsily supplying her wants. Curious how out of place some men seemed at a picnic. He was one of them. If she had known that Lex Carson couldn't be present, she wouldn't have planned the party, it was his pool and his shore, he ought to play host. Perhaps he was side-stepping it, perhaps it was out of tune with the problems he was facing! Problems! What a load he was carrying. On top of his love affair with Madge Millard and the financial mess of his uncle's estate, had fallen the trusteeship of her legacy, and the hunt for the counterfeiters. As if those were not enough for any one man, along had come the threatened walk-out.

"Ahem!"

Fenton, with a rattle of shells, stopped beside her, Fenton in a chef's white uniform. He had a flair for theatrical effects. He held out a green tray on which was a paper plate heaped with clams.

"Do sit down, Miss. You've been busy about this bake all day and with Mrs. Simonds here to take charge of unpacking the barrels, you needn't do anything more."

"Has she plenty of help?"

"Yes, Miss. Captain Ozias is cracking the lobsters, there are two maids from the house, two men unpacking the barrels besides that Italian from Red Chimneys who's getting under everybody's feet. I don't know who invited him, Miss."

"That Italian from Red Chimneys"—the words clanged through Lissa's mind. With them came the memory of Nino's face as he had leered at her from the door of the lighthouse. Was it possible that he had stolen the Red Chimneys' lease and the Packards' references? What possible use could he make of them?

"Ahem—as I was saying, Miss—"

"I'm sorry, Fenton. What were you saying?"

"That's quite all right, Miss. I know you have much on your mind. I was saying that there's a lot of strangers about. Look at those two automobiles parked on the road to the island. It's indecent for them to stay there and watch while you are entertaining, Miss."

"That is public land, Fenton. I doubt if they are paying any attention to us. A short time ago, I saw two persons walking on the island."

"But that's not public land, it's yours, Miss Lissa."

"What harm can they do? The lighthouse is locked." She dropped to a rug. "Give me the tray. Those clams are cooked to perfection. Is there enough of everything?"

"Yes, Miss. There'll be plenty of food after everyone here has eaten all he can."

"I'm glad the provisions are holding out. The leftovers won't be wasted. The men will take them home to their families." She asked in a low voice; "Are they helping willingly, Fenton? You know what they have threatened?"

"I do, Miss Lissa, but they aren't growling. Oh, no, they're just tumbling over each other to help. Act to me like parties who've been shaken up a bit and set down hard. I suppose Mr. Carson will be back before they—they walk out, Miss?"

"He expected to get here in time for the lobster-bake. If he doesn't come, you and I will have to carry on, Fenton."

"We can do it, Miss. It's a pity Master Andy wasn't allowed to come. He would have liked this, but I suppose they have to be very careful of him. He's a wonderful boy, Miss Lissa. He and I are great friends, if it's not presuming of me to say so. I'll serve the mackerel, Miss."

He walked away with his long white apron flapping against his ankles. Lissa dangled a clam in melted butter and dropped it into her mouth.

"Aren't you a course behind, Miss Barclay?" Major Fane inquired and carefully lowered himself to the rug beside her.

"I am. Aren't these clams luscious? I've never tasted plumper ones. Forgive me if I neglect the gentle art of conversation while I catch up, will you, Major Fane?"

"Go on, eat. Wish I could, the smell of the steaming seaweed and cooking shell fish is likely to bring on one of my dizzy spells. I wish I'd stayed home. The doctors have put me on a strict diet. I've been a sick man."

Was he about to repeat the Inside Story of his body, Lissa wondered. He had given it in such detail once that she had felt like nothing so much as an X-Ray on an exploring expedition. She said hurriedly;

"If you can't eat, you can feast on the beauty of the world, though that's not particularly satisfying to a hungry man. The gold rim of sun capping that purple hill makes me think of the tiaras women were wearing a few years ago. There's just enough of a shore breeze to bring the scent of the pines and spruces. The sea is quiet except for an occasional swell. Looks as if it had had a permanent wave. I miss the floats of the lobster-pots that tossed like little white boats. Ozy has moved his traps to the other side of the island."

"Why?" the sharpness of the Major's voice was in startling contrast to his dull eyes.

"More lobsters, of course. Here come the gulls! Gray. Brown. White. The air beats with the whir and flap of wings. Curious how they know when food is about. They are flocking from all directions like mammoth snow flakes in a blizzard. The white ones are the old fellows. The men must have thrown bread on the water to attract them."

Major Fane watched the soaring, diving, floating birds.

"Lucky devils to be able to eat."

"Cheerio, Major, after a month or two more in this glorious air, you'll be able to eat anything you want. Wasn't that kingfisher that flew by, blue? Do you recognize the tune Johnny Grant is playing? It's the latest smash-hit. There goes the sun in a blaze of color. It's a gorgeous world!"

Major Fane grunted skeptically;

"It may be to those who have digestions." He shook his head at Fenton who was tempting him with a small, plump mackerel, flanked by a potato whose snowy interior, dusted with paprika, was bursting through its thin pink skin.

"New potatoes," the Major groaned. "I love 'em."

He drew a small box from his pocket and extracted a white tablet. He chewed on it solemnly as he watched Lissa daintily de-bone the fish.

"Good?" he asked and swallowed hard.

"Perfect. Can't you eat anything, Major?"

"I'll have some of the watermelon when it comes along. They're cutting it now! I never saw anything so pink and crisp." He crunched his teeth in anticipation.

"I'm glad there is something you can enjoy. Ozy cracked this lobster to perfection, Fenton," she approved as she accepted the tin plate with its crimson cargo the butler offered.

"Who's Ozy?" the Major demanded testily as Fenton turned away. "I understood when I accepted the invitation that only the family from the big house, Kent and his guests and the tenants would be present. I don't like strangers." He was shaky with resentment.

"Don't be disturbed, Major. Is it possible that you have been here for weeks and haven't heard of Captain Ozias who does any kind of an errand, for anybody? You may need him yourself some time. I hope your digestion has improved since you came to Pirates' Den?"

His answer was good for a five minute monologue at

least. The tide swished a soft accompaniment to the drone of his voice and Lissa's thoughts as her eyes traveled from group to group seated on rugs flung on the pebbly shore. Everyone seemed content. Fenton was helping Ozy carve the melons. Lex hadn't come.

"And he was paying just as much attention to what I was saying as you are paying now," Major Fane reminded pointedly.

Startled, Lissa met his eyes. They were strange, sharp eyes, eyes she never had seen before. Even as she stared back at them, they dulled. Had they changed at all, or had she imagined it? She apologized;

"I'm sorry, Major. My attention did wander. You see, I feel the responsibility of this party as the host isn't here. I—"

"What's that dog dragging down the garden path? Where'd he get that?" The Major demanded as the Irish terrier proudly laid a coat at Lissa's feet. It was a man's tweed coat, much the worse for wear.

"G-Man, where did you get this?" she demanded sternly.

The dog looked up at her with beady, brown eyes that twinkled, opened his mouth and ran out a pink tongue.

The Major caught the coat from her hand, scowled at it, turned it insideout, examined the lining. Returned it.

"Thought it might be mine. I like old coats. But it isn't. Shall I take charge of it for you?"

The hint of restrained eagerness in his voice had the effect of a red Stop! signal on Lissa's mind. The Major wanted that coat. All the more reason why only Lex should have it. Apparently none of the other guests had seen G-Man bring it. Fenton, who might know to whom it belonged, was talking with Ozy. She would make no inquiries about it until Lex had seen it. She tucked it securely under her arm.

"Nice of you, Major, to offer, but as my dog stole it, I feel the responsibility of returning it. At last! Here comes Lex Carson!"

xviii

"Come over and enjoy your melon with Mrs. Barclay, Major," Lissa suggested in an effort to divert his attention from the coat. "She told me she liked you. What's the secret of your devastating fascination for women?"

"You're laughing at me, Miss Melissa. Nobody loves a dyspeptic."

"But apparently most of them marry," Lissa responded dryly.

She left him seated on a rug beside her stepmother and heard him launch into a description of his late operation before she turned away. A hand caught her arm.

"Watch your step, beautiful! You'd have plunged into that pan of clam shells in a minute!"

She looked up and met Lex Carson's eyes. Why, why should they set her heart aflame when she knew that he loved Madge Millard? For an instant she saw the gorgeous western sky through a mist, had to steady her voice before she answered;

"I've had the responsibility of this party on my mind, Lex. Atlas upholding the heavens on his shoulders and hands had nothing on me, and to add the last perfect touch, G-Man stole this coat."

He took it, looked it over, frowned intently at the lining.

"No tailor's name on it. Any idea where it came from?"

"Not the slightest. That bad dog was three quarters of the way down the garden path before we saw him. He might have brought it from a neighbor's, the big house, or the Packards'. Your guess is as good as mine. G-Man moves in a mysterious way, his snitching to perform. Major Fane looked it over just as you did. He offered to take charge of it till the owner was found." She added the last sentence in a lowered voice. Lex Carson's eyes questioned hers.

"He did? Nice of him, but as the coat was deposited on my land, I'm responsible for it." He dropped it behind a boulder. "I'll pick it up later. Realize I haven't seen you for three days, Lissa? What have you been doing?"

"Writing every morning."

"How's the old imagination working?"

"Overtime. Better plots and more of them is its slogan. I've been doing some village visiting and each family suggested a story. I love people. They're my assets. They are interesting to me even when they're shallow and inconsequential. Maupassant and O. Henry would have written masterpieces from some of the things I saw and heard."

"If you get ideas here, you'll get a kick from living in Washington. There's a story to every square inch there."

Lissa's eyes were wide with surprise as she looked at him. A smile lurked in the depths of his.

"But I'm not going to Washington."

"Oh yes, you are. You don't know it, but you are. I'm psychic!" he added in a perfect imitation of her voice and inflection. Before she could reply, he asked confidentially;

"Any news about the proposed walk-out?"

"Nothing definite. I talked with Marty Simonds today. I think she'll stop it."

"More power to her. I don't want things stirred up here now, if I can prevent it. By the way, I'm through my estate business for the present, if nothing breaks, I've put across a deal. I'll take two weeks vacation before I return to Washington. You and I are going places, beautiful. We'll begin to celebrate tonight. Tod wants us to wind up this party on his boat. I'll take you out."

Lissa quickly turned away. She flung over her shoulder; "Sorry. I have a date!"

"Perhaps now Lex will understand that I won't pinch-hit for Madge Millard," she told herself.

"G-Man, why are you such a bad boy?" she demanded of the Irish terrier, who trotted along beside her.

The dog sniffed, put his forepaws on her knees and looked up with adoring eyes. She pulled his ears.

"Old splendid! You know I'm crazy about you. You know while you've been helping Andy get well, I've missed you, don't you? You may stay if you won't beg for anything to eat. Remember the last picnic? I was up with you all night. Come on! Let's speak to Marty." She raced along the shore with the dog at her heels.

"Lands sake how red your cheeks are, child," Marty Simonds exclaimed. "Look as if you'd been bending over these steaming barrels, but I know you haven't." She lowered her voice. "I called on all the wives today and you may tell Mr. Carson that there won't be a walk-out."

"Really? What magic did you use?"

Marty Simonds cocked her head. Her eyes snapped like those of an angry sparrow.

" 'Twasn't magic. It was only my tongue and their common sense. I told them that the men were going to give up their pay rather than take a cut in wages—they didn't know about the planned walk-out—and I guessed they'd better make the most of those dresses they were knitting as it would be a long time before they bought so much as a shoe-lace. They just firmed their jaws and said, 'There won't be a walk-out.' And if I know women, and I do, there won't be one. Ozy is wig-wagging to you, child. Be sure you don't let on to him a word of what I told you."

"I won't, Marty."

Lissa crossed the beach to Captain Ozias. Whispered;

"Did you want me, Ozy?"

He handed her a pie-shaped slice of melon. She bit deep into its pink lusciousness. The dog whined suggestively.

"No. Not even a scrap, G-Man. Thanks ever so much for helping, Ozy."

The Captain pushed back the brim of his hat, sniffed like a hound, flashed his ferret-like eyes around before he warned;

"Don't grin at me like that, folks'll suspect something. Is the light unlocked, Lissa?"

"You mean the lighthouse on my island? No, but I have the key in my pocket. I'm planning to stop on my way to the cruiser to get some papers I left there. Do you want it?"

"Shsh! Keep the key but when you shut the lighthouse door, leave the latch up, so's I can git in later. Tell Lex I got to talk with him. Tell him to stay behind after the others have gone."

"I will, but—"

"Git goin'! Git goin'! Here comes Tod. Don't let him come now. I can't be bothered."

Lissa slipped her hand under Kent's arm.

"You'll take your life in your hands, Tod, if you approach the melon carver. I asked him a simple question and he did everything to discourage me but brandish his knife. Bend your head as if you were looking at my sports bracelet. Lex told me why The Sphinx is here. Ozy wants to speak to him. Tell him to wait after the others have gone to the cruiser. Tell him also that I think there's something queer about Major Fane."

"Why?"

"Haven't time to explain. The Major is looking at us." She raised her voice.

"I'm going to the cruiser in our small motorboat. I have to stop at the island and I'm taking Mr. Packard along."

It took some diplomacy and a certain amount of dodging of Johnny Grant before, with Ralph Packard in the stern, Lissa swung the wheel of the motorboat for the island. She had a feeling that if Lex had not been talking to Ozy, she wouldn't have gotten away, no matter how much she dodged.

"What's on your mind, Miss Barclay?" Ralph Packard asked. "You haven't smiled since we left the pier."

"Nothing on my mind, now that the lobster-bake is behind me. I did want it to be a success and I think it was. Isn't The Sphinx a beauty? Already it is strung with lights. See the shimmery reflections."

The man in the stern did not answer. Hands on the wheel, she turned to look at him. He was regarding the rocky, white fringed shore ahead. Her eyes followed his.

"Perfect, isn't it? I never approach the island without being thrilled that it is mine. I love every inch of it. Aunt Hetty asked me not to sell it, except under dire necessity, but, if editors remain firm in their refusal to see in me a potential best-seller and to assist in a wider distribution of the fruits of my industry—that last is a quotation, in case you care—I may have to. That topmost ridge looks like the back of a seamonster rising from the water. The shallows and tide-pools have been dyed claret by the afterglow. Here we are."

The boat slid into a sheltered cove and along the side of the float. G-Man jumped out and dashed away. Packard took the painter from the girl's hand.

"I'll fasten it."

"Thanks. When I come ashore here, I can't decide whether I feel more like Robinson Crusoe or the-world-is-mine Monte Cristo."

They mounted the runway, crossed the pier and followed the path to the light. Lissa called;

"What are you digging at, G-Man? Did you cache a bone the last time we were here?"

She dropped to her knees beside the dog who was pawing furiously in a bed of hardy pink and red Shirley poppies beneath a window of the white house. She pulled him away by the collar.

"You're ruining my flowers. My word—there is something."

She pulled at a scrap of black oilcloth sticking up from the damp earth. She dug around it with a sharp flat stone.

"Help, Mr. Packard! Buried treasure!"

He stood behind her with his hands in his pockets.

"Take care! You may pull up something infernally unpleasant, perhaps a skull."

She sank back on her heels and pushed her hair away from her eyes.

"Think I'm afraid of an old skull?" she demanded scornfully. "Where's your spirit of adventure? I intended to go fifty-fifty with you," her words came breathlessly as she dug, "but if you won't help—hooray! I have it!"

She sank back on her heels and raised a heavy pouch of black oilcloth, the size of an able-bodied coconut. G-Man sniffed at it, lost interest and rolled on his back on the pebbly walk that circled the light.

Now that she had the thing in her hand, Lissa's heart

beat uncomfortably fast. What was inside? Not a skull. It was too heavy for that. She looked up at the man who was staring at the black oilskin pouch in her hand. She shook it.

"Listen! It sounds like money!"

"Better put it back where you found it, Miss Barclay. Whatever is in it may have belonged to a pirate—pirates were a dirty lot—the man who buried it may have had scarlet-fever or—"

"Scarlet-fever! I believe you are frightened, your voice is shaky. If you're imagining horrors, think of something worse than scarlet-fever. Have you a knife? Cut the cord for me, will you?"

"I will not. I won't help you. I don't believe in touching that dirty thing."

"All right, if you feel that way about it, I'll untie the cord. I won't be stumped."

Lissa tugged at the tarred twine. Stopped to flex her fingers and tugged again.

"Darn! There goes my pet fingernail! It's coming! It's untied! Stand back! This is the dramatic moment for the cameras to start turning. Pandora loosed a wicked genie when she opened a buried box, I may loose a demon germ. I—"

One corner of the pouch slipped from her fingers. A stream of silver poured forth and scattered on the ground. She stared at the coins incredulously.

"That hasn't been buried here since piracy was in flower. It's nothing but a lot of our own money, half dollars, quarters."

She dropped to one knee and picked up a coin. She turned it over.

"It's new money! Brand new money!"

She looked from the scattered coins up into the eyes of the silent man frowning down at them.

"Who could have put it here?"

Even as she asked the question she remembered the automobiles parked on the road which connected mainland and island, and saw as plainly as if pictured on a screen, two figures walking toward the lighthouse. That didn't help. The pouch had been buried more than a few hours.

Packard shrugged and thrust his hands deeper into his blue coat pockets.

"Why ask me who put the money there? You jeered when I told you not to open the pouch. I'd advise you to tie it up and put it back where you found it. We don't need a crystal-gazer to tell us that it is stolen money which has been hidden here till the hue and cry of pursuit dies down. It gives me the creeps to think what may happen to you if the crook who buried it suspects that you've found those coins."

xix

CROOK! Stolen money! The words exploded in Lissa's mind like depth bombs catapulted from the smooth flow of his voice. Coins!

Her heart stopped and raced on. Lex had said that he was after a man who made bogus bills and coins. Ozy had asked her to leave the lighthouse door unlatched! He had had something to tell Lex. Did he know about the money? If he did, ten to one he would mess things up. These might be counterfeit coins! Lex must know of her find. She had promised she would help him and the chance had come. She must be careful that Ralph Packard did not suspect what she was thinking. She said breathlessly;

"Isn't this the most exciting thing? What a story I could make of it! What a grand story! I'm not crazy, though, about your suggestion as to what crooks might do to me. It loosed a million little nerve wigglers up and down my spine. Now that you're sure that this isn't germ-ridden pirate gold, help me put it back, will you?"

"Why put it back? You own this island. If I know my law—and I think I do—anything buried here is yours legally. Let's take the pouch along. Hide it under the seat of your boat and in the morning I'll see that you get it."

"I could do that—but—no, no, I'll leave it here. It might start trouble were I to take it to Tarry Farm."

She scrambled up the coins. Packard dropped to one knee and helped. She pleaded;

"Hurry, please hurry! I'm getting jittery. I read the papers. I know what horrid things happen. Only a few more. Is anyone coming? I'll finish. Is there a boat in sight?"

As he stood up to look at the harbor, she slipped a coin into the pocket of her white frock. If she couldn't get the pouch to Lex, she could produce a sample.

"All in! Help me tie it up. Please! My fingers are thumbs.

Lucky you didn't have a knife with which to cut the cord, isn't it? There! It's back in the hole."

She spread the earth carefully in place and stood up.

"Directly under the kitchen window," she said to herself before she suggested;

"Now we'll pray for rain to cover our tracks. Look at my hands and the dirt on my gown! That will take some explaining when we get to the cruiser."

"Why go to the cruiser? Let's get my manuscript and return to Tarry Farm. We can sit on the terrace and talk writing till the others come. I detest parties."

Something in his voice and eyes sent Lissa's heart to her throat. "Silly," she derided herself. "You like him, don't you?" Aloud she insisted;

"I must go to the cruiser, I promised Tod I would. Hear the woodpecker! He had to start drilling to add to the eeriness of the situation. I wish those gulls we disturbed would stop screaming. I'm on edge. I'll unlock the lighthouse and get your story while you stand guard. The person who buried the coins may have a side-kick who's hiding here."

She put the key in the lock and swung open the door. For an instant the service room was still, uncannily still—then —the wicker chair creaked.

Lissa's heart beat like a drum. Who had been sitting in it? Had Ralph Packard noticed the sound? Apparently not. He was frowning a little as he lighted a cigarette.

She dashed across the room, snatched up the manuscript beside the typewriter and joined him at the door.

"Here's your story. It's good. You have a fine style. Who was it said 'style in writing is like good manners in human intercourse'? It reminds me of one of the big writers. Can't remember which, the resemblance keeps teasing at my mind. Let's go."

"Why hurry? I'd like to see the lamp-room again. Want to use it—for atmosphere. May I?"

"Of course. Meanwhile I'll get some of this grime off my hands in the kitchen."

The sound of his footsteps clanged through the still tower as he ran up the narrow circular iron stairway. Lissa bathed her hands hurriedly and returned to the entrance door. She heard the swish, swish, of the tide against the rocky shore. The music of Johnny's ukulele and Jack Millard's voice singing came from the cruiser;

" 'You are my lucky star
    I saw you from afar—' "

Green and red lights had blossomed on boats swinging with the tide. A pale egg-shaped moon was tip-tilted above a hill like Humpty Dumpty peering with owlish eyes above his wall. Tiny white ruffles rimmed the ledges. A brilliant star pricked through the darkening sky. The juniper scented air was like wine, it left a salty taste on her lips.

Ralph Packard was coming down the stairs. Cautiously she adjusted the door-latch. What curious impulse had prompted her to make him believe that she was frightened? There had been something in his expression as he had looked down at the scattered coins, a flash of triumph that went as quickly as a flash of lightning—that had caught at her breath. He had been almost eager when he had suggested that she take the pouch with her. She'd better make sure that the coin was secure. If by mistake, she pulled it from her pocket it would take some explaining.

Quickly she tied the bright quarter in the corner of her handkerchief and thrust it in her blouse.

"Ready to go?" she asked eagerly as Packard crossed the room.

His eyes sharpened.

"All over your attack of jitters, aren't you?"

She wished he wouldn't stand so near. Only yesterday she had read an article on thought transmission, how minute electric waves, constantly being produced by the brain, will respond to suggestion. The writer was all for it. Ralph Packard must not suspect that she was planning somehow, someway, to get that pouch to Lex. She corrected;

"Attack of imagination expresses it better. You, if anyone, ought to realize that my imagination is my fortune, kind sir, she said. I haven't recovered so entirely that I want to hang around this light with dusk coming on. Enter Jupiter, the brightest star to become visible in the twilight. Look at the fireflies in that dark clump of arborvitae darting and flashing for all the world like a lot of fallen stars making whoopee. Scram, G-Man and don't stop to dig up any more buried treasure."

Packard followed as she and the dog ran ahead. She was on the float untying the painter when he came up.

"Why didn't you wait and let me do that?" he demanded. "I'm crew."

"He's too slow to be crew for us, isn't he, G-Man?" she inquired of the Irish terrier, already sprawled on the bow of the motorboat. She frowned at the dog. "What shall I do with you? I forgot when I brought you along, that we were going to the cruiser. You'll have to go home across the bar. Come here!"

The dog jumped to the float. As he sat back stubbornly on his haunches, she caught his collar and dragged him up the incline to the pier and into the road. She pointed.

"Go home, G-Man. You know the way, you've walked across the bar with me often enough. Go! I can't take you with me."

She watched him as he trotted forward a few feet, stopped and looked back.

"Go on!" she called.

Lissa followed him with her eyes until he reached the bar road. She returned to the float.

"He'll go home now. Let's go!"

Packard stood beside her as the boat glided through a smooth sea toward the cruiser. He suggested;

"Why mention the coins you found? Let's keep the buried treasure a secret between us. Finding that pouch and working out the mystery of its being there will make a grand story. You and I will collaborate, make a hit with it and sell it to the movies. No danger that you will have to sell your island after that."

"You must believe in fairies. If we are going to do all that, perhaps we should have brought along the coins, instead of leaving them behind us on the island."

She glanced back over the white wake the boat was kicking up.

"Look! See that speck on the pier? It's G-Man, bad boy! I won't go back for him. If he doesn't cross the bar road before the tide turns he'll have to stay there. It will be good discipline. Here we are at The Sphinx. Isn't she a beauty!"

The white-capped sailors with boat-hooks were posted at the head of the boarding ladder to catch the motorboat as it drew alongside the cruiser. Ralph Packard warned quickly;

"Don't mention the coins. Mum's the word or someone may steal our plot stuff. Is it a bargain? Shake on it." He held out his hand.

"Hi, you two!" Tod Kent hailed from the forward cockpit. "Get a hustle on, will you? What's the big idea standing there holding hands? We've been waiting for you. Now that my guests have inspected the refrigerating system, engines, radio, housekeeping and living quarters, they're frothing at the mouth to be off on a cruise down the bay."

Lissa hastened on board. Good old Tod! His hail had come just in time. She hadn't promised Ralph Packard that she wouldn't tell about the coins. He had a reason for wanting to keep secret the finding of them besides using the buried pouch for plot material, she was sure of it. She must tell Lex. She apologized eagerly;

"I'm sorry to have held up the party, terribly sorry, Tod. We were detained by—"

"My awkwardness, Kent," Ralph Packard's smooth voice took up the explanation. "I fumbled the painter, my burned fingers are still all thumbs—and the rope got mixed up in the propeller."

There was warning in his eyes as they met Lissa's. How silly for him to tell that rigmarole about the rope and the propeller, she thought.

"Glad to know why you were so late. I was just coming after you," announced Lex Carson, who was standing behind Kent.

"Why should you feel anxious about Miss Barclay when she is with me?" Ralph Packard questioned aggressively as he stood at the girl's shoulder.

"I've told you before, my sense of responsibility. Tod, the launch has been hoisted aboard and your guests are clamoring to start."

Lissa's mind was in a tumult as she passed along the wide side deck to the after cockpit. Was Ralph Packard really a writer? For the first time she doubted it. There had been something familiar about his stories which teased at her memory.

"Sit here, Lissa." Jack Millard rose from one of the gayly cushioned wicker chairs. Cleo detained Packard by a white hand.

"Thanks no, Jack. I'll sit at the stern. I love the smooth motion of the boat, love to hear and see the water rush by, especially when there's phosphorescence as there is tonight. Johnny, bring your ukulele over here. The night and the boat were made for it. Jack, if you want to add the perfect touch to Tod's party you'll sit here and sing for us. Johnny, don't scowl. It's frightfully unbecoming."

Jack Millard perched beside her. They sat with their feet on the great circular leather seat in the stern. His blue eyes were alight with laughter. He took one gray flannel knee into his embrace.

"Am I unpopular with the gentleman on your left? I'll say I am. But when an old married man like myself is singled out to sit beside a swell girl, like you, does he hesitate? He does not." He added so that Lissa alone could hear; "Has Packard been annoying you? You were a long time on that island."

"How did you know where I was?"

"Lex had to go to the big house and was the last to come aboard. When he found that you and Packard hadn't arrived, Tod and I had all we could do to keep him from

oing after you. For some reason he doesn't like your glossy
riend. I don't either. Know what I suspect, that he's looking
or a wife to help him socially. Apparently, he doesn't need
noney, but he needs social backing, there's a suggestion of
oughness under his gloss."

"He may be glossy but he's interesting to me."

"But you tried to shake him a few minutes ago, didn't
ou? You didn't ask me to sit here because of my irresistible
harm, did you now?"

"You're too modest," Lissa retorted gaily. "I do like you
immensely. When the world seems topsy-turvy I look at you
nd your wife and things steady. You seem so honestly in
ove after fifteen years of marriage. You are so—so cour-
eous to one another."

"Why that word, 'seem'? I don't like it. We are. What
did you expect, that I would beat her? Sounds as if you'd
been unfortunate in the husbands and wives you've met."
The laughter left his voice and eyes; "No one could help
adoring Madge, she has such a lovely soul. She is looking a
ot better, isn't she? She's coming out of the fog of fear
she has lived in since Andy's illness. She has plenty of time
for me, now. With the crushing anxiety of the boy off our
minds, we're honeymooning a bit. You've helped tremendously, Lissa."

As if she felt that he was speaking of her, his wife turned
her head and smiled. Soft color mounted to her forehead
as her eyes met her husband's. That didn't look as if she
were in love with Lex. Evidently he was doing the loving,
Lissa decided.

"Why is your world topsy-turvy tonight?" Jack Millard
asked.

"Can't tell you why, it just was. It isn't now. Do you get
the scent of flowers from shore? Reminds me of the fra-
grance that drifted toward us from Flores, an island miles
away, when my father and I were sailing past the Azores.
Isn't Jupiter brilliant? How red Mars looks. I've never seen
them so close together. The Milky Way makes me think of
a bride's veil of malines being trailed across the sky, it is
made of star dust and thousands of baby stars, isn't it?
See the dark patches? Until recently, they were thought to
be holes into the atmosphere. Now astronomers have discovered that they are collections of nebulae that do not shine.
Those fleecy clouds sailing along look like a fleet of airships
with silver-tipped wings. Truly 'The heavens declare the
glory of God; and the firmament showeth his handiwork.' "

"You'd get a better effect from the bow cockpit, Miss
Barclay."

Ralph Packard's suggestion broke into Lissa's rapturou study of the heavens with the devastating effect of an ele phant plunging through a rose garden.

"She will not," Johnny Grant declined for her belligerent ly. "She asked me to park beside her, and she's spent ever moment since either monologuing about the perfect hus band at her right, discoursing on the heavens, or quotin, Shakespeare. I'll bet she's practicing on us in the hope o landing a job as lecturer in a planetarium. Scram, Packard She now talks to me. Jack may keep his seat if he wants to but the girl is mine."

"In that case, 'The Captains and the Kings depart,'— that isn't Shakespeare, Johnny, I'll go too." Jack Millar linked his arm in Packard's. "It has been subtly indicate that we are not wanted. Come on. I need a smoke."

✗✗

As the two men walked forward, Lissa's glance lingered on Sidonie Packard who was talking to Lex Carson. It could hardly be called talking, she was looking glamorous and seductive and he appeared as fascinated as a gentleman-spider gazing at a lady-spider's web. Men certainly were easy marks. Johnny Grant twanged a few soft notes.

"Why that impatient sigh, sweet thing? You're right, about Millard, he and his wife do restore one's faith in the honor-able estate of matrimony, and they have a great kid. I've never cared much for small boys, but I like that one. Jack and Madge are corking together, not mushy, but somehow you just know that their love is the real stuff, though he did do a bit of hovering about Cleo. I'm willing to bet my road-ster that she did the hovering. Packard's her love interest at present and he seems that way about her. Watch Sidonie the Dumb angling for Lex Carson. She isn't the first woman who's tried for him. There was a story going the rounds in Washington that his heart is buried in the grave of his first love, as if that happened in this age and generation."

"Cynicism in tweeds! What a gossip you are, Johnny!"

"Perhaps I am, but I noticed you listened with all your ears. I wouldn't be a cynic with you, and I'm not so dumb as you and Jack Millard think I am, either. I knew you were quoting the nineteenth Psalm, took a course in Bible Lit in college. I called it Shakespeare to get a rise out of you. Marry me, will you?"

Lissa shook her head.

"Why—because of Cleo?"

"No. I've had days and years in which to think since we were engaged, Johnny. I've been growing a lot of principles for living. In my travels I've had a chance to play round with the sort of people you like, the 'restless moderns' someone called them, people who rush from one social date to another, who dally with thoughts of tawdry infidelities and tarnished adventures until they slip into fact. I've also met the normal healthy-minded people—I don't mean that they're perfect—who still believe in the Ten Commandments; the comfort and healing of prayer; in large doses of humor in their daily lives and the working efficacy of the Golden Rule. I like them best and they would bore you to death."

"Straight from the shoulder! Got anything else against me except the set I run around with?"

"Not much. I like you, Johnny, I've grown to like you more than ever this summer, but liking isn't loving, besides, I won't marry a man who gets even a little drunk. It will get him down after a while and I don't want a husband who is down."

"How long since you've been a teetotaler?"

"I've always been a teetotaler for myself, you know that. I hate cheapness, and if you could see and more particularly hear yourself—you've made my face burn like fire—when you are in what you call an 'incandescent glow,' you'd know what I mean by cheap."

"Thanks for them kind words. I suppose you picked up your anti-glow ideas from your trustee, Carson. I've never seen him drink anything stronger than coffee. I've wondered a lot about that lad. He's a lawyer, he has an office and I know some of his clients, but, sometimes I suspect that's not all of it."

"What else could there be?"

"Don't get excited. I don't mean anything shady. I like him even if he is inclined to be high-handed with me and treat me as if I were a kid—he's the straightest-shooter I know—but, when the modern man doesn't drink, it makes one suspect he may be keeping his head clear for a purpose. I know an actor who won't touch sherry even for fear it might crack up his memory while he's in the midst of a speech on the stage. Must be wearing to have a job like that."

Lissa looked at him incredulously. Johnny Grant was the last person she would have supposed would see below the surface of a personality. It would be wise to get off the subject of Lex. She said quickly;

"I wonder why Fenton is here. In his Tarry Farm regalia, too. He must have been a lightning-change artist at some time in his career. I've never yet found out what that lavish sprinkle of silver buttons on the tail of his dark green coat means."

"They're as big as quarters, aren't they, and as bright as new money."

New money! The words flashed a picture of the buried coins. Lissa put her hand to her breast. The coin was there. She could feel its hardness against her flesh. She had been foolish to leave that pouch behind. Hadn't Ralph Packard said that it was hers legally? Of course it wasn't and she wouldn't touch the money, but how stunned Lex and Tod would be if she produced it and told where she had found it. She must get it. How?

"When stuck go into reverse."

The words echoed through her mind as clearly as if broadcast from a radio. Why? She had sent her hero into reverse when she had pulled her novel out of a threatened impasse. Was it an answer to her quandary about the coins? Go into reverse. She had left the island. Did that mean that she was to return to it? If she didn't heed that inner voice it might be discouraged and never help her again. G-Man might not have crossed the bar. She could use him as an excuse for returning to the island.

It wouldn't do to start back alone. She must have someone with her. Not Lex nor Tod, she wanted to stage a surprise. Why not Johnny? Perfect! She whispered;

"My own motorboat, the one Aunt Hetty willed to me, is at The Sphinx mooring. When we get back to it, insist upon taking me home, then we'll slip over to the island, will you, Johnny?"

Johnny Grant stared at her as if doubting his ears.

"Have you gone haywire or have I, sweet thing? Of course I'll take you, but—"

"Shsh! Miss Packard is looking at us—"

"Ahem!"

Fenton, who had appeared with the suddenness of a rabbit prestidigitated from the air, presented a tray.

"I opened some sparkling catawba for you, Miss Lissa." He lowered his voice; "I hope you don't mind my coming on board, but Mr. Kent's steward is indisposed and Mr. Kent asked me if I would help out. I was very glad to be of service. It's a beautiful boat. Quite the last word in cruisers, I'd say, Miss Lissa."

"Why should I mind, Fenton? Mr. Carson is your employer, not I."

"Of course, Miss, but I've taken orders from you for so long, it seems natural to ask you. I hope the punch is quite as you like it, Mr. Grant?"

"Quite, Fenton. What this country needs is more butlers like you. If you mixed that, you may have a job with me any time you're out of one."

"Thank you, sir, but I don't expect to be out of one. I'm hoping that Mr. Carson will need me in Washington, sir." He moved on with the tray.

"Isn't he ripping? Quite the last word in butlers, I'd say, Miss Lissa."

"You've missed your vocation, Johnny. You should be giving impersonations before a mike. That was Fenton's voice to a tone. Does—does Lex Carson keep house in Washington?"

"I think not. I know that he gives small, select parties at his club. I met him the first time at a dinner. As he and I are both bachelors, we are invited out a lot. Now what's coming? Fenton's setting up a table and Kent is producing a book and a fountain pen. Let's go see."

Lissa caught his sleeve.

"Johnny! Wait! You will take me to the island, won't you? I've left G-Man there. I can't bear the thought of his spending the night alone."

"Sure, I'll take you, but you make a baby of that dog. Do him good to be lonesome."

"I know it would, but I love him. Don't let anyone know we are going. We might be stopped."

The cruiser, trailing a wake like a coiling, fiery serpent all shimmering scales, glided through a smooth sea, past wooded islands, a ghostly beach and an anchored vessel loaded to the gunwales with lumber. Washing on lines strung from cabin to mast hung limp and motionless like bodies with the filling gone out of them. The port light peered into the night like a great red eye. From the ship drifted a bar of dance music.

The wash of the cruiser roused the buoy. It moaned faintly. The moon hung in the heavens like a gleaming one-sided twenty-dollar gold piece. The stars of the Great Dipper shone steadily. Polaris, which tipped the handle of the Little Dipper, glowed like a jewel in a spangled canopy. A flaming meteor hissed through the purple velvet sky and vanished.

Tod Kent picked up a book and opened it to show a page.

"Fingerprints! Now what do you know about that," Johnny

123

Grant exclaimed. "Quite the last word in autograph albums, I'd say, old boy. What?"

Lissa pinched his arm as Fenton, who was holding a tray with the rigidity of a cigar-store wooden Indian, glanced at him from between narrowed lids. Apparently the imperturbable calm of the butler could be pricked, he knew that he was being mimicked. Tod Kent laid the open book on the table.

"It's an original with me, Johnny, and am I proud of it? Got the idea when I heard that the precinct stations alone are registering about three hundred civilian fingerprint volunteers a day. Most of the high-bracket income lads are on file. It's a fool-proof method of identification. I've got the prints of the great, near-great and not great-at-all within those covers. So far everyone who has sailed on this boat, even to the crew and Jap boys, has been willing to come across."

As he talked, he removed a metal ink-pad, a rubber roller, cotton waste and a bottle labeled "alcohol" from the tray Fenton held and laid them on the table.

"I don't want anyone to do it who'd rather not. I've given orders to anchor, the least motion might blur the prints. This way boys and girls! It's quick and painless! Who'll be the first?"

There was an instant of silence broken only by the creak of anchor chains and a splash, before Lissa Barclay held up her hand as if she were a school girl answering, "Present!"

"Good little sport! Come on!"

Kent pulled out a chair at the table.

"I don't know why the thought of pressing inky fingers on that blank page should set little shivers tobogganing down my spine, but it does," Lissa confided as she sat down. "Hope my hand won't be shaky, and blur the prints. The rest of you have the advantage of watching me. You'll know just how to do it."

She looked up at the faces about the table. They had the intent look of persons expecting something, they knew not what, to jump from a box. Ralph Packard's eyes were narrowed, his lips were touched with a cynical smile. His sister's face was expressionless, as arm linked in his, she looked down. Cleo stood beside Johnny Grant, arm in arm the Millards smiled at Lissa.

"Jack and I have done it, it doesn't hurt," Madge encouraged.

"Hurry, Melissa! I'm so anxious to try it," Mrs. Barclay twittered, "aren't you, Major?"

Major Fane, perched on the rail, shook his head.

"Don't believe in it! Wouldn't have come aboard if I'd

thought I'd be asked to do such a darnfool thing." He puffed out his lips with little explosive breaths.

Tod Kent grinned at him.

"Calm yourself, Major, as has been said before, nothing obligatory about this. You'd better come off that rail or resentment may pitch you overboard." He held out a pen.

"Put your name and the date at the bottom of the page, Lissa. All set? Here goes."

He ran the roller over the pad and then over her hands. "There you are! Nicely inked. Lay the fingers of your right hand, one at a time, on the page. Don't press hard! Now all the fingers at once. That-a-girl! Repeat with the left. Perfect! Lex, I'll appoint you hand-cleaner extraordinary."

That, Carson acknowledged, was handsome of him. He picked up some cotton waste and the alcohol bottle.

"Come over here, Lissa, and get your hands cleaned."

"But, I want to see someone else do it. Johnny's sitting down."

He led her to the stern before she could protest.

"Sit up here with your feet on the seat and you can see your adored Johnny. Is he your adored Johnny?"

He looked up from the hand he was swabbing with alcohol-soaked waste. She kept her eyes on her inky fingers.

"Who are you to probe the secrets of a maiden's heart?" she demanded flippantly.

"The man who loves you."

Her lashes flew up.

"Loves me! Who's fiction-minded, now? Hero rescues lovely girl from watery grave—that's me, in case you don't recognize the description—and embraces wife of friend."

"I can explain that, Lissa."

"You're crushing my hand. Now Mother Barclay is being fingerprinted. I want to see it done."

"Forget the fingerprinting. Look at me! Straight! Do you think I'd tell you I loved you if I were even pretending to love another woman? Something happened to me that never had happened before as my eyes met yours when I pulled you from the water. Believe me, darling?"

Lissa's heart soared with the speed and lightness of a runaway balloon. He mustn't know it, though. He had said that he could explain about Madge but he hadn't. "Remember Johnny, my girl, remember Johnny," she prodded herself. She veiled her eyes from the ardor in his.

"I don't believe you or any man. You're not an expert de-inker, are you? If Tod intends to take up fingerprinting as a leisure industry, he'd better get another helper. I wish Major Fane would come off that rail. If he were to have one of his dizzy spells, he'd go overboard. Fenton is standing beside him, but I doubt if he'd be much good pulling him out of the water."

The hard pressure on her hands sent her eyes to Carson's. "Why are you scowling at me like that?"

His unsteady laugh tightened her throat.

"You'll have to read expressions better than that before you'll make good as a writer. That wasn't a scowl, that was concentration. I was deciding whether to shake you or kiss you. Tod Kent saved you that night in my study, but now I've decided—"

"Our genial host is calling for the alcohol bottle," Ralph Packard's smooth voice flowed between them. "There are other hands to be cleaned, Carson. Much ink has rolled over fingers since Miss Barclay's were printed. Did he do a good job?"

Lissa held out smooched fingers.

"Not what you'd call perfect, but they'll do. Better hurry on to the next clean-up, Lex."

"Remember, I've come to a decision," he reminded and returned to the table.

"Did you tell him about the coins?" Ralph Packard demanded.

"Coins? What—" Lissa regarded with amazed eyes the man frowning at her. "Would you believe it? This finger-printing drove that buried loot completely from my mind. Not only I haven't told anyone about the coins, I haven't thought of them."

"Now, Sidonie, it's your turn. After your fingerprints, we'll get Fenton's if he doesn't mind." Kent sent his voice over the heads of the group about the table to the butler who stood beside Major Fane perched on the rail. "You don't mind, do you, Fenton?"

Fenton put his fingers to his lips.

"Ahem! I should be proud to have my hands in such company, sir. I—My God, sir, am I losing my mind? Is that a flash from the lighthouse off the left side, sir?"

Everyone turned to look in the direction of the butler's pointing finger. The Major leaned backward. Ralph Packard rushed to his side and stared at the island. Lissa's heart pounded in her throat. A flash! From her light. Was someone signalling about the buried coins? Fenton wasn't imaginative. He was leaning over the rail straining his eyes—Oh—

"Quick! Quick!" she called. "The Major's overboard!"

LEX CARSON flung off his coat. Kicked off his shoes. Dove from the rail. The boarding ladder was lowered. In a moment it was all over but the exclamations. White and shaky the Major was boosted to the deck. Between shivers he spluttered;

"Must have been one of my dizzy spells. Get me home, quick."

The order was given to make all speed ahead to The Sphinx's mooring. The Major was bundled in blankets and given something hot to drink. Ten minutes later in the shadow of the wheel house, Kent advised Carson, wrapped in a woolly top-coat;

"Better take the Major home, it will give you a chance to go ahead of the rest and change to dry clothes. Be at Tarry Farm float half an hour after the launch drops you. The wind has shifted. Those dark clouds rolling up mean a thunder storm. I've carried out your orders. The 'electrical engineers' have the coat you brought aboard. Ozy and I couldn't wait for you to get back from Boston so we went ahead and planned. If that infernal Major hadn't gone overboard, I would have had all the finger—"

"Of course Lex is all right, Sidonie," he answered the question of the woman who had appeared suddenly beside them. "He's going ashore with the Major as soon as we get back to our mooring. That officer and gentleman certainly smashed up my little party. It's gone cold. I'll never get the other fingerprints for my book now. Perhaps though, you'll let me have yours at some later date when you're on board?"

"I will, Tod. I wouldn't miss having my hands in such distinguished company. Will you mind if Ralph and I go ashore when the Major goes? I'm tired. I'll call this a day."

"Sure, you may go. They can land you on the way to the Major's. Pick up your things. There go the anchor chains."

As she turned away, he said in a low voice;

"Taking the Packards will delay you a little, Lex, but it's a break for me. I'll go with the second load and pretend to come back to the cruiser. I won't. I'll wait in the lee of the boathouse for Ozy."

As the launch got under way, Lex Carson spoke to the man at the wheel;

"To Red Chimneys first, Prescott."

He was aware of the brother and sister side by side in the stern, the murmur of their voices. They did not speak to him until the launch drew alongside the Red Chimneys float. As she stepped out of the boat, Sidonie Packard extended her hand;

"Thanks for bringing us home, Mr. Carson. I hope you've come to Tarry Farm to stay. It's your duty to devote some time to becoming acquainted with your tenants, isn't it, Major Fane?"

The Major grunted. Carson responded cordially;

"I wouldn't call that a duty, pleasure is the word. I'm through with estate matters now and have two weeks of pure vacation ahead, no work and all play. Good-night. Good-night, Packard. Push off, Prescott. If we don't get the Major home quick, we'll have a sick man on our hands."

He looked over his shoulder as the launch shot ahead through water which rippled darkly. The motorboat which Lissa had said was part of the equipment of Red Chimneys was not at its mooring. Where was it?

The moon was as indistinct as a face behind a veil of cigarette smoke. The same haze dulled mountains and islands. The tower of the lighthouse was faintly luminous as if it had been coated with radium that no amount of darkness could quite dim. The lights on the cruiser were chunks of clouded amber.

"Tune her up, Prescott, looks like rain. Not that a little more water in our clothing would make much difference to you and me, eh Major?"

Major Fane's reply was muttered into the blanket muffled about his chin. As the launch slid up to the Pirates' Den landing, Carson jumped ashore and held out his hand.

"Here we are. I'll go to the house with you, Major. You might be dizzy again. I'm afraid you looked too long upon the lobster when it was red."

Major Fane glared from beneath shaggy brows.

"Didn't touch the lobster," he growled. "Wasn't dizzy. Someone pushed me."

"Who pushed you?" Lex Carson demanded sharply.

"It was either the butler or Packard. I don't like that brother and sister. I don't like their Italian houseman, either. He's always snooping round my place. Next time I hire a cottage, I'll find a landlord who's careful about his tenants. It's the last time you'll ever get me on a boat. Here come my houseboys. Must have been watching for me."

128

He climbed clumsily to the float and joined the gesticulating Filipinos. Carson frowned as he watched the three cross the landing.

"He doesn't like the Packards, the oily Nino snoops around his cottage and he thinks Fenton or Packard pushed him overboard," he said to himself. "It wouldn't be Fenton's technic and Packard has too much at stake to risk an investigation. Get under way!" he ordered. "I felt a drop of rain."

Prescott tipped his white cap to a sharper angle;

"The Major certainly gave you an earful. Grateful, ain't he, Mr. Carson. Never said so much as 'Thank you'! for pulling him out of the water. Next time you'd better let him drown, and not risk your life, sir."

"There was no danger for me in that smooth sea. The Major is subject to dizzy spells and I feared he wouldn't be able to help himself."

"Dizzy, is it? Huh! I guess he's an old kill-joy from what I hear. They tell me he's got a radio outfit that's so powerful he could send or receive messages from the moon, if he wanted to. Something to do with the Army, he's a radio expert keeping in practice while on sick leave, folks in the village say. The other launch from the cruiser is at Tarry Farm pier, sir. See the dark figures skurrying to the Treasure Chest and up to the big house?"

"Here we are," he announced five minutes later as the boat slid alongside the lighted float. "Better hustle before you get caught in the rain, sir, there's a thunder-storm on the way."

Carson hustled, not because he cared about the rain—he couldn't be much wetter than he was—but because he wanted to speak to Lissa before she reached her room. When on the beach she had flung over her shoulder, "Sorry, I have a date," he had flamed with fury. At that moment he had been in perfect accord with the primitive man who dragged the woman he wanted off to his cave.

As he entered the hall, Cleo ran half way down the curving staircase. She stopped with one hand on the banister, the other over her heart. The hammered satin of her pale blue pajamas reflected the light in the sconce above her, her hair was a fluff of gold about her head.

"Where's Lissa?" she demanded.

"Lissa! Didn't she come home with you?"

She descended a few stairs, her gold sandals gleaming against the Oriental rug that covered them.

"No, she and Johnny Grant left the cruiser in her motor-

boat. They were very secret about it, acted as if afraid someone would notice them."

Carson's heart contracted unbearably.

"Sure she's not in her room?"

"I'm sure. She's been trying to get Johnny back all summer.
She has probably persuaded him to elope with her."

Carson's laugh didn't ring with mirth but it served.

"Lissa persuade Grant! That's the funniest thing I ever
heard, Cleo. You're fooling yourself if you can't see that he
is doing the persuading. They've probably stopped at the
Treasure Chest for a bite. Excuse me, if I dash past you. I'm
wet to the skin. Good-night."

He took the stairs two at a time. As he opened his door,
G-Man brushed by him into the room, flung himself to the
hearthrug and gazed up with beseeching eyes.

Carson closed the door and looked down at the Irish
terrier.

"Where's Lissa?" he demanded.

There was a faint rumble of thunder in the distance. The
dog whined.

"Afraid of the storm, are you? All right, stay here. Make
yourself at home."

Speedily he changed to dry clothing. As he brushed his wet
hair furiously before the mirror, Cleo's intimation that Lissa
and Johnny Grant had fared forth on a clandestine adventure pricked unbearably at his mind. Of course it wasn't
true. If they wanted to be married, why should they make a
secret of it? Lissa marry the man who had jilted her? It
was unbelievable. Cleo was a cat. She was trying to make
trouble. Of course the two were at the Treasure Chest.

He'd better stop worrying about Lissa—pronto—and concentrate on the job ahead. His pulses thrummed. This
promised to be an exciting night. It had started off at high
with the Major's plunge overboard. So even the crew aboard
the cruiser knew that he had a high-power radio. He, himself,
had known it weeks ago. It was his business—as a landlord
—to know what went on in the cottages he leased. Something
to do with the army, a radio expert keeping in practice while
on sick leave, Prescott had said. That explanation would keep
the curious from snooping around Pirates' Den for the present. After tomorrow—

Tomorrow! The blood raced through his veins and set his
pulses quickstepping. If nothing broke, the last link in his
chain would fit into place tomorrow. Meanwhile—

He glanced at his wrist watch. Time for him to start. He
went to the window. Pitch dark outside. He shrugged into
a Burberry, thrust an electric torch into one pocket. He felt

for an automatic in a drawer of the desk. Should he take it? This was only a reconnaissance trip, if they were in luck, they'd get out and back without interference. Suppose they didn't have luck? Suppose there was rough stuff? Even so, he wouldn't take the gun. Guns bred trouble. He looked at the Irish terrier curled up on the hearthrug.

"Where did you get the coat you dragged down the garden path, G-Man?" he demanded. The dog opened one eye and with a beatific sigh rolled over on his side.

"You're the world's No. 1 helper, aren't you, boy?" Carson laughed and closed the door.

He descended the stairs cautiously. Why the dickens did they have to creak? Was that furtive sound behind the wainscotting a mouse? The hall was faintly fragrant of wood fires. The old clock ticked loudly enough to waken the Seven Sleepers. As he reached the hall the overhead light flashed on. His heart stopped for an instant and raced on. Fenton stepped from the living room.

"Oh, is it you, sir? I thought I heard someone coming down secret-like. For three years I was the only man in the house, and I've felt the care of the place, sir."

"I appreciate your interest, Fenton. As I went up to change my wet clothes—" Carson glanced over his shoulder and lowered his voice, "Miss Lissa told me that Miss Lissa had not returned, even suggested that she and Mr. Grant had eloped. I'm going out to find her. Understand, Fenton?"

"I do, sir. It wouldn't be like Miss Lissa to do that, sir. Wouldn't you like me to phone round the neighborhood?"

"No, Fenton. That would start gossip. I'm sure they've stopped at the Millards'. I want to find her myself. Perhaps you understand that, too?"

"Yes, sir, I do, sir. Miss Lissa is a beautiful character, if I'm not presuming to say it, sir."

"She is, Fenton. Leave the terrace door unlocked. Don't wait up. I shall go back to the cruiser after I find Miss Lissa. Mr. Kent wants me to finish up the party."

"I'm afraid I spoiled it, sir. For a minute I thought I saw a flash from the lighthouse. Of course it couldn't have been, the light hasn't been used for three years, sir, it must have been the reflection of a meteor. Perhaps you noticed that the sky was full of them? If you're late getting home, you'll meet many boats coming into our harbor. They'll begin arriving at midnight to be here for the Fair tomorrow. It's a pretty sight, sir, when they're all lying at anchor."

"It must be. Good-night, Fenton."

"Good-night, sir."

xxii

UNFORTUNATE that he had run into Fenton, Carson thought as he crossed the terrace. Perhaps, though, it wasn't such a bad break. He had learned from the butler that from midnight on, boats would be arriving in the harbor for the Fair. That meant that Tod and he could shoot around in Ozy's dory without attracting attention till the business of the night was finished. Where was Lissa? If only he could be sure that she was with the Millards. If Tod wasn't waiting when he reached the pier, he'd sprint to the Treasure Chest and find out.

He felt his way down the path. The stepping-stones were no longer visible. He stopped. Strained his eyes to make out the path ahead. Went on. Thunder rolled, lightning flashed in the distance. Soughing trees, scattering the smell of the sea with every move, added a touch of somber mystery to the night. Shrubs were but darker blurs in the gloom.

Once he lost the path and found himself waist high in the flower border. It wouldn't do to use the electric torch. There might be eyes watching.

Queer, he thought, as he picked his way cautiously down the path, that this hunt for the man whom the Treasury Department considered one of the largest makers of spurious plates and printers of counterfeit notes and coins in the country, should have fitted in with the settlement of his uncle's estate, which had threatened soon to be operating entirely in the red. That danger was past if the plan he was negotiating went through, he was to know in the morning.

His work for the Government had helped him bear the uncertainty of Lissa's feeling for him, too. Not that he thought she wouldn't be his in the end, but it looked like rough going till he had a chance to explain Madge's collapse against his shoulder. He had two weeks ahead of him in which to do that. Madge had no reason now to fear Cleo. Apparently Jack had become wise to her tactics. This evening he had politely but firmly snubbed her. Ralph Packard had been her shadow on the cruiser. Ought he to warn—

"Sst!"

The sound scattered Carson's thoughts like dry leaves caught in a miniature vortex. Was that a white boar or a shadow swaying at the pier?

"Sst!"

He followed the sound. A hand gripped his arm. A hoarse voice asked;

"Can you see Ozy's dory?"

He caught the odor of dead fish and oil in the moisture-soaked air.

"No, but I smell it, Tod."

"Take care. Don't make a sound."

"Hold on a minute. Seen Lissa?"

"Saw her boat at the Treasure Chest float as we came along. We're crazy to stand here, come on."

With a mind relieved as to Lissa, Carson stepped cautiously into the dory. He could make out a dark form at the wheel. The far off din of the storm sounded like the finale of a fireworks show. He heard a sniff. Ozy was on the job.

"Okay!" Tod Kent called softly and the boat shot forward. He huddled beside Carson in the stern, whispered;

"Doesn't this boat smell like thunder? Had to use it, because if we're seen everyone knows that Ozy pulls his lobster traps at any old time. Had a noiseless engine installed under cover, the very day I got your orders. Guess the old one couldn't have been heard in this storm, though. The tide is high enough on the bar to allow the dory to shoot straight across to the other side of the island. Hope you'll approve of what I've done, Lex?"

"You bet I approve, Tod. I'll recommend you for a G-Man job. Here comes the rain. Hear it hiss!"

The wind increased in violence. Spray broke over the bow of the boat which creaked and strained in all its joints, shuddered and tossed like a chip. The cabin shed Niagaras of water, now to left, now to right.

Tod Kent crept forward and spoke to the man at the wheel.

"Can we make it, Ozy?"

Captain Ozias sniffed.

"Why don't you talk up? Who do you think's goin' to hear you in this blow? Sure we're goin' to make it. Course my lobster-float may be the only one there, but if I yell 'two' you fellas git ready to haul in."

"You're the skipper!" Tod Kent pulled off a slicker. Rain beat through Carson's polo shirt when he flung Burberry and hat on the seat behind him.

"Here we are, fellas! Look sharp! Two floats! Can you see 'em? Reach for both! We ain't got time to waste."

"I've got it," Carson whispered and hauled in a lanyard. "Thunder! No, I haven't. It's a lobster-trap!"

"Don't let that trap scrape against the gunwale! Don't you fellas know nothin'?" The captain's voice cracked from excitement. "We ain't got a minute to waste! Thought I heard an engine on the harbor side of the island. One of you take the wheel, I'll try myself!"

"Don't move, Ozy! Don't move! I've got one!"

"Haul it in! Quick! Can't hold this boat much longer. I'll rap if anything's comin', though I guess I couldn't hear a fleet of planes in this racket."

"Got it, Lex?" Tod Kent's voice rasped.

"Yes."

"Can you lift it?"

"Yes. It's about a foot square."

"All right. Beat it to the cabin. The window is covered and we'll close the door."

"Keep the dory steady, Ozy," Carson cautioned. "We've got to drop the float in the same place."

Kent closed the sliding door of the box-like cabin. Shut in, almost smothered by the smell of oil and dead fish, the two men knelt in water sloshing from side to side on the bottom of the rolling boat. Carson snapped on an electric torch and played the light over a watertight case at the end of the lanyard. He worked at the cord which bound it. Once he stopped to put his hand to his head.

"Go on, Lex, go on! I'm sick as a horse too and I've spent my life in boats. We've got to open it boy, we've got to."

"Sure we have! What else are we here for? For the love of Pete, give us a little air!"

"Can't! While we have the light. Keep on!"

"Okay, but if this boat doesn't stop rolling—" he swallowed hard. "It's untied. Unclamp the cover! Don't bend it! We've got to put it back, remember."

The rolling boat, the sickening odor, were forgotten as the two men stared down at the contents of the watertight case. Greenbacks. Tied and labeled. Carson looked at Kent whose face was ghastly in the faint light.

"They've gone into big money, Tod." His voice broke from excitement. "One hundred dollar notes on a Federal Bank in—"

Rap! Rap! Rap!

"Ozy's signal! Something's coming!" He drew on a pair of cotton gloves. Slipped off the top note of a package of greenbacks.

"Take it, Tod! We'll get the fingerprints on it tonight Quick!"

Kent drew an oiled silk folder from his trousers' pocket. Carson laid the bill in it.

"Pull the roll from my pocket, Tod. Tuck one of the bills from it among these. It will keep the count correct. They won't miss the one we've taken till they check up."

Rap! Rap! Rap! Rap! Rap! Rap!

"Hurry! Okay! Looks just as we found it, doesn't it?"

Carson drew off his gloves, clamped on the lid of the case. "We've got to get this thing tied up!" he muttered. Black spots danced before his eyes, his fingers slipped as he tried to tie the wet cord in the exact pattern in which he had found it.

"Don't fumble! Don't fumble, Lex!" Tod Kent wailed.

Rap! Rap! Rap! Rap! Rap! Rap!

"Hustle, Lex! We've got to get that thing back!"

"You're telling me, fella! Try it yourself!"

"Don't get sore, boy. You're the boss, but since you asked me to help I haven't slept nights I've been so excited! Hurry! It will give the show away if they find they're one case short. Got it? Got it?"

Carson nodded. Speech was beyond him. He soundlessly slid back the cabin door, took a long breath, staggered to the side of the boat. The dory dipped to the gunwale as he and Kent paid out the lanyard.

"Careful, Tod! Don't let it splash. Someone may be watching! Pay out the line. It's down!"

He flung the float over and dropped to the stern seat. The rainy air was as cooling as a drink of spring water. There had been an instant when his one burning desire had been to follow that watertight case into the sea. A spear of red flame slashed the sky. Thunder reverberated among the hills. Tod Kent crept back from a whispered conference with Captain Ozias.

"He didn't rap because of a boat. It was to hurry us. He was afraid we might be seen when lightning flashed. Wants to know if he'll take us to the other floats?"

"No. One's enough. Tell him to shoot for the island."

"Jiminy, what a flash! It crackled like a forest fire. The lighthouse looked like a pink ghost. Hear the thunder bump away among the hills! This isn't rain. It's a flood. Something burst overhead. I'll—"

His sentence was drowned in a crash which shook the heavens.

"I wonder where that hit? Gosh, when I was in that cabin—"

"If you mention cabin, I'll strangle you, Tod."

"My mistake. One hundred dollar notes! Those boys are

135

flying high. Ozy'll land us near the light and if we hav
luck, we'll see the airtight cases picked up."

"If someone doesn't beat us to it and reach the lamp
room first. Did you arrange to have the lighthouse un
locked?"

"I did. Ozy asked Lissa to leave the latch up. When I go
your message that his yarn about the extra floats had set yo
thinking that two mugs of beer were not a reasonable ex
planation of his double vision, I got hold of him and tol
him what you suspected. Did you pick that hunch out o
the air, Lex? If you did, I'll believe in the theory of vibra
tions. Ozy's gone sleuth-minded, too. He remembered ther
that there had been a strange vessel which looked like one
of the kind that buy pulpwood anchored beyond the ledge
that night. He was all excitement. Said he'd be on the look-
out."

"He was. This afternoon at the lobster-bake he told me
that a strange vessel had anchored in the same place and
offered to hang round Tarry Farm pier tonight and take us
out to check up on the floats. When your skipper reported
that two red lights, one above the other, had glowed for an
instant on the lumber vessel, I was certain that some funny
business was on foot."

"Who put that bogus money there? Someone near at hand
must have done it."

"If they come in from the vessel for that case, or cases, I
presume there are others, we stand nine chances out of ten
of running into their boat," Carson evaded.

"Ozy's bound for a cove in which he claims the dory will
be as invisible as a gray cat in a fog. There might be a
dozen boats lurking in these coves and we couldn't see them
tonight. He'll wait for us there while we're in the lighthouse. He says we'll have to do the chamois act climbing
the rocks."

The chamois act was a perfect description of their climb
up the rocky side of the island. Breathless, dripping, with
hands scratched and numb from pelting hail, they stole and
stumbled toward the lighthouse. It seemed miles. At each
flash they crouched and ran forward. Then waited for another glare to show them the location of the ghostly tower.

"Let's make a break for it in the dark," Kent whispered,
ran and came down with a crash.

Carson helped him up. He controlled a frantic desire to
shout with laughter as lightning showed Kent's grieved expression. This night of adventure was doing things to his
nerves.

"Here we are, Tod. Blind luck. We've landed at the door."

He put his hand on the knob. Jerked it back. Caught Kent's arm. Whispered;

"Someone ahead of us! Listen!"

They put their ears close to the door. A flash revealed Tod Kent's bulging eyes as he choked;

"Boy! It's Fenton talking!"

xxiii

IT had been a simple matter to slip away from The Sphinx in the motorboat, to linger in the shadow of the float at the Treasure Chest until the launch from the cruiser had landed its second load of passengers and gone back, then to steal away. Lucky the engine was almost noiseless, Lissa exulted as she steered for her island. Common sense tugged at her complacence to remind that the get-away would not have been so simple had not Lex Carson gone ahead with Major Fane and the Packards. She had been throbbingly conscious of him while on the cruiser, had felt his eyes on her, had—

"Hi, sweet thing!"

Coat collar turned up, Johnny Grant stood beside her.

"Is this little excursion the reason you invited me to the lobster-bake?"

"I didn't invite you, Johnny."

"Aha! Methinks I detect the fine Italian hand of my former fiancée. I had a hunch to that effect when she asked for a loan."

"Did she get it?"

"She did not. She had the nerve to tell me when she broke our engagement that she never had cared for me, had thought it amusing to try to get me away from you. She did it. A girl like that couldn't chisel a cent from me if she were starving. Why spend a minute talking about Cleo? Did you hear that roll of thunder? Thought I felt a drop of rain. The sky's gone black. We're in for a storm. We'd better come about and run ahead of it to Tarry Farm."

Lissa looked up at the spongey mass of sky. Not a star to be seen. How the gloom dramatized this ordinarily sleepy harbor. The lighthouse loomed like the tower of the Empire State Building and the cruiser took on the proportions of the Queen Mary. The air was saturated with moisture. A perfect night for someone to retrieve those coins. She'd get them first.

"I must go, Johnny. I wouldn't sleep a wink if I knew that G-Man was alone on the island tonight. Storms frighten him. He'll probably be curled up in a sheltered corner of the porch at the lighthouse. Besides, there's another reason. I'm after buried treasure."

She swore him to secrecy, told him of the pouch of coins she had found. Instead of sympathizing with her, he was furious.

"You're crazy! We may get mixed up with the guy who put them there."

"We'll scout around first, Johnny. They are directly beneath the kitchen window. I have a reason, a very serious reason for wanting them. Listen! Thought I heard a boat the other side of the island. Hear it?"

"No. You heard the echo of the launch returning to the cruiser probably. You don't think people are sailing round this bay tonight for pleasure, or treasure, do you? They're not so crazy."

"Cheerio, Johnny, it won't take us ten minutes from the time we leave the island pier for the lighthouse till we get back to it."

"All right. You may bet your last dollar I wouldn't have come had I known what you were after. It's a fool stunt but you're the captain. Better let me take the wheel. Felt another drop of rain."

"What's a drop of rain to a couple of adventurers en route to Treasure Island?" She sang a snatch of the song. "A thunder storm always sets me a-tingle. I'll stick to the wheel. I know the location of every ledge in this bay. I've run into them in the outboard times enough, and the outboard finished its career by smashing into one all by its lonesome. See that sudden glow of light behind the hills! Looks as if someone had hung up an arras of copper-gold lame. That storm is coming up fast. Here we are!"

She stepped to the float. With the painter in his hand, Grant scrambled after her.

"How hushed the world seems. It's weird—"

With a snarl and a shriek the wind swept down on them and wrenched Lissa's soft hat from her head. She clutched the air.

"Johnny! My hat! Catch it!"

Grant lunged, tripped, dropped the painter. He grabbed for it, but with a demoniac howl the wind whirled the boat out of his reach. A crackling blaze split the sky. A tree-crested ledge stood out in sharp relief. The great eye of the light shimmered in the unearthly glow. The tower shrank to half its size. Brasses on the runaway boat, tossing like a cockleshell, were tiny flames. The world went black. With a noise like the turning on of a Gargantuan hose, the torrent burst. The rain Lissa had wished for to cover the roughened earth above the buried pouch had come, buckets of it. She clutched Grant's sleeve.

"Where do we go from here, Johnny?"

He patted her wet hand.

"Good little sport. You take life on the chin, don't you? I'm terribly sorry, Lissa. Honest I didn't mean to let that boat get away."

"Of course you didn't. You have your faults, Johnny, but they're not in that class. Hear the rain hiss-s-s!"

For the first time, the consequences of the loss of the boat flooded Lissa's mind with dismay. She swallowed hard. It wouldn't help to get panicky.

"Let's make one try for the pouch, Johnny, I didn't bury it deep. We can't be any wetter than we are." She put her mouth close to his ear to make herself heard above the rain and wind. "Ooch! What a flash! Smell the sulphur! The lighthouse stood out like a close-up. Now it has disappeared. The thunder's deafening. Here comes another crack! Quick! While the sky's like a sheet of brass. Run for the light!"

Hand in hand they ran while the storm turned its light on and off as if it were manipulating giant push buttons. The tops of tall pines and cedars beyond the lighthouse twisted and bent and writhed in the fury of the wind.

Lissa stopped under a window. Whispered;

"Dig among those poppies, Johnny. Dig! Where is it? Oh, where is it? Someone's taken it! There's the hole!"

"I'm glad of it! Beat it for the house, you crazy nut."

At the door of the lighthouse, Lissa panted;

"Where do you suppose G-Man is? I tried to whistle as I ran but my throat was too dry. Find—the knob. I left—the latch up—this afternoon. That last flash—stung my eyes. I can see only two great gold discs."

They stumbled into the chintz-hung service room and with difficulty closed the door against the wind. Rain beat upon the roof, streamed down the windows, made little pink rivers when lightning slashed the sky. It poured from a broken spout outside with the roar of a miniature Niagara.

"At the next flash, pull down the shades, Johnny. I've found the lamp. I'll light it as soon as we've shut out the storm. I feel as if I were in a nightmare, as if in a minute I'd wake and find myself in my own room at home."

"I'd give a fortune to have you in your own room at home, Lissa." Grant's voice choked.

"Someone came for that pouch after Ralph Packard and I left for the cruiser," she whispered. "Who could it have been?"

She touched a match to the wick of the brass lamp which shone like gold. She looked furtively over her shoulder as the room leaped into life and color. The huge hollyhocks on the chintz never had looked so richly crimson and rosily pink, the old map over the fireplace, the brass candlesticks on the mantel, the rhythmic tick-tock of the clock, the book-laden shelves, her typewriter on a table, her knitting bag on a hook, gave her a sense of reality, of safety. She drew a ragged breath of relief.

"There! Now let the storm do its worst. We're safe, but I wish we had what we came for. When I start a thing I like to put it through."

She smiled at Grant, who, white faced, hair drenched, looked back at her gravely.

"You're telling me! As if I didn't know by now that you're the she-died-but-she-did-it type. We're in a jam, Lissa. We both can't stay here all night. Think of your stepmother's tongue and Cleo's. I'm going."

"You're not going out in this storm, Johnny Grant! Listen! Isn't that hail tick-tacking against the windows? It's only a shower. It will be over in a few minutes and the moon and stars will be out. Then we'll go home."

"The boat's gone. Thinking of walking the waves?"

"Goodness, aren't things screwy enough without going sarcastic on me?" She glanced at the brass-framed clock on the wall solemnly ticking off the seconds. "I am thinking of walking, but not on the water. In two more hours we can cross the bar on foot."

Color came back to his face, his eyes sparkled.

"Bar! That word sounds good to me. Got any—"

"Sorry, that shiver and sneeze were well done, Johnny, but the only beverages I have here are tea and coffee. I'll find something dry for us to put on, then we'll remove a large portion of my real estate from our hands."

She lighted one of the candles on the mantel, shaded the flame with her hand and entered the bedroom. A chain of fire crackled through the heavens. Everything in the small room burned red. A crash shook the building and put out the candle. She groped for the closet, pulled two woolly house coats from their hangars. Dashed into the service room.

"That last flash—was ter-rific, J-Johnny. I've always

boasted that I loved—thunder-storms. Never again! I don't —if only I could—find G-Man."

"Don't worry about that terrier. When he decided you weren't coming back for him, he probably beat it across the bar for home. That dog thinks."

"He does, Johnny. If he hadn't gone home, he would have known that I was here, wouldn't he? Put on this blue coat, blue's your color—while I'm in the kitchen slipping into the green one and making coffee, nice strong coffee that will curl our eyelashes. Lucky I had these coats here last fall to bundle up in while I was writing. Even with a big fire on the hearth, my hands would get so numb I could hardly type."

"Let's light the fire now."

"No, no. I think we'd better not, Johnny. The man who took the pouch might smell wood smoke and come bursting in." That wasn't the only reason, she added to herself. Ozy had asked to have the latch left up that he might get in. Wood smoke from the chimney might upset his plan. She smiled at Grant ingratiatingly even while she disciplined a shiver of nerves.

"You wouldn't like to go into the kitchen first and pull down the shades, would you, Johnny?"

He preceded her into the small kitchen, drew the shades at the two windows, waited until she had lighted the lamp and a burner on the oil stove, before he pumped water in a basin and bathed his hands.

"That's better. I felt like a ditch-digger. Golly, that was a crash! The buoy sounds as if it were moaning mad. Hear the waves lash against the ledge. No one will come near this island tonight. Want me to stay here until you've made the coffee?"

"No, I'm all right now. You're sneezing again, Johnny. Go into the other room and get off that wet suit. I'll never forgive myself if you get pneumonia."

"Pneumo-chu! I'll go. You'd better change your clothes, sweet thing."

"I will, Johnny, as soon as I start the coffee."

"What this country needs is more girls like you," he attested gruffly and closed the door.

Lissa scrubbed her hands, pumped water into the glass globe of the percolator, lighted the lamp under it, and measured coffee for the container. She pulled off her one-time white frock, now a pale gray with a cubistic design of green which had run from the leather belt, and draped it over a small clothes horse. A soggy wad dropped to the floor.

"My word, lucky I didn't lose that, now that the pouch

has disappeared," she thought and picked it up. "Just as bright as you were when I found you," she added under her breath as she looked at the silver quarter in the wet handkerchief. She wadded it up again and dropped it into the pocket of the green house-coat as she slipped into it.

She had acquired plot material for a story tonight, for a dozen stories. Noble of Ralph Packard to offer to work with her, but she preferred to depend on herself. If only she were an expert in handling it like Kipling or Stevenson or O. Henry. O. Henry! A close-up of Sidonie Packard shrinking against a background of books flashed on the screen of her mind. The stiffening went out of her knees. She shivered. Now she knew why Ralph Packard's stories had seemed familiar. Those she had copied were O. Henry's with names and locales changed! There was a complete set of O. Henry on a shelf at Red Chimneys.

Dazed, incredulous she stood in the middle of the room while the storm crackled and thundered and howled outside. Why had he done it? What could have been his object in deceiving her? She would tell Lex. Terribly disappointing that she could not help him by producing that pouch.

"If you don't believe him when he tells you he loves you, why believe his story about the counterfeiters?" she asked herself. The shell of disbelief in a man's faithfulness in which she had encased her heart helped mighty little against Lex's demanding eyes, his husky voice.

"Deep down in your soul you do believe him, you know you do. You don't dare meet his eyes because they make you ache to creep into the warmth of his arms," she accused herself passionately.

The vision she had conjured caught at her breath, set her pulses racing. Close on its heels came the memory of Madge sobbing against his shoulder.

She closed her eyes tight to shut out the picture and shut it in. It hurt, hurt unbearably. Only a surgical operation could cut that out. Was getting engaged to Johnny the answer? In an effort to thrust back the thought, she looked about the spotless kitchen. Shining rows of copper pans and pots hung from hooks. Watteau figures on china simpered behind the glass doors of a cupboard. Tin goods by the appetizing half-dozens stood shoulder to shoulder on a shelf.

She prepared a tray with cups and saucers, thin wafers, and the percolator, now sending forth a delicious aroma. She answered an impatient knock on the door.

"Ready, Johnny. Come and take out the tray, will you? My, but you're devastating in blue," she mocked gaily, as she followed him into the chintz-hung room.

"You're not so bad in green, sweet thing, if your head didn't look like a wet-chu!"

"Don't sneeze when you're carrying that coffee perco-lator, Johnny Grant!"

"Think I'm sneezing because I like it? I didn't ask to come on this adven-chu! did I?"

"Give me the tray, Johnny. Quick before you drop it. Pull out that table. There!" She did things to the percolator and poured him a cup of steaming coffee.

"Doesn't the smell of that grow wings on your spirit? That's condensed cream, but what's condensed cream be-tween friends? Drink it quickly, before you sneeze again."

Lissa watched him anxiously as he put the cup to his lips. She would never forgive herself for dragging him to the island on a night like this if he took a serious cold. He grinned at her.

"It's beautiful. Quite the last word in coffee, I'd say, Miss Lissa."

"Johnny, that was Fenton to the life," she gripped his arm, whispered;

"Don't speak! Someone's at the door!"

xxiv

JOHNNY GRANT flung his arm about Lissa as the entrance door banged open and two men burst into the room.

"Lex! Tod!" she whispered.

Her heart, which had stopped, picked up and poured blood through her veins till her face, her finger tips burned. Why was Lex here? His eyes, enormous and black, were burning pools of fury in his livid face, the muscles of his jaw tight-ened and relaxed, tightened again. If Tod's balloon cheeks got much redder, they'd burst. What were they thinking to look at her like that? Condemning her without a hearing because she and Johnny were here together? Well, let them. She freed herself from Grant's arm and said flippantly;

"I suppose, gentlemen, that this is what might be called adult drama. Is it time to warn me that anything I say may be used against me?"

"Lissa—" Carson's voice broke with anger—"Lissa—"

A blinding glare filled the room. Something outside creaked

and tore. A shower of splinters struck roof and window. The building rocked from the crash that followed. Something bumped down the curving iron stairs, something clinked and rolled from step to step. Lissa raised her face which had been crushed against Lex Carson's shoulder. She freed herself from his arms, how had she come in them, she wondered dazedly, as she stared at the heap on the floor, at the river of silver coins pouring down the stairs.

"Nino!" she breathed incredulously.

Carson and Kent bent over the Italian.

"He's only stunned," Carson whispered. "Now that we've found what we came for let's get away. Quick! Where's Fenton, Grant? Don't quibble. We heard his voice."

"You heard me imitating him to amuse Lissa."

"To amuse Lissa! How did you get to the island?"

"In a boat, do you think we swam?"

"Cut the comedy, Johnny," Lex Carson's voice was like a blast of liquefied air against Lissa's heart, it froze it. "Where's the boat?"

"It got away from me when we landed."

"Oh, it got away from you?"

Lissa shook back her wet hair and prepared for battle.

"Don't speak to Johnny like that, Lex. He's not to blame because we are here. He didn't want to come. I persuaded him."

"Oh, you persuaded him."

"Stop echoing my words! When Ralph Packard and I started from the island for the cruiser this afternoon, I told G-Man to go home, waited until he reached the bar. Half way across the harbor, I looked toward the island and saw that bad dog on the pier. I couldn't go back for him then and when I saw the storm coming I knew he'd be frightened and persuaded Johnny to come here with me to get him. I—came for something else, too, but the moment we landed, the storm burst and my hat blew off—Johnny, don't interrupt—and when Johnny tried to catch it, he dropped the painter and the boat got away and—and here we are."

Kent gripped Carson's arm. "Let's go. Quick! We don't want that—" he nodded in the direction of the unconscious Italian—"to know we saw him."

"You're right, Tod! Got a coat, Lissa? Get it."

His tone infuriated her. He didn't believe what she had told him about her reason for coming to the island. She defied;

"Just because you have the right to dole out my money, Lex, doesn't mean that you have the right to order me about, does it?"

144

"Get that coat."

"I won't—" Lissa met Grant's eyes. What was he trying to tell her? Why were the two men here? They hadn't come for her or they wouldn't have been dumb with surprise when they saw her. They had been on the trail of someone, of course. Nino? Had she messed things up hopelessly? As if answering her question, Carson snapped;

"Lissa, get that coat."

She dashed into the bedroom. Pulled a sports coat from its hanger. Changed to old dry shoes. How quiet the world seemed after that world-shaking crash.

When she returned to the service room, Nino had been lifted to a chair. The tray with the coffee percolator was on the table beside him. Johnny had changed to his wet suit. Lex Carson seized her arm.

"Come along!" he ordered in a voice which suggested pent-up explosives.

"Will he—he be all right?" She nodded toward the lax figure in the chair.

"He's coming out of it." Carson flung open the door. "We must get away before he sees us. Where's the key to this door?"

Lissa took a key from a nail on the wall.

"I keep an extra one here in case the one I carry is lost."

"Don't stop to explain. Lock the door, Johnny—on the outside! Put the key on that right-hand window-ledge. Step on it, all of you!"

The storm had passed, all that remained of it were pale flashes and the distant sound as of giants bowling. The mouth of the moon tipped up at the corners as it gazed down upon a gigantic pine which had been stripped open from tip to root; its light laid a quivering trail of quicksilver across the water, turned boulders to platinum; arborvitae, spruce and clumps of juniper to dusky purple, and dropped a bridal veil of silver over the lighthouse tower. A chorus of crickets serenaded the stars which spangled the sky. The buoy moaned. Somewhere a cow-bell tinkled. The air was crystalline and fragrant with the pungent scent of wet juniper.

"Gorgeous night isn't it?" Lissa whispered. She laughed softly. "I've seen a prisoner on the screen, gripped on each side by an officer being rushed along as you and Lex are rushing me, Tod. What's the idea? 'Fraid Johnny and I will escape the strong arm of the law? Have you forgotten we haven't a boat?"

"We've forgotten nothing," Lex Carson reminded icily.

"Do you know, Lex, the more I see you, the more convinced I am that you are wasted in this country, you should

145

get into the Dictator business," Lissa asserted flippantly. "Can't you stop sneezing, Johnny? You've advertised every step we've taken."

"Why not advert-chu! it? Is this a secret expedition?"

"It was, until you joined it," Lex Carson answered drily.

"I knew you were something besides a law-chu! Carson. Didn't I tell you so, Lissa?"

"Whatever you think I am, keep it to yourself till after tomorrow, Grant. Beat it, Tod. Locate Ozy and the dory. I'll look after Lissa." As Kent disappeared beyond a clump of scrub pines, Lissa confided;

"Believe it or not, Lex, Johnny and I came to the island to help you."

"What do you mean, help me?"

His thoughts ran on a double track as she gave him the coin from her pocket, told of her discovery of the pouch; of her determination to return to the island for it. A ton of depression slid from his heart. She had not come to be with Johnny Grant.

One part of his mind was engaged with speculation as to who had buried the coins, the other concerned with a plan to get Lissa home. If it had been a tough climb for Tod and him coming up, what would it be for her going down? She would have to make it. There was no other way. The road across the bar wouldn't be clear again for an hour. It would be like her stepmother and Cleo to find out that she had gone to the island with Johnny Grant. His heart had been so numbed by the sight of them together at the light, that he had forgotten for a moment why he was there. The crash had sent her straight into his arms. In danger she had turned from Grant to him. The memory of the confiding unrestraint of her body set his pulses quickstepping. If she—

He'd better keep Lissa out of his mind until the business of the night was finished. The question as to who would signal the waiting vessel had been answered when Nino pitched down the iron stairs in that flood of silver coins. Undoubtedly they had been given him in payment for buoying the watertight cases of bogus bills and signalling from the light to the dark vessel anchored off shore. He must be spirited away from the island before the man whose tool he was could learn what had happened. A radio message from the cruiser would take care of that.

"It may be your idea of a fitting finale for the evening to pitch off this bank—" Lissa's voice cut into his planning— "but I've had water enough, if you ask me."

Carson ignored her jibe.

"Ozy's below in a boat. Grant, the trail down is a tough

146

one. I'll go ahead. Grab Lissa's left hand, I'll take her right. If she slips, hold her with all your strength, understand? Ready, Lissa?"

She nodded. Good little sport not to make a fuss about it, he thought, and felt for a footing in the jagged rock. Step by careful step they descended. Once Lissa slipped and fell heavily against him, pine needles above them rained a shower of crystal drops. He felt the rock crumble under his foot, grabbed at a stout trunk of creeping cedar, bent flat by winter winds, and prayed that it would hold.

"I'm sorry," she breathed.

"Don't move! Hold her, Johnny!"

"I've got her, but I'm hanging on by a twig myself."

"I'll get a foothold in a minute. Don't be frightened, Lissa."

"I'm not frightened, I'm thrilled," the catch in her voice belied its lightness.

Johnny Grant sniffed. "You may be, but if ever I get back to the mainland, me an' the island is done."

Grant wasn't such a bad sport himself, Carson thought, as Lissa chuckled at his imitation of Ozy. For a youth who spent his days and most of his nights speeding in a fire-engine-red roadster, he was doing this chamois act without a protest.

"Wait! Don't move!" Carson warned. "Crouch behind those junipers! Quick!"

"Look, Lex! That's Ozy's boat! He's going to his lobster-traps," Lissa whispered. "Why don't you call?"

"Ssh!" Carson gripped her arm. He watched a white dory with a shoebox cabin steal cautiously along a ledge and stop. A search light from it played along the shore.

"Lie flat! Both of you! If you sneeze, Grant, I'll choke you!" Carson threatened.

From behind a clump of junipers he watched the light. It was coming nearer. It lingered on the bushes above them! Had they been seen? Whoever was handling that search light would not have dared use it on the Tarry Farm side of the island. Nothing but ledges and ocean between them and Europe this side.

After what seemed ages the light went out. The dory was a blur of white. From it came the sound of wood scraping. Lissa shook Carson's sleeve;

"Someone's stealing Ozy's lobsters!" she whispered. "Shout and stop them, Lex!"

"No! No! They're not stealing lobsters. They are after something else. Don't move!"

From behind the shelter of the junipers, he watched the

white dory move from ledge to ledge. Must have come from the lumber vessel. Clever idea to make it a dead ringer for Ozy's. Anyone seeing it would think that the Captain was pulling his traps after the storm. Were there five of those watertight cases? He must get to the cruiser's radio. He couldn't move until that dory finished its collections, though. It was going! Going fast! Running straight for that dark hulk with the red eye on the horizon.

"We can go now. Come on," he called softly into the shadows behind him and stood up.

"Come on! Just like that! I'm so stiff I can hear my joints crack when I move." Lissa rose slowly and stretched her arms above her head. "Are you dead or only sleeping, Johnny?"

"I'm-chu!"

"Stop sneezing, Grant. Grab Lissa's hand," Carson commanded. "I'm stepping down."

He caught at the creeping cedar to steady himself. Went on. Step by cautious step the two above followed. This wasn't the way he had come. The cliff was almost perpendicular. He'd taken the wrong trail. They'd have to go on now.

"Look out for the wet moss," he warned. "The rain has soaked it."

He slipped and slid holding Lissa tightly with one hand and grabbing at wet rocks with the other.

"Not much farther to go. I can see a narrow beach below. Don't let Lissa slip, Grant. I'll drop. When I hold out my arms, let her go and I'll catch her. Ready!"

Carson had to twist his hand from the girl's clutch before he dropped. It seemed as if he slid miles down the cliff— though it couldn't have been more than twelve feet—before he landed on a pebbly beach. He called;

"Come!"

Lissa jumped. He caught her before her feet could touch the beach. Held her close.

"All right?"

She nodded and freed herself.

"Can't we help Johnny?" she asked breathless from her plunge.

"Always and forever 'Johnny' with you, isn't it? He seems to be doing extremely well without help," Carson observed drily as Grant contacted the beach with a crashing impact. He looked up at Lissa and blinked;

"Are my lower teeth protruding through the top of my head, sweet thing? I felt them sky-rocket when I landed."

Lissa leaned weakly against the cliff and shook with laughter.

"I don't see anything so hilariously funny," Grant growled and pulled himself stiffly to his feet.

"I'm not laughing at you, Johnny, it's—it's just everything. What a night! What a night!"

"Pull yourself together, Lissa," Carson commanded unfeelingly—she mustn't suspect that he was anxious about her—"or we'll have an hysterical girl on our hands and that would be the last straw."

"I'm not hysterical. I'm—"

"All right, you're not hysterical. Prove it. Stop laughing. We'll have to follow the shore till we find Tod and Ozy."

Curious what had become of the Captain's dory, he thought, as the three splashed into water in coves, ploughed through wet pebbles, slipped and slid over boulders. They must realize that he had mistaken the trail. This side of the island wasn't so long that the white boat couldn't be seen. Perhaps they were in some dark cove and had seen the cases picked up. The man, Nino, must have been leaning over the stairs listening, when that world-rocking crash came. Had he heard their voices? And if he had, before morning he would be where what he suspected or said would do no harm.

It was almost as light as day. The stars looked as if the rain had polished them and hung them up to dry. The sea rolled in noisily, dashed against boulders, receded with a swish, dragging pebbles and foam with it, like a dainty woman trailing fluffy white ruffles behind her. The moon was slanting now and lighting every crack and cranny among the ledges. There must be a million or two crickets chirping.

Carson's thoughts kept pace as he hurried on. His work on the estate was finished for the present. If the agreement he had signed yesterday went through, he could handle the rest of the business from Washington. If his program for tomorrow—it was today, now—went through—if—the word beat in his mind like a muted drum. There shouldn't be an "if"—it must go through.

XXV

"ARE you sure we haven't hiked along the whole Maine coast, Lex?" Lissa asked breathlessly. "All these coves and boulders I've slipped and slid over can't belong to my island."

"Your treasure island," Grant puffed. "You'll never get me on one of your excursions again, sweet-chu!"

"There's Ozy's dory!" Carson exclaimed. "If you two are as glad as I am to see that white boat, it makes it unanimous!"

In a dark cove Kent and the Captain stood in water to their waists holding the gunwale of the dory at the stern of which a motorboat took the wash sidelong.

"For Pete's sake where've you been?" Tod Kent demanded.

"Keep your voice down. Took the wrong path over the ledge. Where'd you get that motorboat?"

"It was beached in one of the coves so we towed it along. Decided it belonged to the man we left behind us. See the name, Red Chimneys, on the side? What shall we do with it, Lex? He isn't going to need it for the present." Kent chuckled.

"But you and I are."

Captain Ozias sniffed, jerked Carson's sleeve, and pointed at the wet line on the shore that showed the drop of the tide.

"Say, Lex, if you folks don't get started we won't git this boat over the bar, the tide's ebbin' fast. I guess you don't want to give yerselves away by going round the light, do ye? Thet's the only other way to git back to Tarry Farm landin'."

"Tod and I are not going back with you, Ozy. Take Lissa home. Grant, go with her, will you, and see that she gets to the house safely?"

"Sure, I'll take her home. Left my roadster there when I came to the lobster-bake. Golly, that seems years ago. Aren't you coming, Carson?"

"No. Kent and I are going to the cruiser to finish a job. After that—" he looked at Lissa standing in the shadow of a huge boulder. "I shall devote all my time to settling another matter."

"Say, if you folks expect me to git this boat over the bar—" rasped Captain Ozias.

Carson caught Lissa by the elbows and swung her into the dory. "Hop aboard, Grant. All set, Ozy!"

"Good-night, Lissa," he called softly as the dory nosed its way out of the cove.

"Good-night!" her voice came faintly across the fast-widening strip of water, came also a loud, "Chu!"

"When you can take time off from watching that boat out of sight, perhaps you'll tell me what we do next," Kent suggested crisply.

Carson turned his back on the dory.

"Next, we'll push this motorboat out where we can start it. We're both wet to the skin now, a little dampness won't hurt us. There she goes! Jump in, Tod!"

He swung himself aboard, seized the wheel, and switched

on the engine. Kent caught his arm. Pointed to a dark hulk, with one red eye, which was moving slowly toward the open sea.

"Suppose she's got those bogus bills aboard?" he whispered.

"Sure of it." As he swung the wheel to avoid a whirl of white water, Carson told of the dory he had watched hover about the ledges. He concluded;

"From the cruiser we'll radio the revenue cutter that's standing by to help us, to board that lumber vessel, seize the crew and those bogus bills before they flood the country."

"I didn't know there was a revenue cutter in the offing. Think of everything, don't you, Lex?"

"I haven't had a chance to tell you before, Tod. I've worked at white heat since I had the hunch where to locate the Ace. I'll bet I've been over every square foot of the area pegged off on the map. No, I haven't thought of everything. We'll radio the revenue officers to send a gig to the island to pick up the Italian and the coins, but what's to prevent the man whose tool he is, from suspecting when Nino doesn't report in the morning, that there's something in the air and making his get-away? I can see all our summer's work cracking-up."

"Course it won't crack-up. You're having an attack of the jitters, Lex. The moan of that confounded buoy is enough to send one's spirit into low. Taking it by and large, you've had a tough night. Seeing Lissa in that room with Grant's arms about her gave me an awful jolt for a minute. Only for a minute, though, you can't look at that girl without knowing she's about as fine as they come."

"You're not apologizing for Lissa to me, are you?" Carson demanded savagely.

Kent chuckled;

"That-a-boy, bite the hand that feeds you. I was merely trying to pull your spirits out of a nose-dive. To return to the slick Nino. I have an idea. This is his boat, the Red Chimneys' boat, isn't it?"

"Yes."

"We'll have Prescott tow it to the bar, beach it and turn it upside down. Conclusion: that Nino was swept overboard in the storm. Get it?"

"Sure, I get it. You're a wonder, Tod."

"I'm good when I put my mind to it. Grand night after the storm. We'll take it as an omen that we'll pull off our coup without a hitch."

Carson nodded and looked up at the silvery mackerel clouds. Patches of indigo sky were dotted with stars which twinkled like gold sequins on a lacy dance frock. In the east where sea and sky met spread a rosy glow. A pale moon was riding westward. A drift of mist lay on a hillside like a film of chiffon against a rich fur. The cool smell of pines drifted from the shore.

As the boat shouldered her way heavily through the rough sea, he looked toward Tarry Farm. No lights in the cottages. Had the Major put himself and his radio to bed or was he reaching out into the night to contact with a ship? Had the Packards discovered that their houseman was missing?

The house at the crest of the slope was dark except for one lighted window in the ell. Fenton's room? Lissa had said that he kept late hours reading. Would she get into the house without being heard by him? Did she love Grant? He felt again the pressure of her head against his shoulder, the pulsing warmth of her. If she loved Johnny, would she have flung herself into another man's arms when frightened? That question, along with one or two others, would be answered within twenty-four hours. Meanwhile, he had the message to the revenue cutter to code. The cruiser at last.

With heavy top coats over their damp clothing, he and Kent paced the forward cockpit smoking, waiting for an answer to his call. The radio operator lowered his window and held out a slip of paper.

"Here it is, Mr. Carson. Had some difficulty getting it through. The static witches are riding the air on their broomsticks tonight good and plenty. It's the storm in the distance I suppose, but I've never before heard such weird wails and shrieks.

"Thank you, Connor."

Carson read the slip of paper. Kent looking over his shoulder, nodded.

"Okay? Well, that's that. Now for the boys."

Carson had believed that the last weeks had taught him all he ever could know of suspense; he knew now, that he had but touched the surface of it. As he followed Kent along the companionway, it played wild tricks with his imagination, chilled his blood, turned his fingertips to ice. Only a few hours more, but empires and governments had crumbled in a few hours.

The tense muscle in his cheek was the only surface sign of his turmoil of spirit as he entered the pine-paneled cabin and questioned the two men tilted back in their chairs.

"Well?" The word cracked like a ring-master's whip.

The black haired man with light gray eyes and the light haired man with dark eyes, nodded. Before they could speak Carson held up his hand.

"I understand. Don't say a word. Words get into the air."

He stood at the window for an instant looking at a bright star, hearing the wash of waves against the side of the cruiser and the incessant moan of the buoy. The last link in his chain of evidence had been forged. Now, if there were no weak links—

"If you were in the army you'd get a D. S. C. for this job, Lex," the dark haired man said.

Carson turned.

"The job isn't finished yet. If you can honestly say that to me tonight, I shall be inclined to agree with you."

xxvi

LISSA crossed the sunny breakfast room to the open French windows. Above the terrace, the sky was pure turquoise patched with a few clouds delicate as new-spun cobwebs. Hills, stretching ridge by dusky ridge, towered into infinite space. Some of them were green at the base, marked off like checker-boards by stone walls. The sapphire water of the harbor was dotted with anchored crafts of many sizes and varieties and blotched with ultramarine and malachite where cloud shadows darkened it. A fragrant breeze stirred the mauve hangings. A bird poked a red-topped head from a vine, regarded the girl with bead-like eyes and chirped a greeting.

Gorgeous day after last night's shower. Life is like that after showers, she thought. Storm and stress and the rain of tears followed by clearing skies and the sunshine of hope and joy and courage. It all made for living. The days of this summer had been vivid days, so different from those she had spent as companion and comfort—she hoped—to an ill woman.

"Hello, Lissa!"

Lex Carson greeted her from the threshold as she sat down at the table. He dropped on a chair the coat G-Man had stolen.

"I like you in that green linen. Makes me think of a cool cucumber. Grand day for the Fair."

His voice was buoyant. Some quality in it set her pulses quickstepping. Was it suppressed excitement? She was imagining. There was no excitement in the eyes that met hers, they were quizzically friendly. No hint in his manner that he remembered the unceremonious way in which he had swung her aboard Ozy's dory last night, or his anger when he had seen her with Johnny at the light, or that she had flung herself in his arms when the crash came that had seemed like the end of the world. She hadn't been aware that she had run to him, she'd just found herself there. She agreed;

"It's a gorgeous day and the World and his Wife will be at the Fair. We always give the house-staff the day off, and have our luncheon at the Country Club. Will that be all right with you, Lex?"

"Okay. I shan't get round for lunch. The top of the morning to you, Mrs. Barclay. Morning, Cleo," he greeted the mother and daughter who appeared in the doorway. They looked like sisters in their linen frocks, one amethyst one orchid.

"Good morning, Lex. Well, Lissa, you didn't elope with Johnny?" Cleo asked as she peered under the cover of a silver chafing-dish. There was a glint of blue steel in her eyes as she glanced over her shoulder. "Perhaps you did elope, after all. Perhaps the happy bridegroom is concealed somewhere about the place?"

"An imagination like yours ought to get you a Hollywood job as scenario writer, Cleo," Lex Carson cut in before Lissa had recovered sufficiently from her surprise at the suggestion to answer. "When I ran her down there was no bridegroom among those present nor in the offing, so far as I could see."

"Then you went for her after I left you in the hall?" Cleo asked as he drew out a chair for her at the table.

"Sure, I went for her. You gave me a jolt when you suggested that she had run off with Johnny Grant. Isn't she my ward? No wonder you didn't hear us come in, the thunder made such a racket. Good morning, Fenton," he turned to the butler who entered from the pantry. "That was some storm last night. Do you have many like it here?"

"Not often, sir. We got back from the cruiser just in time, didn't we, sir, though you went out again. It was a busy harbor after that, sir, with boats arriving from everywhere for the Fair. I sent down to inquire for the Major this morning, sir. His Filipino boy reported that he was none the worse for his ducking. There's been a sad accident, sir." Fenton's tone was lachrymose.

"Accident!"

Carson joined in the chorus of exclamations. He stood close behind Lissa's chair as he asked;

"What happened?"

"It's the Italian houseman at Red Chimneys, sir. This morning the Red Chimneys' motorboat was found turned over on the bar road. Mr. and Miss Packard haven't seen him since he asked them at the lobster-bake if he might take the boat to the village. I believe he's quite a movie-fan. They think he was caught in the storm and was washed overboard. Very sad. Shall I pour your coffee, sir?"

Lissa knew now why Lex stood behind her chair. It was a warning to her not to exclaim. Nino had been left at the light. Ozy and Tod had picked up his boat. Did Lex want the story to get about that he had been lost in the storm? She asked breathlessly;

"Have they—have they looked for the—for him, Fenton?"

"Not yet, Miss. The boat has just been found. I'm sorry I spoke of it, Miss Lissa. I'm afraid I've spoiled your breakfast."

"You've spoiled all our breakfasts, Fenton," Cleo flared. "And because of a sneaky houseman. Nino gave me the shivers. Let's talk about something else, Lex."

"I'll see Mr. Packard after breakfast, Fenton. Miss Lissa tells me that the house-staff usually has Fair Day off."

"Yes, sir. It's usual, sir, but if you want me—"

"No. No. Enjoy the holiday. I'm on vacation myself." He backed up before the mantel. "By the way, Fenton, I rescued that coat on the chair from G-Man—you'll have to do something about that dog, Lissa, if he doesn't stop robbing clotheslines. Perhaps you can find the owner, Fenton."

The butler picked up the coat.

"Why that's mine, sir. It's old and comfortable and I wear it in my room. I hung it on the line yesterday to freshen it. Sorry you've been troubled with it, sir."

What was there about that old coat to send a faint wave of color to Lex's hair, Lissa wondered.

"Nothing like an old coat for comfort, Fenton. Glad you have it back. What's the rest of the program for Fair Day? I'm new to it, remember. Do we dine here?"

"Mother and I don't, Lex." Cleo flung her napkin on the table. "The Packards are giving a small dinner at the Club before the ball. We are invited." Her voice was not so cool and indifferent as usual. Was she also caught in the undercurrent of excitement sweeping through the house? Lissa asked herself.

"What ball?"

"The County ball. Everyone goes. Mixed party, but something to kill time," Cleo shrugged.

"Are you dining with the Packards, Lissa?"

"No, Lex. I was not invited to the dinner, but I've accepted an invitation to lead the opening march at the ball with the chairman of the Board of Selectmen. Doesn't that sound exciting?"

"It does. The ball sounds festive to me, as has been said before, I'm on vacation, now. I may be late, but I'll get there. Save me some dances, Lissa."

"The phone is ringing in the sports-room, sir."

Lissa's eyes followed Lex Carson as he left the room. A certain timbre in his voice had confirmed her in her belief that he was rigidly controlling inner excitement.

"Where were you last evening, Lissa?" Cleo's voice was as sweetly acid as a lemon drop. "I saw you leave the cruiser in your own boat with Johnny Grant."

"Why not cross-examine Johnny?" Lissa flung over her shoulder from the threshold. "He knows where I was."

Would Cleo question Johnny about last night, she asked herself as with Andy Millard squirming with excitement beside her, she drove the yellow roadster along roads bordered with feathery purple and white asters, goldenrod and a tangle of ferns and shrubs. Above them an occasional flame of scarlet and crimson maple press-agented the approach of autumn. Sunlight on the chromium trim of the car dazzled her eyes as she followed closely in the wake of crowds of people, vehicles, automobiles, farmtrucks, motoring tourists stopping over, a yoke of oxen, all converging on the County Fair.

It was the first moment she had had in which to review the hours which had passed since the conversation in the breakfast room. There had been flowers to arrange for exhibition at the Fair; telephone calls for the employees to answer; water had stopped running at Pirates' Den. The Major had gone for the day, the excited Filipinos had reported, and because neither plumbers nor electricians would work on Fair Day, she had labored side by side with them until the temperamental engine had coughed a speck of dust from its larynx and started.

She had been quite alone in the house when Lex had arrived with two genial, interesting looking men.

"They've come to look over the property," he had said to her in an aside. His voice had been strained as he added, "I think I've sold it, Lissa. It will be like dropping the Empire State Building off my shoulders, if I have. Wish me luck."

For lunch she had made herself a sandwich in the pantry at Tarry Farm. No time for the Club. She had heard the voices of Lex and the men in the conservatory balcony as she slipped into an exotic print frock. Then the Millards' maid had arrived with the boy—and here she was.

Andy bounced in his seat. His white suit accentuated his faint coat of tan.

"Hear the music, Lissa! Isn't it 'citing? I smell popcorn and molasses boiling. Do you think Fenton will be here to take me on the merry-go-round? He said he would."

"Then he will," Lissa answered and devoutly hoped that she was right. Merry-go-rounding as a sport, left her cold. "You like Fenton, don't you?"

"Rath-er—Johnny Grant taught me that—rath-er. When I'm big I'm going to be a butler and stand straight and wear a coat with silver buttons on the tail. Look! The plane! Flies like a gull, doesn't it? See its wings shine. Can't you drive faster, Lissa? Mother is coming for me in an hour. She said I mustn't stay longer. I have two half dollars to spend. Lex gave them to me. See?"

Lissa pressed the accelerator with a slim green shoe as he clinked the silver in a hand grown slightly plump and in a palm more than slightly grimy. She remembered the white, emaciated fingers he had laid on G-Man's head, not so many weeks ago. Living down by the sea and tender care had worked a miracle of healing. She hugged him.

"Andy, you're sweet, I love you."

"All right, but gee, can't you hurry?"

Quickly she folded the wings of sentiment.

"Sorry, I bubbled over. Suppose we leave the roadster in this parking place and walk the rest of the way. We'll get along faster."

"Okay with me—Johnny taught me that, too. What's the man shouting?"

"Mr. Alexander Carson is wanted at the judges' stand! Mr. Carson wanted at the judges' stand," a megaphoned voice proclaimed.

"Does he mean Lex?" Andy asked. "Is he coming to the Fair?"

"He'll be here later. Are you still clutching those half dollars? Better put them deep into a pocket of your shorts or you may lose them. Let's go."

Hand in hers the boy hopped and skipped beside her as they were swept to the gate by the crowd. He wriggled with impatience while she bought tickets at something which looked like a sentry box.

They passed through the turn-stile and stepped at once into a haze of dust, into the midway broiling under a hot early afternoon sun. A potpourri of smells greeted them, frying hot dogs, popping corn, boiling coffee, crisping fat from roasting beef turning slowly on a spit. From the big barn drifted the scent of hay tinted by the strong smell from the bodies of cattle, the lowing of cows, punctuated by an occasional bellow; the grunt of pigs, the ba-a-a of sheep, the crow of cocks, the cackle of hens.

Behind tents and booths the old sedans of the concessionaires sagged as if inexpressibly weary of the welter of shabby household goods spread on the ground about them. The sounds would have put to shame those of the Tower of Babel. Shrill cries of innumerable vendors, "Lemonade! Five cents!" clashed with the barking of showmen, "Step in and see the Wild man! He eats raw meat!" "The Wonder of the World! Molly, the calf with two heads and three tails!" "Hit the chink's head and you get a cane!"; the distant pounding of horses' hoofs on tan bark, mingled with the tin-panny music, the shrill whistle of the merry-go-round, and a radioed voice singing the latest popular song.

Swinging slim black canes she had bought at Andy's insistence, Lissa and the boy made their way through the milling crowd which mopped its brow with one hand and risked its money on chances with the other. She nodded to summer residents who hailed her; stopped to speak to villagers who smiled at her; edged by rough looking men who ogled her; shook her head at vendors who importuned her. The boy tugged like a dog on leash.

"We'll never get to the merry-go-round if you stop to talk to everybody in the world, Lissa," he protested. "Here's Fenton! Here's Fenton!" he shouted.

He hopped up and down with excitement as the butler approached. He was a stranger to Lissa in his tweed suit and straw hat which last could be described best as "natty." The combination of hat and sideburns tickled Lissa's funnybone. She bit her lips to keep back a laugh. Fenton held the hat in his hand as he greeted her.

"Good afternoon, Miss. Sorry if I've kept Master Andy waiting, but, the house-staff and I have been having our lunch in the grove outside the Fair grounds and it took me sometime to get back. A mixed crowd, Miss, a very mixed crowd. All sorts of riff-raff comes to a place like this, if you get what I mean, Miss." He cast a scathing glance at a man with burning eyes and an out-at-elbows coat, who lingered near.

Lissa's hand tightened on the boy's, until the man slouched away.

"I understand, Fenton. We—"

Andy tugged.

"Lissa! Lissa! Why do you and Fenton talk so much? If we don't go to the merry-go-round, we'll never get there and I only have an hour."

"He's right, Miss. I'll take him along now, Miss, if you'll trust him with me."

A distant trumpet sounded a fan-fare. "The races are on, Miss. You'll want to see the horses run, I know, and you really should take a look at our cattle. They've won the blue ribbon, Miss. The late Madam would have been proud."

"Lissa! Please let me go!"

"All right, Andy. Don't let him ride too long, Fenton. They've been broadcasting for Mr. Carson, doubtless to inform him about the ribbons. I'll look at the Tarry Farm cattle then I'll come to the merry-go-round tent. Mrs. Millard may get there first, she's driving over for Andy."

Lissa watched the tall man in the jaunty straw hat with the small boy hopping and skipping beside him until they were lost in the crowd. She had a curious feeling, a sort of why-did-I-let-him-go sinking of the heart. The old imagination working overtime again she jeered at herself, hadn't Madge told her that Andy might ride with Fenton?

She stopped at the rail of the track. Between races a red-headed woman in a spangled green velvet dress was walking a tight-rope. The rope snapped. The woman fell. "Oh!" moaned the crowd. The sound swept the air like the soughing of the wind.

The tight-rope walker, ghastly under the rouged spots on her cheeks, picked herself up, gallantly threw kisses and limped to a tent. Her audience cheered and one by one and in groups drifted on to fresh fields of entertainment.

As Lissa approached the cattle barn she saw Ralph Packard with Cleo in a blue frock and floppy matching hat. She dodged into a food booth to avoid them. A man with a double gap in his upper teeth set in a moon-shaped face grinned at her in friendly inquiry;

"What'll you have, Miss?"

Lissa looked up but she wasn't seeing him, she was seeing Lex Carson's white face as he had stared incredulously at her as she had stood with Johnny Grant's arm about her in the service room at the light. What had he thought? He had asked Johnny to take her home. He had been too disgusted to think she would run around with the man who had jilted her to care who took her home, probably. She had fought back the memory for hours and now here it was without any warning, to submerge her.

"What'll you have, Miss?"

The concessionaire's question, tinged with impatience, snapped Lissa out of her abstraction. She looked about the tent with its small tables set close to the canvas wall, before she smiled and asked;

"What can I have?"

The moon-face melted into mushy admiration.

"Ice-cream cone? Root-beer?" He winked. "Real beer, if you like."

"Coffee ice-cream, please."

Cone in hand, she retreated to a small table as a group of customers entered the tent. She would remain here until Ralph Packard and Cleo had passed. Since she had discovered his deception about the short stories, she couldn't bear to look at him, much less speak to him. What had been his object in deceiving her? When the coast was clear, she would pick up Andy and meet Madge Millard.

"Say, listen! Did you see the Ace?"

The low, sinister question broke into Lissa's troubled thoughts. It came from one or two shadows on the canvas wall beside her. The man outside who had asked the question must be sitting almost shoulder to shoulder with her. The Ace! The words slashed her mind wide open. The Ace was the man Lex was looking for! The counterfeiter! He was here? At this Fair? Never again would she believe that a mind couldn't rock from shock. Hers was swaying. She mustn't lose a word.

She nibbled at the cone. Leaned closer to the canvas wall. Not too close; she might touch the shoulder of the man outside.

"Say, are you seeing things?" another low voice jeered. "The Ace made his get away out of this country four years ago. Do you think if he'd come back, we wouldn't have knowed it? Slick as he is, he wouldn't got by us, not with what we have on him."

Slick. The word flashed a close-up of Ralph Packard on Lissa's mind. Ralph Packard and his man Nino. Absurd, hadn't the Packards had A 1 references? Those references had been stolen! Was she about to find out why?

"I tell you he's here," the sinister voice insisted. "I had a tip he's been living in this hick town lately. That's why I came. I saw him talkin' to a dame. He got away before I got close. Me not know the Ace! You make me sick! Come on. We'll find him! We'll stick him for a grand."

The Ace! at the Fair! The words whirled round and round in Lissa's mind. She tried to stop them. He had been talking with a dame! That was a help. There were at least a thousand men among those present talking with women. What should she do? Find Lex, of course. Wherever he was, she must find him. Perhaps he was still at Tarry Farm with the men who were looking over the property but if she left the Fair grounds, she might miss him.

If, as the man outside the canvas wall had said, the "Ace" had been living in this town lately, the counterfeiting plates also were here. No time to waste. The men she had overheard might warn the hunted man. She must find Lex. What should she do about Andy? She'd think up a reason to cut his merry-go-rounding short and find someone with whom to leave him until his mother came. Too bad to burden Fenton with him, the butler doubtless had plans of his own. She mustn't sit here, the two men who had been outside might enter and see her.

She pulled her soft green hat rakishly over one eye and approached the counter. She smiled at the moon-faced man.

"Your ice-cream is wonderful."

He leaned on his elbows and invited;

"Say, girlie, have one on me, now."

"Thanks, I couldn't eat another mouthful," Lissa responded and forced herself to make a leisurely exit.

She wanted to run, go somewhere, anywhere to find Lex. How could she walk? "Walk you will, my girl," she disciplined herself and serpentined her way through the crowds. Once she met burning eyes. Were they the eyes of the man whose whispered words she had overheard? Ice feathered through her veins. Did he know that she had been on the other side of that canvas wall when he had hissed his discovery? Was he following her? If only she hadn't worn such a gayly printed frock. Why worry? The Fair grounds were a riot of color from gayly printed frocks.

The raucous music was thinning to a finale when she reached the opening of the merry-go-round tent, chariots, prancing horses, lions and tigers, revolved more and more slowly. In spite of her burning impatience to get away, Lissa bit back a laugh. Fenton in straw hat and sideburns sat stiff-spined as a riding-master on a wooden white charger and on a high-stepping bay beside him rode Andy Millard.

The machinery creaked to a stand-still. The music faded away. Fenton swung the boy to the ground. Andy ran ahead to Lissa. His eyes sparkled with excitement, his cheeks were red as if rouged.

"Lissa, it was grand! May I go round again? Fenton said he would take me if you said I could. Please, Lissa! Please!"

They were outside the tent now, a tent deserted by the crowd which had flocked to the aviation field. She looked at the boy hopping up and down, then at the butler who had joined them.

"I'll be glad to take him again, Miss. I—"

He snapped up his head to look at the genial, ruddy man who tapped his shoulder. His skin turned the color of yellowed ivory, lines cut deep in his face, his eyes chilled, his lips thinned and hardened, his hand shot to his left breast.

Another man caught his arm and held it. A voice behind him warned;

"Take it easy, Mr. Fenton. No shooting allowed in the Fair grounds. Say good-afternoon to the boy. You're late for an engagement, several years late if you ask me."

"You've made a mistake—" the butler's protest was strident, disjointed.

"Oh, no. Your stooge, Nino, is waiting to tell you we haven't."

Fenton looked behind him. His eyes turned, his voice snarled; "Major Fane! I thought there was something phoney about you. It's a pity I didn't drown you when I pushed you overboard last night."

Major Fane! Lissa stared at the short, stocky man incredulously. His eyes were not opaque now. They were keen, cold steel. He poked Fenton in the back.

"Get going!"

Andy, who had been listening and looking up with puzzled eyes, twitched a corner of the butler's coat.

"Aren't we going on the merry-go-round again, Fenton?"

The man looked down at him. "Not again today, Master Andy—but sometime." He cleared his throat. Nodded to the man beside him. "You win. Let's go."

Lissa watched the four walk toward the gate in close formation. Two of them were the men who had come to the big house with Lex to look over the "property." What did it mean?

"Quite the last word in arrests, I'd say, Miss," observed a perfect imitation of Fenton's voice.

Lissa wheeled. Johnny Grant stood behind her.

"Arrest! Was Fenton arrested, Johnny?"

"Sure, 'twas an arrest. Modern methods. No melodrama. No shooting. No yelling. Just a hand on the shoulder— 'You're late for an engagement, Mr. Fenton!'—and there you are. Remember I told you that butler was too English to be genuine? Hi! Hold everything! You're chalky! For the love of Mike, don't pass out here, sweet thing!"

Lissa clutched the sleeve of his blue coat to steady herself. She smiled with stiff lips.

"I'm not faint, Johnny. Just thought of something. I'll be all right in a min—"

"Lissa! Lissa!" Andy tugged at her hand. There was a hint of tears in his voice and in his startled eyes;

"What does arrest mean? Why couldn't Fenton take me on the merry-go-round again?"

Johnny Grant caught his shoulder.

"Fenton had to keep a date but I'll take you, stout fella. Am I good on horseback? You ain't seen nothin' yet! You ought to see me at a rodeo if you want to know how good I am. What the country needs is more riders like us fellas, you and me. Come on!"

Andy's face was radiant. His laugh was like a peal of silver bells. "You're awful funny, Johnny. Funnier than Fenton. Okay, I'm ready." He turned to Lissa. "Don't let mother stop me if she comes before we've been around a lot of times, will you?"

Lissa nodded. She couldn't speak. Her mind was a-whirl. No need now to rush to Tarry Farm to find Lex, Fenton was the Ace!

xxvii

THE orchestra in the red, white and blue draped Town Hall was playing a request number, "Beautiful Lady In Blue," a hit of several seasons past, when Lex Carson appeared in the doorway. Lissa's heart stopped and raced on. He was evidently looking for someone. His white dinner-jacket was conspicuous against the tweed and blue coats of the men standing behind him.

Madge Millard and Tod Kent stopped beside her and immediately Lex started forward. He was coming for Madge, of course. Lissa reminded;

"You haven't asked me to dance tonight, Tod."

"And why? You've had 'em in swarms about you. Perhaps it's that silver tissue thing you're wearing. It floats. Of course it may be—"

"Oh, I got charm!" Lissa laughed. "Come on, Tod. Must I beg you to dance with me?"

"Wait a minute, Lissa," Madge pleaded. "Lex is coming. Before he gets here, I want to thank you for being so wonderful to Andy this afternoon. He'll never forget it. His hero-worship is divided now. He had almost as much to say about Johnny Grant as about Fenton when he came home."

"What's that about Fenton?" Lex Carson inquired sharply

as he joined them. Lissa's smile in return for his was faint and fleet. Did he know about Fenton? Of course.

Madge Millard's eyes were brimful of tenderness, her mouth unsteady as she smiled at him;

"I was telling Lissa about Andy's afternoon. He didn't seem a bit tired when he got home. I'm a happy woman, Lex, not much like the woe-begone creature who flung herself in your arms that day in the sports-room, and cried her heart out. I burn with shame when I think of it."

"Don't think of it, Madge, mine's a sort of community shoulder. They're playing the Beautiful Blue Danube. Come on, Lissa, this is our dance, isn't it?"

Lissa turned away from the demanding question in his smiling eyes.

"I had promised Tod—"

"Tod can wait, I won't."

He put his arm about her and swung her among the dancers. A goodly number of summer-residents in gala attire danced elbow to elbow with native sons and daughters also dressed for an occasion, their faces dim in the amber light.

"Realize that this is the first time we've danced together, beautiful?" His arm tightened about her until she looked up. "You got wings, chile."

Lissa couldn't tell him that when Madge had smilingly explained that episode in the sports-room, that wings had lifted her heart until they beat in her throat. She glanced up;

"Good, aren't we? There's always the movies for talent like ours." A voice which came from her lips but didn't seem to be hers, asked wistfully;

"Is your heart buried in a grave, Lex?"

He looked at her as if he couldn't believe his ears.

"Is my heart—what?" His arm tightened. "I'll show you where my heart is. Here comes Grant. He can't have you. You're mine. The other girls will have more chance if I take you off the floor. Get your wrap."

He waited for her to get her flame-colored Mandarin coat. In the corridor Simonds stopped them, Simonds glowering and beet-red with suppressed anger, twirling the pencil at the end of his chain, till it cast off golden sparks like a fiery pin-wheel.

"Just a minute, Mr. Carson. I don't believe in it but the men asked me to tell you they'd take that cut."

Carson's eyes narrowed. "They took till the last minute to make up their minds, didn't they, Simonds? Come to the house tomorrow morning. I have something for you to tell them."

In the metallic brilliance of the light from half a moon, Lissa, nestled in the deep leather cushions of Carson's roadster, could see the firm line of his mouth. A man of power, someone to hold to in time of trouble, she thought, as she had thought once before. Why, why had she asked that silly question about his heart?

"Where are we going?" she inquired, to break the silence broken only by the purr of the engine and a crooning surf. A salty breeze blew her hair in a red-gold aureole.

"Want to know what happened this afternoon?"

"Oh, yes. Yes."

"Then we'll go home. I have something to show you. Warm enough? There's a touch of autumn in this crisp air."

"Yes."

He didn't speak again until they were in the library at Tarry Farm. The room was fragrant with the warm scent of smoldering birch logs and the breath of red Radiance roses in a tall silver vase. He poked up the dozing fire. She established herself in a deep chair and faced him as he stood before the mantel. The firelight touched her tender eyes, tinted the smooth curves of her throat, rouged her gallant mouth.

"Now for the story of this summer," he said and plunged his hands into the pockets of his coat. "Do you realize how tempting you are, beautiful?" he asked huskily.

Lissa hurriedly avoided his disturbing eyes and suggested;

"Let me tell my story first."

She told of the conversation she had overheard in the tent; of her determination to reach him before he left Tarry Farm; of meeting Fenton and Andy, of the men who had personally conducted the butler from the Fair. Long before she had finished, she was standing looking up at him. She concluded breathlessly;

"Not until Johnny spoke did I realize that it was Fenton —Fenton whom you wanted. When did you know?"

"Sit in the big chair again, Lissa, I can't think when you're so near. That's better."

She looked away from the dark intensity of his eyes, watched for an instant the tropical fish flash and flame in the crystal cylinder in the wrought iron sconce against the wall. Her eager eyes came back to him as he went on;

"Tod, the criminologists—known hereafter in my story as 'the boys'—and I, had come to this harbor with no expectation that our man was here. My inheritance seemed an excellent excuse for us to use it as a base from which to forward our investigations. When, the day of our arrival, you said that you imagined you had seen a flash from that abandoned light, even the roots of my hair tingled. The next days, perhaps you remember, I stopped to buckle my shoe in the lamp-room, at the same time I picked up a cigarette stub. You may remember also that I relaid the fire in the service room. Sticking from between the logs was a newspaper with a portion torn out. You said you hadn't torn it, that you cut items from a paper. Anyone might have torn out that scrap, but, when one is on a hunt, one doesn't let a straw of a clue escape, and there was the flash and cigarette stub to be explained. I sent for a copy of the newspaper of the same February date, finally fitted this into the torn place. Read it aloud."

Lissa read from the diamond shaped piece of paper he dropped into her lap;

"FRENCH FISHERMAN'S FEAR CLUE TO A SMUG-GLING PLOT. SEEING TWO LOBSTER-TRAP FLOATS WHERE HE PUT ONE CAUSES HIM TO REFUSE DRINK AND THE CUSTOM OFFICERS TO INVESTI-GATE. MERCHANDISE OF A HIGHLY DUTIABLE CHARACTER WAS FOUND IN WATERTIGHT CASES AT THE END OF LANYARDS ATTACHED TO FLOATS."

"Was that what you and Tod were doing in the storm, pulling up lobster traps?" Lissa asked in a thrilled whisper.

"Not lobster traps. We pulled up a watertight case full of bogus bills." He returned the clipping to his breast pocket. "A few minutes before the newspaper for which I had sent came, Ozy had told Tod and me that one night he had found two lobster-trap floats where he had buoyed one."

"Did you suspect then that Fenton was the Ace?"

"No, I liked Fenton. But when, that very day, you told me that he had done all the buying for the place, that your Aunt Hetty gave him cheques and he would pay cash—something clicked in my mind. It works that way, some-times. I made you think I had heard a suspicious sound out-side the door. My hunch seemed too improbable to believe, but I followed it. I didn't dare search Fenton's rooms for fear he would find out and disappear. The Ace had slipped away so many times when the authorities thought they had him. That fingerprint party on the cruiser was to get his but he was too smart for us, he pushed the Major overboard.

"For weeks I have followed signposts pointing to his trail, oftentimes such a faint trail, that I was tempted to think that my hunch was nothing but a brainsquall, but I kept on and on, as it twisted and turned until it ended under this roof. Even then I wasn't sure I had the Ace. Last night we found his fingerprints on one of the bills. The boys on the cruiser vacuumed the coat G-Man stole and found in the bag, tin, antimony and lead dusts, the metals counterfeiters use. You heard Fenton claim the coat. Today while he was at the Fair a photo-engraving and printing plant, with any number of bogus bills, was uncovered behind the bookshelves your aunt had had built into his room."

"Fenton has been making counterfeit money in this house! I can't believe it. No wonder he was content to stay here three years. How did he dispose of it?"

"Cautiously. An occasional bill tucked in with a payment made around here, but, recently, most of it on his week-end trips to different places. He has sizable sums of real money cozily tucked away in real banks under different names."

"Do you remember that Fenton called Simonds a specked-apple—I thought for a minute that the dour foreman was your man—Remember when he said, 'There's something in the world besides money'? What a hypocrite!"

"What an actor, I'd say. I thought he was about to burst into tears when he proclaimed his passion for cows. He has been so secure that he got careless and ambitious. When back in February he read in the paper of the way in which dutiable merchandise had been smuggled, he must have thought up the plan of having watertight cases filled with his bogus money picked up by an alleged lumber vessel and dared make the bills bigger. The fact that I worked on the case must not be known. It would destroy my usefulness to the Treasury Department. You understand that, Lissa?"

"Yes. Instead of a G-Man, you're a T-Man, aren't you? Do you like unearthing criminals?"

"No! No! But, it is like spy service in war—it has to be done. It is part of the battle against crime which cannot be won unless every citizen does his part."

Lissa's silver frock shimmered with little pink rivers of reflected firelight as she clasped her hands about one knee. She said thoughtfully;

"Each year I have wished that one of the tenants would provide a plot for a story and all the time a mammoth plot was being hatched under this roof. I'll confess now, that deep down in my mind, I've suspected Ralph Packard. I can't understand why he posed as a writer."

"You suggested the idea to him by assuming that he came here to write, didn't you? He jumped at the chance to hold your interest by posing as an author. I eliminated him as a suspect, when you told me that he was beating at those blazing curtains. No counterfeiter would risk his fingers. Even after I found that the stub in the lamp-room, the cigarette his houseman dropped on your doorstep, had his monogram I knew that he was not our man, that Nino had been helping himself to his employer's cigarettes."

"And Major Fane? Is he really a dyspeptic? I suspected him, too."

"He's another good actor. He eats anything and everything. It must have been torture for him to pass up that lobster-bake. He was here to help me, though we communicated only through headquarters. I'll answer the phone.

"Carson speaking—Mrs. Barclay! Where are you?—She has! Oh, No! No!—of course I'm not jealous. I was surprised, that's all. I hope she'll be happy—That was generous of him—Okay. Be as late as you like getting home. I'll sit up to let you in." He cradled the phone.

"What's happened? What did Mother Barclay tell you, Lex?" Lissa's voice broke from excitement.

"Cleo married Packard tonight! Your stepmother's voice shook with triumph."

"Married! Cleo married! To Ralph Packard? He must be the 'last resort.' Why did you say, 'No! No!'?"

"Because Packard is a millionaire bootlegger-baron gone respectable and—cultured—even Cleo ought to do better than that. I had his record before I had been at Tarry Farm a week. Sidonie is his sister, but she has had no education—grew up with no advantages. She was afraid to talk for fear her deficiencies would betray them both. When she felt she was out of her depths socially, she'd have a headache and go home. The electric shock at the light evidently loosened the screws that held Nino's nerve together for when the revenue men picked him up he babbled that he had been a body-guard for Ralph Packard in his bootlegger days; that Packard had deliberately burned off his fingerprints that he might wipe out the past and marry a girl who was 'a swell' —that's the Italian's word, not mine—that his boss liked the red-headed sister better, but that the blonde had more friends."

"Did he confess about Fenton?"

"Yes, information rattled from his rocking mind like pennies from a bank shaken by a small boy. He whined that last night after he had lowered the watertight cases, he had dug up a pouch of coins he had buried for safekeeping, had flashed a signal to the lumber vessel by inserting an electric torch in the great lens,—as he had done twice before —and was about to make his get-away forever with the pouch and a pocketful of bills Fenton had paid him, when you and Grant burst into the lighthouse and he was trapped in the lamp-room."

"Then I did help you! I so wanted to! My writing has accomplished something. I wouldn't have gone back to the island if memory hadn't flashed 'When stuck go into reverse,' on the screen of my mind."

"I'll say you helped, you and G-Man. The Treasury Department ought to award that Irish terrier a medal. He was prophetically named. He stepped into a G-Man's role when he produced that coat. It clinched the evidence against Fenton. In some underground way he had heard that the Packards were looking for a summer place, and after he conceived the dazzling plan of buoying the watertight cases beside Ozy's lobster floats, he suggested to Nino that it would be to his advantage to steer them to Red Chimneys. Nino confessed that the references were forged, and that as they were a menace to Fenton's safety, Fenton stole them and destroyed them. Packard must have suspected that his houseman had buried those coins, that he was mixed up in shady doings. He wanted to get hold of the pouch that he might hold it as a threat over his one-time bodyguard."

"Do you think Ralph Packard believes that Nino was drowned?"

"Not for a minute. He probably figures that the man made his get-away for reasons connected with the coins. He may have thought them real money and that Nino stole them. Whatever he suspected he was taking no chance of having his plan to marry Cleo upset by a story the Italian might tell, so persuaded her to marry him before his preprohibition record leaked. I doubt if it ever does. So much has happened since then, that that era is almost forgotten. He made correct tax-returns and had no criminal record. He was a product of his times. He gave his bride a cheque for a hundred thousand dollars."

"Now she can pay her bills. I'm dazed. What a plot for a story. Perhaps Cleo will establish Ralph Packard socially, she has a lot of friends and you say he has heaps of money. That's an unbeatable combination these days. Cleo is proud. It will hurt her terribly if ever she finds out what he has been. I'm sorry, terribly sorry for her. I'll send her Aunt Hetty's aquamarines and diamonds for a wedding present."

"Lissa, as has been said before, you're adorable. Prepare for more shock. I've sold this house."

"How grand! To those men who were here yesterday?"

"No, they were here to check-up on Fenton. I've sold it to a summer resident. He has had his eye on Tarry Farm for years. I sacrificed it, but, I won't have it to carry and the money will pay off some of the mortgages on the other property. This summer has done so much for Andy that Jack Millard has bought the Treasure Chest."

"Really, Lex? I'm so glad for you. Have you sold the other cottages?"

"No. You said Red Chimneys was your favorite. I'm keeping that for—us. I asked you to give me one summer—now—I want all your summers. Don't back away. Come here!" He caught her hands. "You can write, just the same. 'Melissa Carson' will be a lot better looking on the cover of a book than Melissa Barclay."

"Not above bribery are you?" she teased with breathless gaiety.

His look set her heart pounding.

"I'm not bribing, I'm just telling you that you're going to Washington with me as my wife, beautiful."

He drew her into his arms, tipped her head back against his shoulder, kissed her tenderly. Then as if the touch set him ablaze, his mouth crushed down on her throat, her eyes. Her lips burned under his, her blood raced through her veins. He said huskily;

"Any doubt now where my heart is?"

His arms stripped away her defense, his voice banished the faint phantom of Johnny Grant's faithlessness.

"No. I know. I know also that I've never been kissed before,—really kissed, I mean."

"You don't mind, do you?" Laughter pricked through his unsteady voice.

She rumpled her red-gold hair against his shoulder. Lifted eager tempting lips to his, reminded softly;

"You do ask foolish questions, don't you?"